THE DEMON'S BEAUTY

TATI B. ALVAREZ

ISBN:

E-book: 978-1-968095-04-8

Paperback: 978-1-968095-07-9

Edited By: On the Same Page Editing and Mountains Wanted

Cover Designer: Coffin Print Designs

For those who wanted Belle to end up with the Beast, not the human prince.

AUTHOR'S NOTE

This book contains elements of:

- Death of a loved one (off page)
- Mentions of Suicide
- Explicit sexual scenes
- Domestic violence (off page)
- Stabbing
- Combat scenes (physical, magical, supernatural)
- Fantasy War

Please make sure you are protecting your mental health. If you need more information send me a message on any of my socials. Otherwise, happy reading!

Kraken
Lagoon
Nephilim
Land
Dragon's
Keep

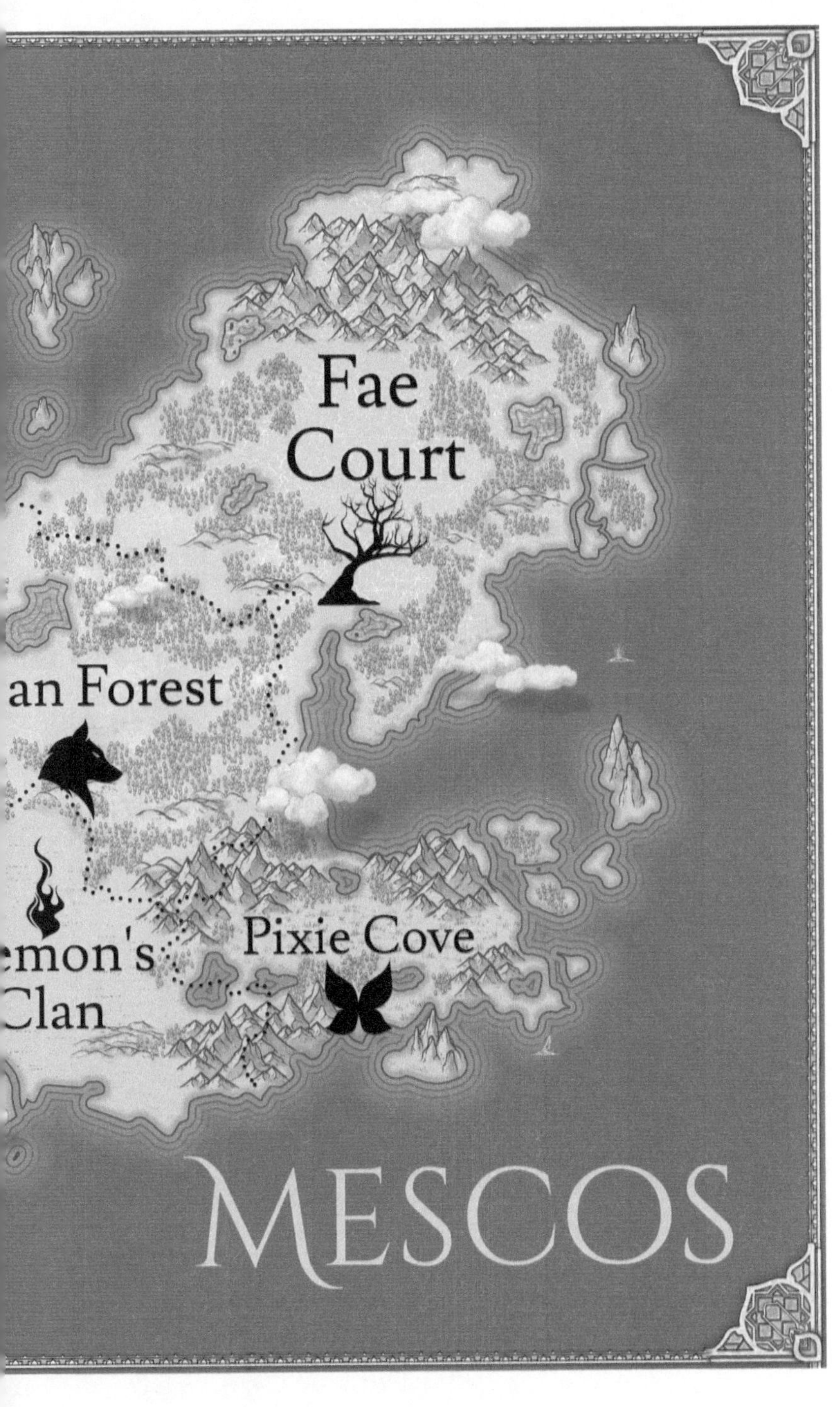

Fae Court
an Forest
emon's Clan
Pixie Cove
MESCOS

PROLOGUE

According to historians of times before, Mescos was once a thriving country full of supernatural creatures and their human companions. In Mescos, humans held their own power, given to them by their god to ensure peace amongst the supernaturals and humans. Humans strengthened their lands and provided immense strength to the supernaturals they mated. Together, their lands, kingdoms, and people thrived.

The time for peace was short-lived, though, as a new danger emerged.

Nephilim, giant winged creatures born from greed and hatred, appeared seemingly overnight. Historians differ in opinion on how these creatures came to be. Some historians argue Nephilim were sent by angry gods, while others say Nephilim traveled from lands far from Mescos. Their origins are still unknown.

The Nephilim brought darkness to the kingdoms. Their leader, Gadreel, led the slaughter of humans to gain their magic. Thousands of humans and supernaturals died in what historians call The Great War. Each human death brought power to the hellish winged creatures.

Knowing they had very little time before the Nephilim became too powerful, the six rulers of Mescos—dragon, pixie, fae, wolf, demon, and kraken—agreed to work together in order to take down the common enemy.

The war between the rulers of Mescos and the Nephilim happened at Dragon's Keep. The rulers of Mescos, their armies, and their human mates fought countless hours against Gadreel's people. Many fell in an attempt to rid Mescos of the vile creatures.

Knowing they were unprepared to slaughter the Nephilim, the Pixie King and his human queen came together, combining their magic as one. Upon seeing this, the other rulers followed suit and, within the mountains east of Dragon's Keep, a magical prison took form.

One by one, Nephilim were captured by the magic and imprisoned within the mountains. Gadreel, knowing his army would not win this war, cursed the rulers of Mescos before he was imprisoned. He damned the kingdoms: in one hundred years, if the rulers did not find their human mates, disaster would fall upon their people, and the Nephilim would rise again.

In his final act of rebellion, Gadreel used the last bit of stolen magic he absorbed from the deaths of humans and destroyed the portal between Mescos and the human world, effectively cutting off access to their human mates.

The leaders of Mescos won that day, but it cost them everything.

Over the next hundred years, the last humans of Mescos died off. With no connection to the human world, the Nephilim rose again, escaping their prison in the mountains. Now the only hope the six new Kings of Mescos have comes from an unexpected ally known as Ender The Guardian. He alone possesses the power to travel between worlds and bring humans to their super-natural mates.

Little is known about The Guardian.

Today, the safety and future of Mescos hang in the balance. History is being written in real time. These accounts will be updated as necessary.

CHAPTER 1

ISABELLE

I don't seek redemption.

I'll look upon the sharp blade of the swinging pendulum with a smile on my face, knowing I delivered justice when others refused. The police, the very people who were supposed to protect the community, ignored us during our time of need. What other choice did I have? When those in power turned their back on me, I took measures into my own hands. And where did that land me?

In county jail awaiting my trial. Or something. I don't fucking know. Everything has been a blur since it happened. I'm not even sure how long I've been here. The only light comes from the humming fluorescent above me, flickering precariously each time a door opens or closes.

The only escape I have from this cell is my wandering mind. The sterile, concrete walls fade around me, and I'm once again at home in my living room. It looks like any other day.

My yellow love seat is stacked high with assorted pillows. The old coffee table I inherited from my grandmother, with more sentimental than monetary value, is cluttered with mugs and last night's dishes. The too small TV on an otherwise bare, gray wall could only handle one streaming service, and even that is questionable.

But every time I think of home, I think of *that* day. It started like any other day. I brewed my morning coffee. I had to drink it black because I was out of creamer and hadn't been to the store in weeks. I remember glancing at the clock above the stove. It was barely three in the morning. A time when most people would be snuggled into bed, deep in REM sleep. But not me, of course. I was on a mission.

A mission to end the terror known as James.

For the last year, I had followed this man's movements, festering in my hate for him until I could bear it no longer. I was his shadow, lurking in the darkness. Watching. Learning. Waiting.

My hatred for this man only grew stronger by the day, consuming me until he occupied every waking hour and my nightmares. I thought of my sweet, brown-eyed sister. She was beautiful and so incredibly smart. Far too kind, even to people who didn't deserve it. She wanted to be a school teacher and mold the minds of the next generation. Because that's who Anna was. Love incarnate. A genuinely good person.

Her only flaw was loving a monster.

In the end, it quite literally killed her.

James took away my sister. My best friend. It was

slow, torturous, and lasted months. I watched my sister wither away until nothing but a shell of her remained. Her beautiful black hair had once been silky and shiny. Toward the end of her life, it was dull and knotted, matching the rest of her haggard appearance. She had even taken scissors and chopped off most of it. The sparkle and life in her eyes dimmed, and I watched my sister die.

All because of James. He didn't stop there, though. He sank his claws into another woman named Erin. Apparently, he had been dating her while he was dating my sister, but Erin was saved by The Guardian. Erin was just another woman James kept on the precipice of death.

Death is funny, though. It gives you clarity in its finality.

As far as I'm concerned, my sister's blood is not only on James, but also on the hands of every officer who didn't listen to us. They valued an abusive man's life over Anna's, and that is something I will never forgive.

It's why I had to do it. Why I killed him, and I'll never regret that.

I could have run after all was said and done. Maybe I would have gotten far, and no one would have ever discovered it was me who killed James. But that's the thing. I *wanted* people to know it was me. That I took care of the problem when no one else would, and I would do it all again in a heartbeat. This didn't bring Anna back, but revenge helped me feel marginally better.

I don't remember much after the event. Getting caught at the gas station and arrested, that is. I think I tuned it all out. All I remember were rough hands.

Choice, angry words. Handcuffs being slapped around my wrist far too tightly.

It was like I blinked and ended up in this cold cell. You'd think they'd at least give me a fucking blanket to cover up with, but apparently I'm far too dangerous to even have one. I might strangle someone with it. They wouldn't be too far off-base with that assumption, considering blood is on my hands. They don't need to worry though; James was my only target.

Soft footfalls from somewhere drag me out of my thoughts. They grow louder and louder until two pristinely polished tactical boots stand outside my cell. My gaze travels up to see an irate-looking officer. He's bald. I wonder if he lost his hair from the stress of the job. Probably not, since they don't seem to do a damn thing but imprison women seeking justice or the dangerous jaywalker. You know, priorities.

The officer—I can't see his name tag—stares at me. I think he's waiting for me to say something, but I know my rights. I don't have to say a damn thing, and I haven't. Mostly because I don't wish to waste my breath on these people. They didn't want to listen to me before, and I'd be damned if they'll listen to me now.

Officer Friendly scowls and reaches for something on his belt. At first, I think he's reaching for a weapon, but then I catch the unmistakable glint of a key, which he uses to open my cell. "Miss Sinclair, looks like you've been released on bail," he says begrudgingly.

This man doesn't want me out in public, and honestly, I'm not even certain murderers are allowed bail. Luckily, I literally have a "get out of jail free" card up my sleeve.

Officer Friendly has little to fear. Because if the person who has come to bail me out is who I think it is, I won't be Grym Hollow's problem for much longer.

Pushing myself off the cold, hard ground, I stretch my muscles, wondering if I'll see a certain gray-horned man waiting for me. Before I can even walk out of my cell, Officer Friendly starts walking away. Not wanting to spend another minute in this cold cell, I hurry and jog after him, eager to get the hell out of here.

CHAPTER 2
ISABELLE

I don't remember this many twists and turns when I arrived. Each time I think we're nearing freedom, Officer Friendly turns and pivots when we reach the end of a hall. It's a labyrinth, but I'm certain the design is on purpose. Wouldn't want us criminals seeing the light of day. Not that anyone would be able to get out of here if they tried. There are far too many cameras, and even though I'm only with one officer, I sense there are more watching me, just waiting for their chance to raise their guns if I step out of line.

We finally reach a desk with a middle-aged woman sitting behind a computer. She looks up through her wire-rimmed glasses, mouth pressed in a tight line as if she's just sucked on a particularly sour lemon. "Officer Canto, can I help you?" she asks in a thick Southern accent. You don't hear that much in Grym Hollow, which means it's probably fake. Just something to make her stand out amongst the sea of carbon copies that populate this godforsaken town.

"Isabelle Sinclair is being released on bond. We need to process her," Officer Friendly—or rather, Officer Canto—grunts like the troll he is.

We stand awkwardly as the woman types on her computer. She asks me basic questions they already know the answer to—my name, birth date, and address—but then otherwise ignores me. It's hard not to feel small and insignificant here. Where my life and freedom aren't my own, but in the hands of people who don't give a shit about me or the reason why I did what I did. They see life in black and white with no room for gray areas. You're either innocent or guilty, and the reasons don't matter.

Soon the woman stands and beckons us to follow. Officer Canto makes me walk in front of him this time as we follow the woman to a room filled with lockers. She glances down at a sticky note she wrote something on before leaving her station, then walks over to a locker, typing in a code I can't see.

With a soft click, the locker door opens, and inside is my backpack, the only personal item I had on me when I was arrested.

"This has been thoroughly searched, and anything deemed a weapon was taken." She hands me the backpack. It's just as heavy as it was when I packed it, so I'm not sure how "thorough" they actually were. Another shitty job executed by the Grym Hollow PD.

"Let's go, Miss Sinclair." Officer Canto grabs my upper arm and leads me down the white hallway to a large black door with a keypad. He swipes his badge, and there's another audible click before the door opens.

Standing on the other side is my ticket out of jail.

The Guardian.

A tall, inhuman...*thing*. I can't call him a man because no man I've ever come across looks like they were carved from stone. His gray skin and piercing blue eyes are beautiful but terrifying. Two horns protrude from the top of his head, curling slightly in at the end.

Officer Canto tenses beside me. If he could, I think he'd use me as a shield against The Guardian.

Coward.

The Guardian's presence isn't any less intimidating than the first time I encountered him, months ago when I sought him out. I hadn't yet developed my plan to kill James, but I knew I would need a way out of jail. I had—and still have—no intentions of rotting in prison.

My freedom comes at a price, though. I exchanged one prison for another, but The Guardian's deal sounded much more appealing. Marry someone who calls himself a demon king and help restore his kingdom. It's vague and, frankly, unbelievable, but I'd rather live in a supposed mythical land with a man I don't know than stay here behind bars until I die.

I need out. And it has to be now.

Officer Canto clears his throat, eyes darting around the room as if looking for the nearest escape route. He drops his hand from my shoulder, and I scowl. Though kicking him in the balls would probably only get me in more trouble and prevent me from leaving.

"She must appear in court next week. Officers will check in daily to make sure she hasn't fled. Is she...

staying with you?" The last question is laced with disdain and perhaps fear?

Good. It's not enough.

The Guardian reaches out. At first, I think he wants to shake hands, but then he gestures to my backpack. "Allow me to carry it, Miss Sinclair."

I'm not sure I trust The Guardian, but I also don't want to fuck up my one chance at escape. I'm hesitant to hand it over, seeing as it's the last of my possessions after going through my house one last time. I couldn't take everything, but I found the most important things I couldn't part with. To outsiders, it looks like an old, dingy backpack that has seen better days. But to me, it's priceless because it was Anna's.

Reluctantly, I hand it over. The Guardian takes the backpack, and in his hands, it looks like it was made for a toddler. He flings it over one arm, muscles bulging as he secures it around one shoulder, and nods. "We must be off."

"Wait, you didn't answer me. Is she staying at your house or not?" Officer Canto's face flushes red, barely concealing his annoyance.

"Or not," The Guardian dismisses him, and before the officer can demand any more, I'm being escorted out of the building with a hand on my shoulder by the scary horned man. I doubt anyone will be knocking down The Guardian's door to try and find me. And if they do? I suspect they won't be breathing for much longer after that.

We don't stop walking until we are out the door, down the steps, and halfway down the street. The

Guardian's long strides force me to jog to keep up with him. "Can you slow down, please? Some of us have normal-sized legs."

The Guardian slows but doesn't stop. He, thankfully, drops his hand from my shoulder. I'm not big on being touched, and I've been touched and patted down enough to last me a lifetime over the past few days.

"My apologies, Miss Sinclair."

"It's Isabelle." He ignores me.

"We must get you to Oziel," The Guardian says. The name doesn't sound familiar, but I'm guessing he has something to do with the contract I signed.

I'm in no position to make any more demands, but I do anyway. "Wait, we can't leave yet."

The scary non-man stops and slowly turns around. I think he's glaring at me, or maybe that's just how he always looks. If so, The Guardian has locked down resting bitch face better than any teenage girl I've met.

"And why can we not leave yet? Are you going back on the contract?" he asks.

I shake my head. "No, nothing like that. I just need..." I take a deep breath, awkwardly shifting my weight from foot to foot. I don't know why asking The Guardian to go see my dead sister one last time is harder than killing James, yet here we are.

"I need to go to the Grym Hollow cemetery." My words are faster than they should be. "I need to say goodbye to someone."

The Guardian doesn't speak for a long time. If he refuses me, then...there's nothing I can do. But I have to see her. Just one last time. If I don't—

"Very well," The Guardian says at last, cutting off my wayward thoughts. "But make it quick."

WE REACH the wrought iron fence that surrounds the perimeter of the cemetery. Two large weeping willows decorate the entrance, their branches cascading down in an array of greens and browns. They appear to be crying, as if the trees themselves are in mourning. The scent of fresh-cut grass and blooming flowers fill the air. The only sound comes from the birds flying overhead and the occasional car passing by.

Aside from a family of three hunched over a grave on the opposite side of where I'll be, The Guardian and I are the only ones here. My horned companion stares upon the graves with melancholy. He makes no attempt to walk inside, instead taking up residence outside the gate.

"I will give you privacy. Ten minutes, and we must go," he warns.

"I only need five." I reach my hand out. "Can I have my backpack?"

With a nod, he slides the backpack off his shoulder and hands it to me. "Thanks," I say before walking in, my body on autopilot. I have walked through those very gates hundreds, if not thousands, of times. The gravel crunches beneath my feet until I veer off toward a grassy area. I pass old and new tombstones. The saddest ones are the ones with birth and death dates close together.

Five. Seven. Three.

I make my way toward the end, near the wrought iron fence directly opposite the entrance. Nestled under an oak tree is a marble tombstone with the name *Anna Sinclair* forever etched into the surface. She sleeps peacefully between our mother, who died of breast cancer when we were teenagers, and our father, who died a year before Anna from a heart attack.

My family together for eternity.

I allow my backpack to fall to the ground next to the tombstones as I sink to my knees. The red roses I brought before finding myself in jail have wilted some but still look beautiful decorating their graves. I think Anna would like them. She always had a thing for roses. Personally, I hated them because of the thorns, and always ended up stabbing my fingers, but when she died, they became my favorite flower.

"Sometimes the most beautiful things in life can hurt you. Unless you know how to tend them," Anna would say each time she brought home a fresh bouquet.

A silent tear rolls down my cheek. You would think after a year without my sister, this would be easier. But that's a lie society tells you so you'll stop grieving the dead. The truth of the matter is that it never gets easier. The pain is still there. Sometimes it lies dormant, and just when you think you have a handle on your emotions, something comes along and slashes right through the box you put them in.

It will never be easier. But if that is the cost of remembrance, then I shall pay it in full.

Before my vision can get too clouded with tears, I

unzip my backpack. The neatly folded clothes I packed are now strewn about. Fucking cops.

Fortunately, the clothes were on top, and the small zippered bags at the bottom seem mostly untouched. I say a silent thank you to the person who "thoroughly" searched the backpack and decided the bottom half wasn't important.

I pull out a leather-bound journal and open it to the first page. A beautiful brunette with a heart-shaped face stares back at me. Many people mistook us for twins, but I always thought my older sister was more beautiful. Her soft brown eyes always held warmness and love, ready to greet anyone as if they were lifelong friends. It's true what they say about eyes being a window to the soul.

Taking a few rocks scattered about, I place her picture near her grave, keeping it pinned down with the rocks and safe from the wind. I hope the tree above the grave will help protect it from the worst of the rain. Anyone who looks down will see her smiling up at them. Just as she always did.

I close the journal back up and then place it next to her photo. I don't need it anymore; I want to share her memory with more people.

"When you died, I wasn't ready to say goodbye." My throat is thick with emotions, tears burning my eyes. If I allow myself, I would curl up in a fetal position atop my family's graves and never leave.

"To be honest, I'm still not ready to say goodbye. But I think I know how to keep you alive, even when I'm gone." I glide my hands over the leather of the journal.

"I've never been one for words. That was more your

thing, but I took your advice and wrote down my feelings. Well, that turned into writing about you and the type of person you are...were."

God, why is this so fucking hard? A blade or bullet to the heart would hurt less than this. But Anna, my big sister, took care of me for years. I have to return the favor, even if it's small compared to everything she did for me and taught me.

"These pages are filled with your story—everything you were and the joy you brought to people. I even included that one night at the bonfire where you accidentally burned the entire bag of marshmallows." I smile at the memory. It was the last winter before our mother died. The last time we were together as a complete family. The last time I remember feeling genuine happiness.

"I'm going to leave this here so anyone who walks by can read your story and know how good a person and big sister you were. I don't know how it will stand up against the weather, but I'm hoping for the best. I love you, Anna, and I'm so sorry I couldn't save you."

This time, the tears fall freely, and I don't try to stop them. I lean forward, placing a kiss to her tombstone and then do the same for my parents. A gentle wind blows, feeling like a caress to the skin, carrying the smell of roses. I imagine it's a sign from Anna that she's still here, and maybe that she forgives me for what I have done.

"Goodbye, Anna. Goodbye, Mom and Dad. I love you all so much." I force myself up and fling my backpack over my arm. I allow myself one last glance at my parents' and Anna's graves before turning my back on them for the last time.

The tears don't completely dry up by the time I make it back to The Guardian, who is still perched in the same spot I left him. I don't have to see myself to know my eyes are puffy and red from crying, but The Guardian doesn't comment.

I'm not sure if I'm thankful or upset about that.

"Before we go," I say at last, "I need to know if there is a woman named Erin Goodwin in Mescos?"

The Guardian gives little away. He's closed-off in emotion and body language. He studies me for what feels likes long minutes, but in reality is only a few seconds, before he nods. "Yes. Ms. Goodwin is in Mescos."

"I want to see her."

"I see." He doesn't ask me why, and I don't offer an explanation. It's not for him to know. He wasn't affected by James like Erin and I were. "I suppose you'll need to ask your husband."

Before I can protest, The Guardian turns and starts to walk away from the cemetery. I hold my tongue for now, silently following behind him, allowing him to take the lead. "Now, let us go to my house," he says. "The portal for us awaits, and so does the demon king. He'll be expecting us."

CHAPTER 3

OZIEL

Flickering lights from sconces illuminate my pathway. The soft, almost imperceptible sound of my footfalls echoes behind me. I've walked this hallway many times, as have many demon kings before me. The hallway is a testament to ancient, malevolent grandeur. The walls are carved with intricate, infernal runes that pulse with a deep crimson glow, casting eerie patterns onto the cold, polished floor. Ruby-red framework adorns the obsidian walls with portraits of my ancestors hanging in each one. I can't help but think that their beady eyes follow my every move, judging me harshly for what has befallen this kingdom during my reign.

Usually, they would give me pause, but today is different.

I reach a set of grand doors with golden accents splashed against the dark wood. The soft sound of hauntingly beautiful music drifts through the air, mingling with the faint scent of burning incense and brimstone. There's something else there too, a heady, musty scent. No longer is the music the only sound emerging from the room, but lustful sighs, moans, and grunts dilute the piano's melody.

My eyes narrow. The party has started without me. I wave my clawed hand, sharp nails scraping the door. They burst open, and the smells and sounds assault my senses. It's intoxicating, a perfect distraction from the curse plaguing my demons.

I pause before stepping inside, surveying the debauchery before me and demons in various states of undress and compromising positions. The ballroom is the largest room in the castle, spanning the size of three formal dining rooms. Much like the rest of the castle, the obsidian-black tiles blend into the walls, making the room feel endless and caving in on you all at the same time.

Floor-to-ceiling windows line one of the walls, bathing the room in starlight. I stalk in, and a few demons engaging in sexual acts meet my gaze. A woman is on her hands and knees, with a male demon thrusting into her from behind and another cock fucking her mouth. She pulls back, a string of saliva hanging from her lips, black claws reaching out, beckoning me.

"My king, join us. Let us serve you," she moans.

The demons never cease their pleasure parties, thriving on sinful temptation. Normally, I would take the succubus up on her offer, but the pleasure she and the male succubi will give me pales in comparison to the news I received earlier. Still, I reach out my claws, sharp nails digging into her skin.

The succubus's eyes roll back, a small gasp leaving her lips.

"Perhaps next time."

"Yes, my king," she manages to say before a cock is thrust back into her mouth at a punishing pace.

I make my way to the chair that awaits me on the far side of the room. A throne made of bones and sinew, polished together, creates a stark reminder of life's fragility and my power here.

But if you ask me, it's a bit much.

I'm not alone when I reach my throne, draping my body over the chair. The piece is more a symbol of power than of comfort, but I don't plan on being here long. It's important I make my presence known, but in the back of my mind, I'm waiting to meet *her*.

"Garvan," I say to my courtier, who has taken up his normal position at my side. "Voyeurism is beneath you. Join in. Indulge."

Just as expected, my courtier blushes. As far as demons go, he's modest and cares too much about his pride and dignity. Makes for a boring advisor but a disciplined one.

"I don't care to participate in such...*follies,* my king." Garvan says "follies" as if the word personally offends him.

I regard my second, a demon I've known most of my life. He was a child when we met—we both were. We grew up, not as friends, because kings rarely have true friends due to the power imbalance, but as confidants. He was an easy choice when I ascended to the throne and had to choose a courtier.

Despite being fully clothed in a room full of nude and mostly nude demons, Garvan stands out. He wears a sharp tailored suit in midnight blue with elongated lapels. His gray horns—smaller than most demons'—are adorned with silver chains. Garvan is slender and tall, awkward in his own body. He wears his meekness like a mask, but it's all a façade. I've seen this man rip heads from bodies and hearts from chests.

People underestimate him, which makes him perfect as my spy and confidant.

"No, I suppose you wouldn't," I murmur, never having seen him do more than kiss another. I don't quite know his preference for male or female. Most demons don't limit themselves to just one gender. Where's the fun in that?

"Are you certain this is appropriate?" Garvan asks. Near him, a rather rambunctious couple slams into a wall, fucking in a frenzy to see who will orgasm faster. It's a game we play, one I find quite fun but have no time to play today.

"I mean, with everything going on, shouldn't we—"

"Whether or not we fuck is not going to stop the curse. Let them indulge while they can." I wave my hand, cutting him off. I grow tired of this conversation. If it were up to Garvan, he'd have the demons locked away in their homes, isolated.

The curse isn't a sickness. It can't be caught from an infected person. No demon is safe. It's a game of chance and not one I like playing. Especially when the odds are stacked against me.

So, no, stopping the sex-induced haze as a form of

escapism will do nothing but leave me with horny and anxious demons. With them occupied, I have been able to put my efforts in other places. And I think I've succeeded, if this morning was any indication.

My lips pull up into a smile, a deep laugh escaping from the back of my throat. Garvan's black eyes bore into me, a burning question on his tongue. My courtier isn't one to stay curious for long though.

"You seem pleased, my king. Is it because Ender is bringing the human here today?"

Ah, yes, that. The entire reason I'm not indulging in tonight's activities.

"Is that today?"

My question doesn't amuse Garvan, and he frowns. His black eyes flash, but not with anger. No, Garvan is smart enough to never show anger toward me in person. Behind my back though...well, he probably still doesn't.

No, there is something akin to fear in his expression, but I don't know why.

Still, I let him stew with his fear for a little while longer. I know quite well my betrothed is on her way to me. I sought out Ender after Malix called a meeting with all the kings in Mescos. I watched from my throne as their people suffered, fed off it, even, but then watched the human women take on the curse and end up victorious each time.

If I want to win—and I always want to win—I know my best chances are with a human mate. It's been months since I've reached out to Ender. So long, in fact, I assumed he forgot about me, until he reached out a week ago and promised to hand-deliver my bride.

Unlike the other kings, I don't plan on sitting around as my kingdom unfolds before me. I will not run away from the dangers but embrace them with open arms. Which is exactly what I'm doing.

And it has worked for me so far.

I got word this morning from a servant that my guards—or rather what remains of them—were successful on their endeavor. The task at hand was to track and locate a Nephilim, horrid and vile creatures set on claiming Mescos as their own. We've been tracking a group that branched off from the others, lurking too close to my border.

My guards tracked one down. But not to kill, no. A dead Nephilim is useless to me. Their instructions were clear. Bring the creature to me. *Alive.*

And now, if the information I was given is to be believed, and I have no reason to think otherwise, a Nephilim is imprisoned in the dungeon below the castle.

Which is a reason to smile.

As eager as I am to visit the cursed beast caged in my dungeon, Ender and my human bride will be here soon. I push myself off the uncomfortable throne, rolling my shoulders.

"Garvan, come with me." I make my way back across the room. More drinks and aphrodisiacs are passed from demon to demon, heightening an already frenzied sex party.

"Where are we going, sir?" Garvan follows behind me like a shadow, mimicking my path to the doors. A man reaches out, running a hand down my courtier's chest. Garvan tenses before pushing off his advance and quickening his step to stay close to me. It would be amusing if it wasn't so pathetic. Garvan's avoidance of touch is part of the reason he's so rigid. A good fuck would loosen him right up, but alas, he seems content with a life of celibacy.

"To meet Ender, of course. You're to be my wife's babysitter."

Garvan stops talking after that and follows me to the courtyard in silence.

CHAPTER 4
ISABELLE

The Guardian's backyard feels like an enchanted forest. Lush green grass softens my footfalls. Rose bushes with blood-red buds line the back of his cottage, creating a cozy atmosphere. Flowers in various shades of blues, pinks, and yellows line his flowerbeds. White trellises with tangled green vines sit behind the beds, acting as a fence for his property.

It's...cute.

But looking at the stone-colored man with horns, it feels out of place.

I keep pace with The Guardian and nearly run into his solid form from behind when he stops abruptly. "This portal is the only way for me to travel and transport you at the same time." His deep timbre sends shivers down my spine, demanding obedience.

The Guardian waves his hand in front of an archway covered in flowers. A white shimmer appears, soft at first before blinking into existence. Despite myself, I gasp. It's one thing knowing The Guardian is supernatural, and an entirely different thing seeing him *be* supernatural.

Better get used to it. This will be my new life.

"Come." With his command, I follow The Guardian through the shimmery veil. A deep chill overcomes my body, and I get a sense of floating. The world changes in rapid succession around me. It's disorienting and confusing. A smoky haze. But just as quickly as it comes, the world around me settles, even as my stomach churns, threatening to be sick.

"Are you well?" The Guardian's voice grounds me, giving me something to focus on other than the nauseated feeling in my belly.

"Never been better." My voice is laced with sarcasm. Either my companion doesn't hear it or ignores it, because he gestures for me to follow.

My eyes dart around my surroundings, taking in my new home. The night sky is painted in darkening shades of blue and purple. A moon sits high in the sky, casting a glow around us, making visibility possible, albeit barely.

The wind nips at my bare arms, making me wish I remembered to grab a coat. Though I doubt it would have fit in my backpack. The air is heavy with the earthy smell of rain tainted by something foul...sulfur, maybe.

We follow a dark brick path up a hill. It's too dark to see what awaits us when we reach the top. Black, twisted trees bent in grotesque shapes with bare branches resembling bony fingers line the path. Yellow and red eyes watch me in the darkness but don't approach. They lie in wait as if they've come here to see the spectacle of me meeting my husband. Fear prickles in the back of my mind, but I push it away. I doubt fear will serve me well here. It seems like the kind of place that feeds off it. Perhaps my husband does too.

Husband. Such a foul thought.

My breaths come in pants as we continue up the narrow, winding path. The demon king couldn't spring for a damn ride? Already, I'm annoyed with him. "How much longer?" I pant, struggling to keep up with The Guardian.

"Nearly there," he replies, not offering any more.

"Nearly there" was another fifteen minutes of hiking up this damn hill until lit torches replaced the trees, illuminating the castle ahead, surrounded by a moat of dark water.

The castle rises at the end of the path, its silhouette a jagged horror against the darkening sky. The outer walls are made of obsidian, with veins of fiery red running through them, like magma caught in stone. In a way, it reminds me of a volcano. Towers pierce the sky, twisted spires that bend in on themselves. The castle feels alive, like a creature more than a structure. The air around it hums with an unsettling energy.

The Guardian approaches the gate, and it opens automatically, revealing a courtyard. The ground is cobbled. The uneven stones are dark with age and slick with moisture from the shadows. Patches of moss sprout between the stones, soft and bright green against the gloom.

In the heart of the courtyard stands a large fountain. It's dry and cracked, nearly eroded, but I make out the grand pillar in the middle. It was probably once beautiful and spouted water but is now overrun with ivy and moss.

What is most unnerving and uninviting, though, are the statues. Not just a few, but many. I lose count after twenty. They range in size and shape but are all people. Some of them have horns while others have tails. Their expressions range from fear, to confusion, to anger. They aren't placed in any particular order, simply scattered about as if someone placed them hastily. Unlike the rest of the courtyard, they aren't covered in moss or vines. None of them have cracks or erosion, so they are a fairly new feature.

The statues' eyes seem to follow my every move, judging each step. I mentally shake myself for getting caught up in the gothic, gloomy feeling of the courtyard. Of course, the statues aren't watching me. They are simply stone.

"What is this place?" My voice echoes around me, disturbing the eerie quiet.

"Demon's Clan. I imagine it's quite different from what you are used to."

I try not to snort at The Guardian's comment. This is a far cry from the one-bedroom apartment I lived in for the last year. "This damn castle feels like I'm walking into Dracula's lair."

"Dracula is not real," he says unhelpfully. "But King Oziel is very real. He's also not a vampire; he's a—"

"Demon, yeah, you've mentioned that," I mumble. "Where is he? Does he know I'm coming?"

"I'm very aware my human bride is here," a deep voice says from behind us, startling me.

I whirl around in time to see two figures seemingly walking out of the shadows. "King Oziel," The Guardian says in greeting.

"Ender," the voice—rich and deep in pitch—says. I guess The Guardian has a name. Should have asked but didn't care enough to.

The shadows part for him, revealing the most terrifyingly beautiful man I have ever encountered. The demon king stands tall and regal, an imposing figure clad fully in black. Pants hug his muscular thighs, and despite myself, I can't help but let my eyes linger before roaming back up his body. Like Ender, this king has two sharp horns protruding from his head. They're black as if dipped in ink and set out to dry. A crown of thorns rests snugly atop his head.

"You must be my human," he purrs, churning something low in my belly. I don't like his possessive nature already. I belong to no one.

Before The Guardian—or rather, Ender—can properly introduce us, I stalk toward the demon king, simmering in my own anger. How presumptuous does one have to be to stake claim to a person as if I were nothing but a shiny new toy? After the last couple of days, my heightened emotions need an outlet.

The man doesn't back up when I approach him. In fact, he appears amused by my action. This close, I can make out every feature of his stupidly handsome face. It's chiseled to perfection—sharp cheekbones, a strong jawline, and full, dark lips that curl into a knowing, predatory smirk. His molten-gold eyes gleam with both intelligence and an undeniable primal hunger, as if they see every secret, every fear, every weakness, and every desire in the soul of anyone who dares meet them.

I decide I don't like him.

"I don't belong to you," I say through my teeth. "I'm here because this"—I gesture to his haunting kingdom—"is better than dying in prison." A decision I'm starting to regret. "I will be your wife in name only, and do what is absolutely necessary, but nothing more. Do you understand?"

The infuriating man ignores my question in favor of his own. "What's your name?"

"Isabelle."

"Isabelle what?"

I huff. "Isabelle Sinclair."

"Why, Miss Sinclair," his predatory smile grows, "I smell sin on you."

That...was not what I was expecting him to say. I don't even know what to make of that.

"Miss Sinclair has had a...challenging few days." Ender comes up behind me. "She will need a hot meal and sleep before she is ready to speak with you about the contract."

I don't particularly like Ender speaking for me as if I'm not here. But he speaks no lies. I'm hungry and need to sleep for twenty-four hours before I have to come to terms with my new home and...husband-to-be.

"Then Garvan will see her safely to her rooms," Oziel says.

The man who has been lingering next to Oziel silently takes a step forward. Unlike the king, this man is gangly—tall and skinny. His features are softer than

Oziel's, and his porcelain skin glows in the moonlight. He stands with poise but lacks the egotistical aura Oziel possesses.

Garvan dips his head in greeting, strands of blond hair falling into his eyes. "Pleasure to meet you, Miss Sinclair."

"It's Isabelle. Nice to meet you too." It's really not, but I'll play nice. I like him more than Oziel right now.

"Make sure Miss Sinclair receives a proper meal. It would be unfortunate if she were to…perish." On the last word, Oziel chuckles, making the hairs on the back of my neck stand on end.

What the hell did he mean by that?

Before I can ask, Ender is gently pushing me toward Garvan. Clearly, his job is complete, and he's eager to leave this place. Lucky bastard.

"Please follow me, Miss Sinclair," Garvan says before walking toward the castle. Unlike Ender, I don't need to jog to keep stride with him.

The last thing I hear before we disappear into the castle is Oziel saying, "Ender, do you have a moment?"

I don't hear The Guardian's answer before I walk through the castle's front doors, and they close with an ominous finality behind me.

CHAPTER 5

OZIEL

Ender bristles at my question, then relaxes his body—as much as he's capable of doing—and nods.

"I won't take up much of your time. I'm certain you are eager to get home, as much as I'm eager to get to know my new wife."

My pretty little human.

Hair the color of shadows and lips the shade of fresh blood. Her skin pale like the moon. A wicked tongue that slices me with her words. She's intriguing and will be fun to torment, but my concern at this time isn't with Isabelle. It's with the creature in front of me.

Ender, or more appropriately, his title, The Guardian, is an enigma to me. As far as I know, he's the only one of his kind and the only person who can pass through the human world into ours. Yet, he never stays in Mescos for long, opting to live in solitude in the human world. He's an ancient creature; power settles dormant over him. We don't know if there were more of him, but most assume there was. The real question is what happened to them, and why is Ender the only one left?

I have questions. Many questions.

"We are in the midst of a war, Ender."

The Guardian nods slowly, showing no emotion. I've seen little from this man and taste nothing but emptiness wafting off him. Demons have a keen awareness of emotions. We feed off them. Use them to our advantage to always have the upper hand. But Ender is giving me nothing. It's as if he's locked his emotions away and sealed them shut.

Curious.

"I have faith the kings of Mescos will prosper against Gadreel and his army," Ender says in a way that's far too casual for talks of wars.

"As long as you continue to bring us our wives," I say.

"Yes, of course."

"Why?"

Something akin to confusion flickers in Ender's smoky eyes. His head tilts slightly, eyes roaming over me. "Why what?"

"Don't play dumb, Ender. We both know you are the furthest thing from it."

Ender balls his hands into fists and then slowly unfurls them. "You will not win this war if you do not have the love of your human. The Great War is proof of that."

"Then help us. You seem to know a lot about a war you have no stakes in. Of course, perhaps you have the most to lose..." I trail off, waiting for his reaction.

A tightening jaw and clenched hands are his only

response. This man is good. Too good. Which means the secret—because there has to be one he's hiding—is big. Life-altering even.

"Are we done here? I must be—"

"We caught a Nephilim," I interrupt him.

Finally, I get a reaction from him. He freezes, mouth slightly agape. He's quick to school his features back to his normal stoic expression, but not before I catch the change. "Have you?"

"Mhm," I hum. "Come with me to visit our captive."

I don't give Ender the opportunity to say no, but he's more than capable of leaving if he chooses to. I can't stop him, but I'm nothing if not a gambling man. I turn my back on Ender and make my way to the castle. The soft crunch of his footfalls behind me says his curiosity won.

We walk in silence through my front entrance. A few of my demons linger in the shadows, their attention focused on the horned stranger at my flank. Ender was a warning whispered in the shadows. A rumor mill with never-ending stories. Now he is flesh and bones. Real. It's easy to see the merit in those stories now.

We reach a curved red door at the end of a dark hall, the only splash of color in an otherwise black palette. I wave my hand, and it clicks twice before opening. Immediately, we're hit with the scent of sulfur and decay. I've smelled it thousands of times, but it never gets pleasant. The prison carries the tang of iron too, from centuries of spilled blood coating the floor.

"This way," I direct and start down the spiral staircase. There are no sconces lighting our way, which is intentional. The prison was designed to confuse the prisoners and play with their senses. It's impossible to navigate unless you know every single inch of this prison like I do.

It takes ten minutes to reach the bottom, far beneath the castle. The prison is a cavernous, sprawling expanse carved deep below the earth, its jagged, uneven walls glistening with a slick sheen of moisture. Torches flicker with an unnatural flame as I pass, casting eerie, shifting shadows. Chains dangle from the ceiling, their metal gleaming faintly in the dim light. The temperature shifts from uncomfortably hot to painfully freezing, never allowing a body to get used to the extremes. Howls and screams from the imprisoned echo off the walls, creating a sinister melody of the damned.

I absolutely love it.

The prison is made up of multiple levels, all dealing different intensities of torture. Other kingdoms send their criminals here when they no longer want to deal with them or when they no longer have the capacity to punish them properly. We take in their prisoners eagerly, feeding on their hatred and fear. It's a game for us. A spectacle.

But I digress into my own thoughts. We've come down for one purpose and one purpose only. The Nephilim. Five guards stand in front of a cage with bars crafted from bones and steel. It's too dark to see inside the cell, but when I clap my hands, fire growls to life around the cell. Violent blue flames dance in the air, licking at the bars of captivity.

At first, the cell looks empty except for a pile of charred remains in the center. I don't remember a burning taking place, but it's not uncommon for my demons to take torture too far. Death happens. It's a mercy, really. They are no longer suffering at our hands, but if these charred remains are the Nephilim I told to keep alive, these men will all die for defying my orders.

Luckily for them, the thing on the floor moves, elongating on the stone floor. What may have once been wings stretch out behind the creature. Black feathers sparsely decorate the appendages, giving hints at what once was. The creature is probably very tall, but the cage only stands at a height of six feet. Even sitting, the creature crouches, blood-red eyes boring into me.

A low hiss leaves the creature's dry lips, followed by a growl that could only be described as frustrated. Possibly pained, or a mixture of the two.

"It has been a long time," Ender says from behind me. His voice is wistful, far away as if thinking of a different time. Oh, to be able to slip into his mind. Even for a second...

"How did you capture it?" I take my eyes off Ender long enough to speak to the demon guard with red skin and emerald-green eyes. Brunoth, I believe.

Brunoth takes a step forward. "The creature was alone, straying away from the others. We did as you instructed, attacked as a group until the Nephilim fell. We drugged it to keep it unconscious until we got it here. It's still drugged, but only enough to keep it docile."

"So, the mighty do fall," I comment. "Has it said anything to you?"

Brunoth nods. "Screamed a lot. But we haven't been able to talk to it."

"And you will not be able to." Both our heads turn to the voice. Ender doesn't meet our stares, continuing to look upon the captured beast. "Only Gadreel can communicate with you. This is just a soldier. They don't communicate in the same way."

"Ah, wonderful. We trapped the Nephilim for nothing." I roll my eyes.

"I didn't say that." Again, his cryptic voice booms around us, drowning out the cries of the others. "I said *you* couldn't communicate with them."

The Guardian speaks in riddles, but there's always truth hiding in his words. I mull them over, tasting them on my tongue. Slowly, I say, "I cannot communicate with them." Ender nods. "But someone else can."

This time, Ender doesn't speak.

Damn him.

"Ender—"

"I must go," The Guardian says, stepping away from the fire. Perhaps it's the lighting, but Ender looks paler than usual. His ashy gray skin is nearly white, and he lacks all decorum as he stumbles back. "Remember your contract with Miss Sinclair. I expect you to uphold it."

I'm a demon. We deal in contracts and bargains. I'm fully aware of what I agreed to.

I don't get the chance to say so because Ender has opened a portal. Magic and something darker hum from the other side. I yearn for the power to open portals to the human world like all kings of Mescos once before. Gadreel and the Nephilim took that away from us.

I watch Ender disappear, the other side engulfing his body until he's nothing but a memory, emptiness where he once stood. Despite his abrupt departure, I got more than I hoped for during this short visit. His words replay in my mind over and over again.

I said you couldn't communicate with them.

Perhaps I can't, but I have a theory of who might.

CHAPTER 6

ISABELLE

Meeting my future demon husband went... fine, I guess. That is definitely not a sentence I ever thought I would say, but here we are. Yet, as I walked away from the demon and Ender, I couldn't help but feel...let down? That's not quite the right word. Maybe underwhelmed.

I just left my perfectly normal world in favor of a supernatural world where demons and who knows what else roams free. Anyone would be feeling a sense of disbelief and tremendous fear. A normal reaction to being a non-powerful human in a world full of powerful creatures.

Except all I feel is numb.

Numb and so very tired.

"Miss Sinclair—"

"Please, if you want to protect your peace and mine, you'll call me Isabelle." I do my best to suppress my mounting frustration due to the headache pounding in my skull. The migraine is coming on with a vengeance, and even the soft footfalls of my companion grate on my nerves.

"Isabelle," Garvan corrects. "Would you care for a tour of the castle?"

"I imagine it's more black furnishings and demons walking around, yeah?" I peer at him through my peripheral vision. I haven't seen any other demons yet, but I'm certain they're here. Somewhere.

Garvan chuckles, his hair bouncing with his movements. He reminds me of a professor, slightly nerdy and kind. Can demons even be kind? I suspect I'll figure that out soon enough.

"Perhaps another time," he says, not deterred by my less than enthusiastic response. "I'll take you to your rooms then."

We walk in silence down the hallway of the massive estate. Garvan's blond hair is a beacon in an otherwise dark space. Light doesn't belong here, and my eyes desperately try to adjust to the darkness. The dark is good for my migraine, but not so good for my sight.

Garvan stops abruptly, and I crash into his back, knocking the air from my lungs. "Fuck." I catch my balance before I fall on my ass.

"Are you okay?" Garvan asks, amusement lacing his words. I think the bastard is laughing at me. I take back my kindness comment from earlier.

"Just peachy, Gar, just peachy," I mumble, pretending I don't hear him laugh as he opens the door to my new room. I'm hit with the smell of burning incense, a mixture of vanilla and wild berries. Garvan steps aside, not passing the threshold into my room, but allowing me to walk past him.

The room is lit by an enormous wrought-iron chandelier, its flickering candles casting eerie shadows that dance across stone walls. A deep crimson canopy bed dominates the chamber. The tall posts are carved with twisting, skeletal forms, and the canopy's velvet drapes pooling onto the black marble floor look like spilled blood. The bed is layered with dark silks and furs, providing a stark contrast to the cold, hard surfaces of the room.

It's...a lot.

But there's more to it. A fire burns in a massive fireplace, heating the room to a near uncomfortable level. The only reprieve comes from the gust of cool air filtering in through an arched window shrouded in heavy black curtains.

"The washroom is just down the hall, and your wardrobe will be delivered later this evening," Garvan says from his perch by the door. "I will have a hot meal sent up and inform King Oziel that you are getting settled in."

"I'm sure the king is very worried about my well-being."

Not catching on to my sarcasm, Garvan nods. "He is. Your presence here is important to us all."

"And what exactly is my presence doing? Why does your all-mighty demon king need a human wife?" I whirl around to face Garvan, crossing my arms over my chest.

To his credit, Garvan doesn't look down at my boobs that I inadvertently pushed up. "I'm afraid that is not my place to tell you. King Oziel will need to be the one to have that discussion with you."

I figured as much, but I had to test the waters. "Fine," I sigh. "Then I want to be left alone. I haven't slept in..." God, I don't even remember. How long ago did I kill James? Two...three days ago? And leading up to his death, I slept like shit, my mind working in overdrive and not allowing me a moment of peace.

"Of course, I'll let you rest." Garvan reaches for the door to pull it shut.

"Is there a lock on the door?" I ask, strolling over to him.

"Yes, but—"

"Perfect, thank you." I cut him off and close the door in his face. I don't have the energy to feel bad about it as I lock the heavy door. There's no way anyone is getting in, at least not without waking me up.

The moment I'm alone, everything I have been running from finally catches up with me. Fear. Anger. Hurt. All the emotions hit me at once, like a heavy load placed upon my shoulders, threatening to pull me under. I let my backpack fall to the ground, relieving my shoulders of some tension.

I left in such a hurry and was so distracted, I didn't pack any clothes to sleep in. So, instead, I undo my jeans and let them pool around my feet before stepping out and kicking them in a pile by the wall. I quickly add my bra to the pile and climb into bed in nothing but my shirt and underwear.

The blankets are soft against my skin, feeling like heaven after being forced to stay in a cold, hard cell. The heat doesn't even bother me as I slip under the mound of blankets into the softest damn mattress I've ever been on. Marrying a demon is worth it if I get this mattress.

The second my head hits the silk pillow, sleep claims me.

That's when the dreams begin.

Rain pelts down on the sidewalk. Leaves from the large oak blow away in the wind, littering the ground. It's late, close to midnight, and yet I can't sleep. My body needs to move, which is why I'm outside in the rain. I don't feel it, though.

The rain, that is.

It's oddly quiet for a storm. No thunder and even the falling rain sounds faint. Like I'm behind a window, watching from the inside.

I have no destination in mind, letting my body tell me where it wants to go. I think I'm searching for something, but I don't know what it is exactly. I haven't lost anything…

My body hits a brick wall, and I go flying back, landing on the sidewalk unceremoniously. The soft tap of boots heads toward me, and I jerk my head up.

I didn't hit a brick wall. I hit…

Brown boots with what looks like dirt on them. My eyes trail up to an old pair of jeans that have been washed one too many times but still hold the stains from their journey. The person wears a plain t-shirt with a dark stain over the chest. Dirt? No…not dirt, something else. Blood?

My eyes widen as I reach the face of this mysterious person. Staring back at me are soulless black eyes and a bloody smile. James laughs, taking a step closer. I desperately search for a weapon, but suddenly the world around me fades to nothing but James and me.

"You killed me." The words come out of James's mouth, but it doesn't sound like James. It sounds like multiple people speaking at once.

I open my mouth to reply, but it's dry, and no words come out. I remind myself I don't regret killing him, because I don't. He needed to die. But I do regret killing him too late. I should have done something before he took my sister.

James laughs again, and then in a speed I can't follow, he pounces on me. Large, rough hands wrap around my neck, cutting off my oxygen. I fight, trying to claw his eyes with my nails. Trying to kick him off. But nothing is working.

And the world is getting darker.

Smaller.

And then...

I shoot up in bed, gripping my neck. My breathing comes out in labored pants as if I just ran a mile in the sun rather than wake up from a bad dream. And that is all it was. A dream.

"Interesting," a masculine voice says from next to me.

I scream and grab the closest weapon I can find, which happens to be a candleholder. I fling it in the direction of the voice, but it misses his body by a few inches, shattering against the wall.

Oziel lurks in the shadows of the bedroom. He looks so natural in the dark, as if he was born from it and commands it. He could, for all I know. My body betrays me as something coils low in my belly. Oziel looks just as good as he did earlier, donning the same black attire.

New silver rings adorn his horns, and I'm tempted to reach out and touch them. I won't though.

"How the hell did you get in here?" I demand, forcing myself to stop ogling him. "I locked the door." I remember specifically turning the latch and making sure it was locked once Garvan left.

"You think a lock will stop me from getting to you?"

His words should not send heat straight to my core. They should piss me off—which they do—but something else stirs within me. Something I don't allow myself to dwell on for too long.

Oziel pushes off the wall and stalks closer. I reach for the blankets and pull them tighter around me, wishing I had more clothes. Not that I'm indecent, but the way Oziel scans my body makes me feel completely exposed to him.

"You need to eat."

"I'm not hungry." Which is a lie. My stomach outs me a moment later, deciding it's the perfect time to growl.

The corners of Oziel's lips twitch up. "You also need to get dressed. I have clothes coming—"

"I don't want your clothes," I snap. "I have my own."

"You mean in that little backpack of yours? I burned it."

"You what?!" I jump out of bed, modesty be damned. I round on him, not stopping until we are chest to chest. Oziel's gaze goes down to my bare legs before meeting my eyes again.

"You had no fucking right," I growl. "Those were my things. Mine!" It wasn't much, just a few clothes and toiletries, but that's not the point. He went through my shit, deemed it junk, and burned it. How dare he take away what little I have. Those were my last connections to Grym Hollow and the family I left behind.

I want to kill him. I've done it before. I sure as hell can do it again. Contracts be damned.

"And now you'll have new clothes. Better suited for a future demon queen," he hums, disregarding me as if I were nothing but an annoying pest in his way.

"I won't wear them."

He laughs, and it lacks all humor. "Are you going to fight me on everything, Miss Sinclair?"

Just like my dream, my mouth goes dry. Only this time, I find a word. "Yes."

Oziel's lips curve up, flashing his white teeth. His eyes shine with mirth, amplifying his predatory nature. "Good." His voice is low, reverberating through the chamber like the growl of an approaching storm.

Oziel steps back, and I gasp softly, not realizing how much his closeness affected me. He turns his back to me, starting for the door. "You will wear the clothes I have selected for you," he says over his shoulder in a tone that leaves no room for negotiation. "Or you will wear nothing at all. Either way, I'll be back in half an hour to fetch you. You have until then to make up your mind."

My heart races, caught between fear and something akin to arousal. Which makes no fucking sense, because I'm fully prepared to murder my husband. Not fuck him.

Oziel walks out of my room without another glance back. The door closes on its own behind him with a resounding thud, leaving me to make a choice.

Which really isn't a choice at all.

CHAPTER 7
ISABELLE

ooking at myself in the mirror, I have never missed my ripped jeans and old, stained shirt more. Oziel's idea of everyday wear leaves much to be desired. The dress was difficult to figure out, and on more than one occasion, I seriously contemplated just leaving naked. Surely that would be easier than stuffing myself into this contraption he set out for me. Granted, I did kick out the maid who brought up the dress for me to put on. She offered to help me get dressed, and I refused. I regret that decision now.

The dress is mostly black, of course. I've yet to see much of any other color besides red, and I'm starting to wonder if color personally offends the demon king. The bodice is form-fitting and adorned with intricate embroidery resembling swirling flames and shadows, stitched in fine silver thread. The neckline sweeps into a heart shape with delicate black lace, teasing the tops of my breasts.

The skirt cascades from the waist in dramatic layers

of velvet and chiffon, each layer edged with glimmering thread. The shoes, at least, are the most sensible part of this ensemble. Plain black heels with enough cushion to help me forget I'm wearing heels in the first place. I opted not to wear the red choker Oziel placed with the dress, my only small act of defiance. I would feel too much like a leashed animal.

"Is this to your liking?" I sneer when he returns exactly thirty minutes later, as he said he would.

Oziel's golden eyes scan every inch of my body, lingering on my chest. I swear his eyes darken, and his pink tongue licks his bottom lip. Thoughts of other things I could put his tongue to good use for plague my mind before I can stop them. The crude image forming has me squeezing my legs together, and I curse my lustful thoughts.

The fantasy shatters when Oziel opens his mouth and reminds me why I can't stand men. Demon men are no exception.

"You look satisfactory. Follow me." He turns on his heels, black coat tails flapping behind him, and storms out of my room as if he didn't just insult me.

Satisfactory? *Satisfactory?*

Satisfactory, my ass. I didn't just spend the last thirty minutes battling layers of fabric to be seen as *satisfactory*. I'm fucking hot, even if I look like an extra member of the Addams Family. Not that I care if my future husband-to-be finds me attractive… I don't care.

I don't care at all.

Mostly.

"You're a real asshole, you know that?" I'm certain he does, but I need to remind him.

"I've been called worse," he says over his shoulder.

Not wanting to be left behind, I reluctantly follow Oziel down the hall. The lack of windows makes it hard to decipher what time of day it is. It's disorienting living in shadows, especially when the shadows feel alive. Invisible eyes feel as if they are boring into my skin, quickening my heartbeat. Blood rushes to my neck and cheeks as I fight to keep my fear at bay.

Despite the pounding of my heart, the castle is eerily quiet and desolate. I know nothing about keeping an estate of this nature running, but it feels as if there should be more people walking around. Cleaning. Catering. Discussing. Unless Oziel has commanded everyone to stay away. Seems like something he'd do—isolate me so I have no choice but to talk to him.

There's nothing save for an occasional demon adorned in crimson armor, standing as still as statues. Some stand taller when Oziel walks by, but all take the time to study me. There's nothing friendly in their gazes either. It's hard not to feel like a sheep in a hungry lion's den. I wonder if they knew of my arrival? If they didn't, they certainly do now. I stand out like a proverbial sore thumb.

I hurry my steps, falling in line right next to Oziel. A twitch of his lips is the only indication he senses my discomfort. "You won't be harmed here."

I scoff. "Yeah, okay." I don't trust him.

Oziel's brow twitches up as he tilts his head to study me. "Do you take me for a liar, Miss Sinclair?"

"How can I take you for anything if I don't know you? And from my experience, you can be harmed anywhere by anyone. Even by people you should be safe with."

Oziel doesn't reply immediately. The pregnant pause ticks by agonizingly slowly as I dare a glance over at him. His lips are pursed together, jaw slack. His demeanor feels...heavier. Like he's consumed by his own thoughts.

Just as I write him off, thinking he won't respond, Oziel says, "I suppose you would know how to handle yourself pretty well."

It's my turn to hold my tongue. Oziel doesn't know my reason for signing the contract, according to Ender, so he would have no way of knowing just how accurate his statement is. I'm not afraid Oziel will scorn me for what I did.

I fear he'd enjoy it too much.

We walk the rest of the way in silence. I recognize the place he takes me to immediately. The courtyard where we met, the one filled with strange-looking statues. Perhaps it's my mind playing tricks on me, but there appears to be more than before. Two new statues surround the forgotten fountain. Both wear a similar expression of pain and confusion.

"You really like your statues," I murmur, reaching out to touch one. My fingertips glide over the cold stone, enthralled by how lifelike it is. When my fingers trail over the statue's chest, something pulses, sending shockwaves into my hand. I gasp at the unexpected sensation and pull away.

"You felt it, didn't you?" Oziel's voice comes from

behind me, hot breath singeing my neck. I shiver, though there's no chill in the air.

"What was that?" I move away from the statue as if it burned me. My back hits a solid chest of well-defined muscles. An impenetrable force. Oziel.

"The curse." Oziel makes no move to pull back. Instead, I feel gentle fingers against my hips. Gentle and Oziel don't seem to go together, but his featherlight touch scorches my skin.

"C...curse?" My voice comes out far too breathy, and Oziel takes notice because a deep laugh reverberates in his chest, churning something low in my belly.

"You know nothing of why you are here, Miss Sinclair, do you?"

My face flushes. "I'm here to help you win a war." Even as I say it, the words don't hold the conviction I want them to.

"A war you know nothing about." His tone is that of scolding a child.

My face heats in embarrassment. I pride myself on being knowledgeable, understanding every angle of a situation. When I went to Ender, my mind was occupied with a murder plot. Still, perhaps I should have paid better attention to the finer details. What use am I if I'm ignorant to the problem?

Ender also wasn't forthcoming with information, so he's partially to blame.

"Demons like torture, Miss Sinclair." Oziel pulls away from me. I immediately feel the absence of his warmth. "We've perfected the art of torture. So good, in fact, other kingdoms send us their vilest creatures for us to play with. And you know what makes our power against them even stronger?"

I shake my head.

"Possessions. Any possession of any value to the poor soul we are torturing. We can easily get the job done without any item belonging to them, but it's so much more fun when we have it. You should thank me for burning your things. Best not to tempt fate."

I ignore the last comment, still planning his murder for what he did to my possessions. "Why are you telling me this?"

Oziel's head snaps up at my question, once-golden eyes now black. "Because you must know." Even though we are outside in the courtyard, his approach feels like the world is crashing down around me, and I'm rooted to the spot. He stands a foot taller than me, and I have to tip my head back to see him.

"Six months ago, I received a strange item at my doorstep. A vase full of roses. A vase that once sat atop my dining room table. Curious as to why it was there, I picked it up and brought it inside. I felt an odd, albeit weak, power emit from the flowers. At first, nothing happened, so I lost interest. Admittedly, I forgot about the entire thing."

"But?" I hear myself asking.

"But." Oziel hums, bringing his hand up to my chin, tipping it up even more. "Then the first petal fell. The server bringing my dinner turned to stone right before my eyes. And then it happened again. Another petal fell—"

"And another turned to stone," I finish for him, looking up at the statue near us.

"Clever girl." Oziel drops his hand from my chin but doesn't move away. "They *were* once alive, and now... they're trapped in stone. When you touched the stone, you felt the pulse of their heart, didn't you? That's how I know my demons are still alive, trapped in a stone prison. I couldn't imagine a worse fate. To be frozen but able to see and feel the world around you. These deadly roses are a reminder of the curse they cast upon our kingdom."

"Who are they?"

Oziel's handsome face contorts into something hideous and nightmarish. Cold fear works its way through my body, reminding me I'm no longer among humans. No, this man before me is a demon, the king of demons at that, and he's showing me just how powerful he can be.

"Are you afraid, Miss Sinclair?" His voice is low and gravelly, more monstrous than before.

"No." My voice wavers, giving me away.

A wicked smile spreads across his lips, showing off his white teeth and two prominent fangs. "Then allow me to show you something even more nightmarish than me. Then you'll understand."

CHAPTER 8
ISABELLE

Every movie and book I've ever consumed has taught me not to go with a demon down a dark passageway leading to a basement. Technically, this "basement" is a dungeon, so I'm not positive the same rules apply. They feel like they should, though.

Except I'm going to be the woman everyone screams at not to go down. Because the moment we walk back into the castle and down the hall, Oziel opens the intimidating red door, reminding me of the elusive and scary door from a supernatural horror film I watched years ago. I have no choice but to follow behind him.

My curiosity has always gotten the best of me. Even now, when I'm about to face a beast scarier than the demon king. Oziel is an imposing force. His strength and power radiate off him in waves, nearly suffocating me with his energy. I have not yet seen his cruelty firsthand, but I believe he is capable of horrific and heinous things. His eyes carry the weight of his sins. They're striking and alluring but also hold unspeakable evils.

"Take my hand, Miss Sinclair." It's not a request. Oziel grabs for my hand, and I'm tempted to pull it away from him, but his grip on me is ironclad.

I quickly become thankful for his presence as we descend the stairs. Maybe it's because I can't see, but it feels like we move in different directions, and at times, it feels like there's nothing underneath my feet at all. That's when I grip his hand tighter. Surely, he wouldn't bring me here to kill me. He needs me.

Fuck, I'm not so certain about that anymore.

The air around us heats up, and sweat gathers at my brow. Low hisses and moans of agony drift around me, sounding both far away and right behind me. An acrid odor reaches my noise, and I cough, trying to block the smell out with my arm. It only gets stronger the farther we walk.

A soft glow of fire soon illuminates the path as we walk and the floor levels out. The cries and screams are louder down here but still masked fairly well. We're standing in a large, open cavernous area with torches on the wall, illuminating it the moment we step inside. A few guards are stationed outside a particular cell, and a familiar face greets us.

"My king." Garvan raises a brow, the only indication that he's surprised Oziel is here. Garvan glances at me and bows his head in silent greeting. He offers me a soft smile before turning back to his king. "Is something amiss?"

"What reason do you have to be here, Garvan?" Oziel ignores the other demon's question in favor of his own.

"It appears we had another casualty to the curse. I was notified ten minutes ago." Garvan steps aside.

I hadn't noticed the statue behind him, mistaking it for part of the prison. But now I can see the obvious features. Horns, smaller in size than both Oziel and Garvan's, with a pinched expression on his face. He had been reaching for the blade at his hip but didn't quite make it before he turned to stone.

Oziel clenches his jaw, eyes blazing with silent hatred. Hatred for what, though, I can't be certain. The curse or his inability to do anything about it. No, that privilege was set aside for me. I might be in way over my head here, but it's too late to do anything about it. *This is better than jail*, I remind myself.

But...is it really?

"Should I take him and place him with the others?" Garvan asks.

Oziel gives him a curt nod, but the demon king's attention is on me. "Step up to the cell," he says, voice low.

My body stiffens. "Why?"

But a loud shriek erupts around us. The sound is high-pitched and feels like needles piercing my eardrums. The demons in the room drop, hands going up to cover their ears. Even Oziel shrinks, gritting his teeth together. The sound is painful for me, but unbearable to the demons. They draw away from the gate, trying to put as much space between them as possible.

Someone shouts my name over the piercing sound, but I ignore it. Despite my better judgment, I step closer to the cage just like Oziel told me to do. Bright blue fire erupts around the cell, encasing the cage and providing enough light for me to see the monster that resides within.

My heart stops.

I scream.

Or I think I scream. The creature tilts its head, soulless sockets where its eyes should be staring back at me. The monster's mouth is twisted up in pain and anger. Darkness surrounds it. Its massively tall yet slender body is forced to crouch low so its head doesn't hit the ceiling.

The creature turns slightly, exposing its scarred, mangled back. What look like two black bones the size of logs jut out of its back, with extra flesh hanging off them. And...are those feathers? The mutilation on its back might have once been wings, but they are now a far cry from anything resembling that. Just shreds of what once was.

Sadness and pain radiate off the monster. Its screams get louder, but they change too. There's a desperate plea in them. A need for someone to understand. Almost as...

Almost as if it is trying to communicate.

As soon as the thought forms, I find myself reaching out. "What are you?" My question is barely above a whisper, not loud enough for anyone—or anything—to hear.

Anguish and detestation coat my tongue like a vile poison. Pain shoots up my spine to my head, feeling like my brain is on the verge of exploding. Then a feeling of something slithering wraps itself around me like a snake, holding me in place.

"*Nnnephilimmm.*"

The word takes up space in my mind. One I'm unfamiliar with in a voice that isn't my own. It's a deep sound, like multiple voices talking at once, hissing the word in my ear.

"*Nnnephilimmm.*"

Again. The same word. *Nephilim.* The word came up in the contract a few times, but I didn't know what it was. My attention was elsewhere, on James. I cared for nothing but his blood painting the road and the life leaving his eyes.

If I knew these were the creatures...

I still would have done it. I don't regret it. James deserved his ending. My only regret is that it wasn't my sister—or hell, even Erin—who pulled the trigger.

"What do you want?" I think I ask the question out loud, but it could have easily been in my mind. Regardless, the pain in my head increases as the creature's answer forms in my head.

"*Deathhh...to...allllll...for HIM.*"

If I didn't know better, I would think the Nephilim is laughing, using the fear and anguish around the room to feed some sick part of it. The same fear threatens to drown me where I stand. The world feels too much, too heavy. The poignant smell of death surrounds me, not just a few, but hundreds of bodies. Blood pools around my feet, soaking into my shoes.

"*Warrr...cominggg...*"

These thoughts of blood and bodies aren't my own. They feel like a memory of the past...but not mine. Clashes of swords strike against metal. There's something I should understand. Something more than what the Nephilim is saying. In the distance, there's someone perched upon the mountains, letting the chaos unfold before them.

In a trance, I move closer, needing to see who this mysterious person is. So familiar and yet different than anything I've ever seen before.

I don't get a chance to see, though, because in the next second, there are arms around my waist, pulling me back against a solid body.

I scream.

CHAPTER 9
OZIEL

The last remaining guard and Garvan drop to their knees the moment the Nephilim's piercing scream reverberates around the room. My body tenses, and I clench my jaw through the pain, forcing my hands to stay balled up at my sides. The demon king can't show weakness, not when my people are always watching and waiting to doubt my ability to lead.

Perhaps bringing Isabelle down here was a mistake.

Isabelle takes a step closer to the cage, just as I asked her to do. Another foolish mistake. The giant beast inside moves to the bars, as if an invisible string connects the two of them. At any moment, the imprisoned Nephilim could reach out and snatch the human, killing her instantly, along with my hopes of defeating our enemies.

I act without further prompting.

The Nephilim's high-pitched wailing becomes more unbearable the closer I get. I bite down on my tongue so hard, my mouth explodes with the taste of my own blood. My powers are waning fast.

Once I'm close enough, my arms snake around Isabelle's torso, bringing the woman back against me. She screams and fights me, a kitten clawing for freedom. If this were any other circumstances, I would call it fore-play. But as it is, I can't enjoy her lithe body moving against mine with pain lacerating my body.

I summon my strength, shadows engulfing us. The sensation of icy water washes over us, and the world around us becomes gloriously silent. That is, until my shadows deposit us in my dining room and Isabelle falls from my arms to the ground. She lands on her hands and knees, retching up the contents of her belly on my newly polished flooring.

Pity.

"What...the...fuck?" Isabelle hisses through panting breaths.

"You're welcome." Did they not teach humans manners in her world? And Mescos thinks demons were rude. I suppose Isabelle fits in perfectly.

"You're welcome?" Her shrill voice does little to ease my spiraling nerves.

Echoes of pain pulse through my body, and my ears still ring with the screams from the Nephilim and my betrothed. My power is all but depleted. I haven't felt my true power for months, ever since the arrival of the rose and curse.

"You had no right to pull me out of there. No fucking right, Oziel." Isabelle rounds on me. The brave—or possibly foolish—woman glares at me through dark, heavy lashes. If black cats were human women, Isabelle would be the leader of them.

"Next time, I'll let the big, bad Nephilim kill you, Kitten. Would you have preferred that?" A smirk tugs at my lips upon seeing her jaw drop, a mixture of shock and anger coloring her pretty face. Makes her even prettier. I so like it when she's angry.

"Kitten?" She spews the word with such detestation, I suddenly became a bigger fan of the nickname. "I'm not your fucking kitten. And why would you pull me away when the Nephilim was talking to me? I could—"

The rest of her words go unheeded as I focus on one part. "What did you say?" Perhaps I misunderstood her. There have never been reports of Nephilim speaking, except for their leader, Gadreel. And even he saves his words for certain occasions.

"I said it was speaking to me."

So, I heard correctly. For once, Ender presented me with vital information. Well, this certainly changes everything. "And what did it say to you? Tell me exactly what it said."

"You were there." She peers at me oddly. "Didn't you hear it?"

I do my best to stay calm, though my patience is delicately balancing on a thin precipice. "I heard screaming. Nothing more."

"Nothing?" she asks, her voice quieting. She studies me, trying to catch me in a lie. I'm many things, but I'm not a liar. Not when the truth is so much more desirable.

"Tell me what you heard, Kitten."

Isabelle shoots me a glare but otherwise ignores the

name. "Well, I didn't know what that thing was, so I asked it. Then I heard a voice in my head telling me it was a Nephilim."

"Correct, it is. Keep going."

"I asked it why it was here, and it said—" Before she gets the words out, the dining door creaks open, and in walks Garvan.

"My lord—"

"Hush, Garvan. I'm in the middle of something." My command makes Garvan pause, stopping short of where I stand with Isabelle. He makes no attempt to leave, but he nods, obeying my order. Slinking back against the wall, Garvan makes himself scarce but still stays close.

"Go on," I urge.

Isabelle's eyes drift over to Garvan before snapping back to meet my gaze. Her cheeks redden, as if she's flustered. "I wanted to know why it was hurting the demons, but I didn't get a clear answer. It said something about how it is bringing death for HIM...but I don't know who he is."

"Perhaps Gadreel."

"I don't know that name." She shakes her head.

"Gadreel is the leader of the Nephilim. They follow his orders," I answer distractedly, my mind racing with possible ways to move forward. It is clear we are at an advantage if the humans can speak to the Nephilim. Or is that power only reserved for Isabelle? There's only one way to test that theory.

"Garvan," I bark, and my courtier stands taller. "Send word to the kraken, wolf, and dragon kings. Request the presence of their wives."

I expect Garvan to bow and carry out my order, but the demon hesitates. "My lord, is this necessary? Perhaps we should put our efforts into finding out who or what is poisoning our river and how we can combat it. It's getting worse."

"Poisoning your river?" Isabelle questions, but I ignore her.

"I gave you an order; go see that it is done."

"But—" Garvan tries to argue, but my patience is worn. Dark shadows surround him, lashing out like invisible whips. He grimaces but finally bows. "I'll send word now."

I call back my shadows. "See that you do."

With another bow, Garvan hurries out of the room, the bitter taste of his poorly concealed anger lingering.

I want to look further into this theory, but for now, it is a waiting game. I clap my hands together, the thunderous sound echoing into the room, causing Isabelle to jump. "Join me for dinner."

"What? Don't you want to figure out what the Nephilim was saying?" she asks incredulously.

I want nothing more than to question the Nephilim further, but I first must know if Isabelle is alone with this ability, and until then, I'm unwilling to risk her. She's too valuable to me to use her as a reckless pawn. Of course, I say none of this and simply gesture for a seat. "Sit. Food will be brought out."

"N...no," she stammers, looking at me as if I asked her to do flips for my entertainment. She must think me unhinged. It isn't a completely inaccurate assumption.

"No?" I raise my brow. "You wound my ego."

She gives a very unladylike snort. "Yeah, fuck that. I doubt I've even put a dent in it. I'm not going to sit here and stroke your ego, Oziel."

"Then perhaps you'd like to stroke something else?"

This time, the red in her cheeks isn't entirely from embarrassment. There's heat there too, if her scent is anything to go by. I'm learning quickly that humans are easy to rile up. A fun game, indeed.

"I'm not fucking eating with you, Oziel. If you don't want to figure out what the Nephilim is saying, I want to go back to my room. *Alone*."

"Fine, if you insist on being a prisoner in the castle, then that's what you shall be." I silently summon a servant, a weak demon, to escort Isabelle back to her room.

The demon woman appears behind Isabelle and takes her arm. She struggles against her, but even a weak demon is stronger than a human. "Take Miss Sinclair to her chambers. Make sure a meal is brought to her. Oh, and don't let her leave until she agrees to sit civilly and have dinner with me."

"Yes, my lord," the woman purrs, her split tongue giving her a snake effect.

"Oziel!" Isabelle shouts, struggling unsuccessfully against the small demon. "Gods, you're such a dick."

Her words ring out, even long after she's gone. I'm left with her sweet and woody cinnamon smell. I sink into the closest chair with a sigh and find myself quite ravenous. As I eat, I find the food does little to soothe my appetite, as my mind wanders to a certain raven-haired human.

CHAPTER 10

OZIEL

Eating dinner alone is no different from any other night, but there's a heaviness in my chest that gives me pause. Feelings and emotions, other than lust and hatred, don't come naturally to demons. Not to say we don't feel other things; it simply is a rarity for our kind.

And Isabelle has me *feeling*.

What, I'm not entirely sure. She's a strange human. Full of anger and reeking of sin. It's potent and consuming, intoxicating for a demon. I've heard stories of the allure of humans, but experiencing it is another thing entirely. A sip of forbidden wine. Isabelle Sinclair is exactly that.

The remnants of my food have gone cold, and I push it aside. My appetite has soured, and I find myself no longer wanting to occupy an empty table. I leave, shadows engulfing the dining room when I walk out.

As I make my way down the hall, I pass the demon

who escorted Isabelle away. "She's in her room. Shall I stand guard?"

"No." Giving her free range of the castle will be interesting. I doubt she'll listen to my prisoner comment from earlier. Isabelle is the furthest thing from a prisoner here. And besides, I have eyes and ears everywhere. There isn't a place she could go I wouldn't know. This castle is an extension of me. I will always be able to find her. Best let her think she has free will.

The demon nods and continues on her way. I pass by Isabelle's door, hearing her move around inside. My room is next door, connected to hers—a small fact I kept to myself, knowing Isabelle wouldn't appreciate the proximity. It's much easier to keep an eye on the human if she's close to me.

My room is untouched when I walk in. No other demon is allowed in here without my permission. That privilege is given to few. It's my only sanctuary within the palace, and even that has become tainted since the arrival of the Nephilim and the curse the creatures bring with them.

The room is massive, with a vaulted ceiling that disappears into shadow, giving an impression of endless height and the dark night sky. Gothic arches and carved stone columns frame the room, and wall sconces are placed strategically to provide a soft glow. I don't like bright lights. Both the bed and furniture are carved from blackened wood and adorned with sharp, angular designs. And sitting atop a small desk in a glass dome is a bouquet of crimson roses.

At first glance, nothing appears amiss. The roses are

vibrant, seemingly glowing within. Each petal is smooth and slightly curled at the end. The stems all have sharp thorns ready to draw blood. To an unsuspecting person, this is simply a beautiful arrangement. No one would even pick up on the sinister nature of it.

My story to Isabelle earlier about demons needing possession of their victims to dole out the most pain is true. Objects belonging to people hold memories. The more significant, the stronger the memories are.

Roses are the only significant items to me.

The Nephilim's message was aimed toward me. A cruel reminder of my failures and the failures yet to come. Each time a demon succumbs to the curse, the roses lose a petal. I fear the day only stems remain. What becomes of my kingdom then?

My mind is occupied with thoughts of my kingdom's impending doom when there is a knock at my door. My shadows see Garvan outside, standing tall with his hands folded in front of him like the perfect lap dog he is. I have half a mind to turn him away because I'm not in the mood for company. But Garvan doesn't stop by for social visits.

"Come in," I call and take a seat upon my cushioned chair. The only seat, other than the bed, in the room.

Garvan enters. His eyes sweep the room, then linger on the glowing roses before meeting my gaze. He gives a formal bow, hair flopping down around his ears. "Word has been sent out to the dragon, wolf, and kraken kings. We await an audience, though I don't believe we will get all the kings here."

"No matter. We only need one and his wife."

"Yes, speaking of wives"—Garvan pointedly looks at the wall separating my room from Isabelle's—"shouldn't you be spending time getting to know yours?"

"Ah, dear Garvan, have you not heard the expression 'absence makes the heart grow fonder'?"

Garvan frowns, clearly not impressed with my sayings. Pity. I like them enough for the both of us.

"I'm not sure that applies when the other person hardly knows you." Garvan steps closer, though he keeps a good distance between him and the glass dome of roses. "She's here to fix that."

"So, you change your tune now?" I raise a brow. When I first brought up the idea of taking a human wife, Garvan was vehemently against it. He said it would make me look like an inept king. Demons were already questioning my role as king because of the curse, and this would cause coups. Fear is a disease and, once caught, breeds insubordination.

But then the reality of our situation came to light. A human mate is needed to win this war. The three kings who found their mates before me are proof of that. I'm a proud demon, but not so proud to deny outside help if it means life or death. Even Garvan could no longer deny I should take a human mate. He was pivotal in helping me speak with Ender.

"This is our only chance." Garvan's cheeks flush at the reminder of his opposition. "You must get the girl to help us."

"Very astute advice," I mock, rolling my eyes. Does he think I'm so dense, I don't know the whole reason she is here? "And how do you propose I do that? What demon should I ask to help me with romancing the human?"

"It's not impossible. Your parents—"

"Are dead," I growl. "They have no relevance in this."

Garvan nods, carefully choosing his next words. "I simply mean it's not impossible to learn to love another."

In fact, it is very unlikely and extremely rare for love matches. Demons aren't—or rather, shouldn't—be capable of love. Obsession and infatuation, definitely. But love? If fear is a disease, then love is a plague. At least fear brings action. Love only results in death. No, I think I'd rather not fall in love with an emotional human.

However, I can't simply ignore her. Isabelle's presence demands attention, and that much I can do. We don't have to love each other, but we could be a team. A strong one if we play our cards correctly. The power a human has in Mescos, according to all ancient texts I've ever come across, is unlimited. As long as they are able to unlock it.

For a demon, Garvan has a bleeding heart. It has always pissed me off, but perhaps today it will be to my benefit. "What do you suggest I do?"

Garvan gets a look on his face that immediately has me regretting my words. Despite there being no available seats, Garvan happily perches himself atop the bedside table, scooting the book sitting on top to my bed. "My lord, I hope you have all night. I have many suggestions."

I will listen to my courtier. Let him speak.

And then I will do the opposite of his suggestions.

With a satisfied smile, I sink back into my chair and

settle in for the rest of the night to listen to Garven drone on and on about the process of courting.

CHAPTER II
ISABELLE

I didn't sleep well last night. Every time I close my eyes, I see the horrid creature. The Nephilim reaches for me and mocks my fear. Even in my dream, I felt the unbridled hatred the creature possesses. Not just for me, but seemingly for the world around it. Its long, bony fingers reached out to grip my shirt and then...

I wake up drenched in my own sweat. These dreams are out of control. Twice I've had vivid dreams since coming here. Before, I could never remember what I ate the night before, let alone my dreams. They were never this vivid. These feel so real.

"Fuck this place." I push myself into a seated position on the bed. Fire crackles from the hearth, splashing the room in a faint glow. The fire has continuously burned since I arrived, making me believe it's some type of magic that keeps it alive. It no longer makes the room feel stifling with its heat. Perhaps I got used to it because it's actually a comfort now, falling asleep to the pops and crackles of the fire.

After I move the furry blankets aside, my feet swing off the bed, landing on the warm stone. Last night's dinner sits mostly untouched on the table beside the bed. It was brought up to me shortly after I was escorted back to my room by the quiet but intimidating demon.

Fine, if you insist on being a prisoner in the castle, then that's what you shall be.

Oziel's words from last night play on repeat in my mind, a cruel reminder that the demon king is not my ally. But I'm not quite sure he's my captor either. I came here willingly and have argued with Oziel every chance I've been given. Instead of getting angry, the demon smirks, finding it nothing more than a game. It's... intriguing.

I'm about to test the prisoner thing because I'm in desperate need of a shower. I wasn't able to check last time, but I hope it's fully stocked with everything I need. I hesitate at the door, seeing the lock still firmly in place. Clearly it does nothing to keep out demons, but it makes me feel better. I turn the bolt, hearing the clicking mechanism of the lock, and turn the handle.

No one greets me on the other side. I half expected random demons to surround my room, forcing me to stay within the confines of these four walls. But there isn't a soul out, and the only light comes from a single candelabra perched on a small table. My first step out of the room feels forbidden, but when I'm not immediately ambushed, I gain the confidence to leave, shutting the door behind me.

I trail my fingers along the wall as I navigate the dim hallway, using it to steady myself. I can't see shit. The air is thick with silence, broken only by the soft scuff of my footsteps. It's unsettling to feel alone in this giant-ass castle. When I reach the first door, I grasp the handle and twist. Locked, of course.

"Damn," I murmur under my breath, moving on to the next one. I try again. Locked.

Frustration coils in my chest as I press forward, but then I come upon a door unlike the others. Instead of dark wood, its surface is rough, cool beneath my fingertips, all made from stone. There's no knob, no visible way to open it, yet something urges me to push.

I press my palm against the heavy slab, bracing for resistance, but it gives way with surprising ease. As it swings open, the faint scent of damp earth fills my nose, followed by the unmistakable sound of rushing water echoing from beyond.

Found it.

But when I round the corner, I realize I'm not alone. Garvan failed to mention the washroom is communal. Like the rest of the decor, the large room is made of polished black flooring that extends up the walls. Showers line the walls, each crafted to resemble demonic mouths or curved horns, from which water pours in steaming cascades, filling the room in a gray haze. Sweat gathers at my brow from the hot mist.

Partitions between showers are sparse, made of dark glass that only partially obscures the view, adding an edge of vulnerability. Meaning I see *everything*.

My face heats. I'm in no way a prude, not thinking

twice about stripping down to shower in front of strangers. I used to do it all the time after long workouts at the gym. The women's locker room was full of naked women, and no one batted an eye. So, I'm used to seeing many different body types and shapes.

However, what didn't happen at gym showers, at least not while I was there, was public sex. Very few shower stalls hold a single demon. Most are occupied by two or three. A woman moans from the shower closest to me. She's not alone. A demon—I can't decipher male or female—kneels at her feet, one of her legs thrown over their shoulder as the demon eats her out in earnest. Another demon stands behind her, an arm wrapped tightly around her torso while his free hand cups her breast. He thrusts shallowly from behind her, the sound of their fucking not muffled by water or the sounds of others.

It's not just them. Most shower stalls are full of demons engaging in various sexual acts. In the center of the room, a communal pool bubbles and churns, filled with milky water, surrounded by carved stone benches. A male demon sits on one of the benches while another male bounces on his lap, crude and dirty words leaving his lips.

My body heats up; being surrounded by so much sex creates an aphrodisiac vibe. Ignoring it is almost impossible. A sultry laugh draws my attention to the back of the washing chamber. Three demons take up the center shower. Two sensually wash each other, their hands and fingers lingering in certain places until they draw a moan from the other demon.

The third demon stands a few feet away, his back toward me. Black shoulder-length hair hangs in spirals with dark horns protruding from his head. His golden-brown skin is flawless, back muscles tensed as he lets the water fall upon him. The curve of his ass should be studied, and his strong thighs look deadly enough to suffocate anyone brave enough to go down on him.

Finally, the man turns.

All color leaves my face, a chill going through my body.

Pearly white teeth peek through his amused smile. I don't mean for my gaze to drift down his body, but like a moth to a light, I can't seem to look away from the indentation of every muscle, to the curve of his hip bone. His heavy cock bobs between his legs, a slight curve at his tip. It hangs like a heavy sword, a weapon to be used to take down his conquests. Probably the only weapon people would beg to be taken down with.

A low chuckle steals my attention. I snap my head up, but it's too late. He saw me looking, and the insufferable ass's giddy smile tells me he's going to be reprehensible.

"Hello, Kitten. Did my bride sleep well?"

Oziel's words have a halting effect on the room, as if everyone is tuned into the show that is Oziel and I. Lewd sounds of bodies slapping together and cries of pleasure all stop. I feel eyes all over my body, and despite being the only dressed person in the room, I've never felt so exposed. The couple next to Oziel takes the opportunity to move closer to their king, not touching him, but it's clear they would leap at the chance.

Out of nowhere, a fiery possessive anger takes over my body. How dare these demons feel so comfortable standing this close to Oziel. My anger flares when he does nothing to separate himself from the demons eager to get into his good graces. I've never been a jealous person before. Vengeful? Clearly. But jealous?

I hate it.

I steel my resolve, pretending I don't have the attention of every demon in the room. "Well enough, *groom*," I snarl, which only seems to excite him.

His cock twitches in interest, and I hate myself for the way my body responds in kind. I have to remind myself I don't like this man. I can barely stand him.

You don't have to like him to fuck him, the unhelpful voice whispers in my mind.

"I did as well," he says as if I asked him. "I had a *very* interesting night." The words are meant to draw a reaction out of me. Besides my body tensing at the implication, I school my face into one of apathy.

"As did I." It's a lie. I did nothing noteworthy, but Oziel doesn't need to know that. His grin only grows larger, as if he knows I'm lying. I pretend to ignore him as I pull the sleeping gown over my head, discarding it into a neat pile on the floor. I try not to dwell on the fact that I'm completely naked in an orgy shower.

By now, the room has lost interest in us, and many have returned to their lustful activities. Only one set of eyes bores into my naked body. It's my turn to catch Oziel looking me over. He doesn't even try to hide it. His gaze sears my flesh, burning me from the inside. There's only one free shower, and it's the one next to Oziel.

Unlike the others, there's only a half wall to separate the two.

Figures.

I keep my head held high as I make my way toward him. Oziel doesn't speak, perhaps the first time I've seen him rendered silent. It's impossible not to feel a sense of pride as I make my way next to him, reaching out to turn on the water.

Hot water, the kind that burns your skin, but in a good way, cascades down around me. I let it hit my face, shoulders, before rolling down my body. My hair grows heavy, and I'm pleased to find an assortment of bottles that must be shampoo and conditioner.

I reach down for the soap, maybe a little more than necessary. Slowly, I straighten my spine, running the soap across my chest until a nice lather forms. Oziel clears his throat next to me, and I turn just in time to see the spiteful looks from the two demons who tried to get my husband-to-be's attention.

The demon king steps out of the shower, but he isn't headed to the door like I thought. No, he does something much worse. Oziel walks out from his stall and moves toward mine.

"What are you doing?" I try to convey my anger, but my question sounds more curious than anything.

"I'm having a conversation with my future queen," he feigns innocence. It doesn't work for him. Even naked, strength and danger surround him. He's an overpowering presence, full of darkness and mystery.

"And we need to have this conversation while I'm naked?"

"I'm naked too, Kitten."

Yeah, I definitely noticed that. It takes all my concentration not to look down at the lengthening member between his legs.

"What do you want?" I turn my back to the king, tossing my hair over my shoulder. I hope it hits him.

"What are your plans today?"

The question catches me off guard in how mundane it sounds. As if we are old friends and not contracted to be married. I'm a stranger in this palace, so my plan is simply to stay alive. So far, so good, for the most part.

"You know damn well I have nothing planned."

He chuckles, and I can just picture the sly smile on his dumb, sexy face. "Then allow me to be your social event coordinator. You'll meet Garvan and me in the dining room in an hour."

"Do you ever ask, or do you simply demand things from people?" I blurt, spinning around to face him. Has he forgotten I have already declined eating with him once? I'm not afraid to do it again.

Somehow, he is closer, his bare chest hovering near mine. My hard nipples are mere centimeters away from touching him.

Or perhaps one meal together wouldn't hurt...

No! Focus.

"I think you know the answer to that, Kitten." Oziel leans down, and my heart speeds up. Out of fear or something else, I'm not sure. "But I do so like our arguments."

His words shouldn't be sexy. Nothing about his sentence is sexy. And yet my core heats. "Must be a kink of yours." Silently, I scold myself. Out of every fucking thing I could say, my brain came up with that?!

Oziel's grin takes on a darker, sultrier vibe. "One of many, Kitten. Perhaps one day you'll learn more."

I feel tongue-tied. Too flustered to produce a good rebuttal. Oziel licks his bottom lip in a suggestive manner before stepping back. "One hour, Miss Sinclair. Don't make me come find you."

With that, he spins on his heels and makes way to a small alcove, grabbing a towel. "Oh, and Miss Sinclair?"

"What?" I snap.

"This was the last towel." Then the bastard laughs darkly, snatching not only the last towel but the night dress I wore here before leaving the washing chamber.

"Fucking ass," I murmur under my breath. Part of me wants to stand him up out of spite, but another part of me is interested in what he has planned.

By the time I'm finished, more demons have made their way to the washroom, and no towels have been brought in to replenish the stash. I use my hands to cover myself, even though it hides nothing, and I half run, half waddle back to my room, cursing Oziel's name the entire way.

I swear I hear laughter in the distance.

OZIEL

Isabelle naked is a glorious sight. One I commit to memory, every dip and curve of her body. Did I detect jealousy from her when she noticed the two demons near me? I paid them no mind, of course, but I admit, I made no effort to move away from them either. Not with her delicious anger permeating the room.

Her beautiful, sinful anger.

I gave Isabelle an hour to meet me. Fifty-five minutes have passed, and the servants have started setting the table, bringing out fruits, pastries, and cinnamon porridge. The gold chalice by my plate is picked up and filled with a sweet wine. I bring the chalice to my lips, letting the sweetness coat my tongue. The watch in my pocket continues to tick away, taunting me with each second that passes.

Perhaps she won't come. I'll be forced to bring her against her will. As fun as that sounds, I don't particularly want to fight with Isabelle. It's fun, sure, but I also must get this woman to like me—or at least tolerate me. More than just lust. It's a task I fear I'm woefully unprepared for. What do I, the demon king, know of love? I have nothing but memories of roses to remind me that love is a sickness, weakening those under its spell.

My parents were proof of that.

Soft footfalls from the entryway seize my attention. Isabelle—no longer naked, sadly—wears a black chiffon gown I had set out for her. She fills it out nicely, looking every inch the queen she is destined to be. Her hair, still slightly damp from the shower, is tossed over one shoulder, a low braid keeping the strands together.

My body moves of its own accord as I stand, gesturing to the spot next to me. "Care for breakfast before we start our day?"

"You sure you don't want to invite the demons you shared your shower with to join you?" Her voice is clipped, and she ignores me when I pull out her chair. Still, she sinks into the seat, helping herself to the food.

"Were there demons with me? Hmm, must not have noticed," I reply before taking my seat. Isabelle huffs and rolls her eyes. "Jealousy is a good look on you, Kitten."

"I'm not jealous."

"Of course you're not. No one who is jealous would bring two irrelevant demons up in conversation," I comment, earning a glare.

Silently, I observe Isabelle fill her plate, what she gravitates toward and what she decides to skip. She pops a strawberry into her mouth, the juices running down her chin. Before she can wipe it away, my thumb swipes her chin, gathering the mess. I pull back, licking the strawberry juice from my fingertip. Isabelle's pupils dilate, and her breathing hitches.

"You'll want this." I hand her the folded black napkin. She snatches it from my grasp, and my lips twitch into an amused smile.

"Are you taking me back to see the Nephilim?" she asks, and the smile drops from my face. "Because I've been thinking, and I want to try talking to it again."

"No."

"No?" She raises a brow, frowning. "What do you mean 'no'? I'm here to help save your people. Or are you no longer concerned with their safety?"

Isabelle realizes her mistake the second the words are out of her mouth. Her eyes widen, and fear seeps into her expression. I pull her chair closer, but she does nothing to stop me. Only once she is up against my chair do I lean over, getting close to her face. "Demon safety is and has always been my top priority, Miss Sinclair. I have never wavered in my vows to protect my people. Not for anything or anyone."

Her bosom rises and falls in quick succession. Her fear, tinged with something else, something sweeter, permeates the air. To her credit, Isabelle straightens in her seat and meets my eyes. Not even the bravest of demons dares to stare me down out of fear I'll take it as a challenge. My cock twitches in my pants, intrigued by this woman more than I should be.

"What do you propose we do then, Oziel? If you didn't want my help, why did you sign the contract in the first place?"

"Because I need your help," I say. Isabelle opens her

mouth to argue with me, so I push on. "But you don't have the whole picture yet."

She closes her mouth; her pouty lips look detectable. Something I want to suck on. Perhaps she'll let me one day.

"Then show me, Oziel. I need to see it all." Isabelle pushes her plate away, no longer interested in the food before her.

"Very well." My chair scratches against the floor when I push up. "You'll need to take my hand." Isabelle scrunches up her nose at the sight of my outstretched hand. "I need to show you something, but you must touch me. I promise not to bite. Unless you ask me to, of course."

My teasing words have the desired effect on her. Her cheeks redden, but she reaches for my hand. The second she does, my shadows surround us. Isabelle lets out a squeak before pressing closer against me. We are engulfed in darkness. A sensation of falling consumes us before the shadows disperse.

No longer are we in the dining room, but outside, near a river. It's eerily quiet, and the air feels heavy with a sense of foreboding. It hasn't always been this way though. Once the water shimmered with an other-worldly iridescence, power radiating all around. But now...

Isabelle pulls away from me, putting distance between us. Her absence in my arms leaves me cold and empty. "Why did you bring me here?" She peers out at the river, which runs the perimeter of the castle, flowing in a steady stream. Or it used to. Now the water is silent and unmoving. The iridescent shimmer dimmed, replaced by streaks of sickly green and inky black that coil like serpents beneath the surface.

"This is the River Hel," I explain, coming up behind her. "It once held pure ancient magic that strengthened the demons." Even now I feel my magic depleting. The usual hum of power is nothing more than a slow, dying pulse.

"River Hel fuels us, cures us of diseases, and will heal a demon on the brink of death. But in its current state, it does little more than parlor tricks."

"Could this cure those who have turned to stone?" Isabella crouches down, getting far too close for my liking. When she reaches out a hand, I stop her.

"I would advise against that." The magic coursing through the river is foreign to me. I fear what may happen if Isabelle touches it. I prepare for a stubborn retort, but instead Isabelle nods and pulls her hand back. An interesting development, but I would have liked to argue with her more. "To answer your question, yes. I believe River Hel could cure those cursed. If it were at its prime, that is."

"Well, have you tried?"

The side of my lip twitches up in a humorless half-smile. I crouch down next to her, using the magic I still possess to part the inky colors momentarily so she can see what sits below.

Isabelle cranes her neck to get a better look. "Is that...?"

"Yes."

Two stone statues sit at the bottom of the river, gathering moss. Their feet are wedged deep into the sand, causing them to stand sideways.

"These were the first two demons that fell to the curse. Back then, the river had been tampered with, but we didn't understand the severity of the toxins plaguing the water. When their bodies were thrown into the water, they should have changed back. Instead, they rest at the bottom until the curse can be reversed."

It doesn't matter that I know very little of the two demons at the bottom of the river except that they work for me. They are *my* demons, and as their king, everyone that falls is an insult to me and my kingdom.

It makes me look weak. Incompetent. This could make the demons start to rebel, misplacing their fear and anger. Not that I can blame them.

"Okay," she says the word slowly, biting her lip in concentration. It's so damn distracting that I miss her words the first time. Naturally, Isabelle huffs. "I asked if the poisoning started when the roses were delivered to your door?"

Ah, I see what she's getting at, but it's another dead end. "Yes. So, we tried destroying the roses."

"And what happened?"

"They all turned to stone. Everyone who touches it. That's why it's in a dome now, so no one else will be tempted to touch the forbidden flower."

"Damn, that was going to be my suggestion," she mumbles under her breath, picking herself up from the ground. She moves away from the edge and starts pacing. "Do you think the Nephilim poisoned the lake?"

"Another great question, Kitten." I push up off the

ground, slide my hands into my pocket and shake my head. "No, it can only be poisoned by someone within because of the protective wards set at our borders. None of the Nephilim have journeyed over the river. They can't. It acts as a barrier to keep them out. However, I fear that won't be the case much longer."

"Are you saying one of your demons is sabotaging River Hel?"

With a sigh that holds all my exhaustion, I nod once again. "Yes, Miss Sinclair. That is exactly what I'm saying."

CHAPTER 13

ISABELLE

"Well, that's fucking unfortunate," I huff, crossing my arms over my chest. I don't miss the way Oziel's gaze dips down to my cleavage. His eyes darken, reminding me of a starless sky, something you could get lost in.

"Well put, Kitten. Very astute observation."

What I just thought about him, I take back. His eyes remind me of garbage. Fat, smelly piles of trash. Why this man insists on that god-awful nickname, I'll never know. Telling him off or showing any negative emotion toward the name would only give him satisfaction, so I try to keep my face as neutral as possible.

Judging by his snicker, it's not working well.

Oziel just burdened me with a lot of pertinent information. My mind is still reeling from everything. Even as I look upon the still river, I can't picture what it once was: a power that sustained demon magic. The air is filled with death and decay, and a heavy sadness washes over me, as if River Hel is crying out, grasping at the last bits of power remaining.

It's hard to be near it. I'm not even a demon—depending on who you ask—but even I can tell how sacred this river is. How can one of Oziel's own want to poison it? What would be in it for them other than the downfall of Oziel?

"Someone hates you very much," I say after a pause.

When he smiles, it doesn't meet his eyes. Oziel does a good job at playing the role of a mighty, unfeeling king, but I think he shoulders every burden and failure. He's just gotten really good at hiding it.

"That does not narrow the list down much, I'm afraid," he says. "Even as we speak, demons plan a coup against me to steal the throne. Perhaps before the curse I would say differently, but now everyone is on edge."

"What? Why?" Something akin to anger and fear—for him?—heats my body. "If you know this, why aren't you doing something?"

He stares pointedly at me. "I am doing something."

Right. I'm the something. It hardly seems like enough, though. This is way out of my skill set. Need me to kill an abusive dick? Done. I'll never regret that choice. But saving an entire kingdom? Saving Oziel from his own people? People who are scared and don't know how to handle that emotion, so it manifests in anger? I believe Oziel is more than capable of taking care of himself. He wouldn't be king in a place like this if he wasn't, but he is still one man.

I didn't like the odds.

"So, what do we do? Obviously, the first thing would be to figure out who is sabotaging your magic supply."

I'm shocked to see Oziel shake his head. "No, the first thing is for us to marry."

He could have sprouted a tail to match his horns, and I would have been less shocked.

"*What?*" My voice reaches octaves I didn't know I was capable of. "After everything you just told me, you would rather focus on our marriage than the real problem?"

"I am focusing on the problem, Miss Sinclair," he growls. I pretend my body doesn't heat at the sound. "And I'll be at my strongest if I'm connected to my human wife. For everything we will endure, I need to be at my strongest."

His words are a stark reminder of why I'm here. For power. For war. To further his kingdom. These are the things I agreed to when I signed the contract. Nothing else can or will come from this arrangement.

However, it's incredibly one-sided. I haven't survived this long on my own without looking out for myself, and even here, in front of the demon king, I will make demands.

"Fine, but I have conditions."

"I would be surprised if you didn't." Oziel crosses his arms over his chest, an amused expression on his face.

"First, there's a woman named Erin Goodwin here. I don't know who Ender paired her with, but I want to speak with her."

Oziel lifts a brow, clearly taken aback by my first demand. He knows nothing of the reason why I'm here.

And although I won't ever regret what I did or seek redemption, I'm also not ready to tell him. Erin deserves to hear the news first. She deserves to know what happened to her abuser. Admittedly, I'm nervous about her reaction. I've never spoken to the woman, so I don't know how she's going to take the news.

"Noted," Oziel says. "What else?"

Nerves get the best of me, and I awkwardly shuffle my weight from foot to foot. My next words could potentially piss him off, and there would be little I could do against a mad king. Still, I don't want to live with the regret of not voicing my needs.

"When this is all over," I gesture around us, "the war, the Nephilim—I want out."

"You can't go back home—"

"I know, and I wouldn't go back there even if you paid me," I interrupt. "But that's not what I'm saying. I want you to let me go when this is all over. I don't wish to stay married because it would feel too much like a prison. I want to leave freely, despite anything that might happen between now and then."

I don't realize I've moved closer to him until I'm a hair's breadth away from him. I see the soft rise and fall of his chest, smell his smoky scent, and feel his power. Despite their poisoned source of magic, Oziel is deadly. I fear what will happen when he truly unleashes himself upon the world.

"Do you think something might happen, Miss Sinclair?" His hot breath heats my neck.

He's trying to get a rise out of me. Or for me to lie. I plan on doing neither. "You're a demon surrounded by lust, and I'm not ignorant of your...charm. If something happens, I need for you to know it changes nothing."

"Charm?" He chuckles as if I told a joke. But then he drops his smile, and a dark cloud lingers over him. "That would be for the best. You are free to leave when this is over. I will not stop you."

"Good." And it is good. I don't know where I'll go yet, but I'll figure it out. Yet, I can't help but feel disappointed he agreed so easily. I expected a little resistance...but this is for the best. I have an aching need to reach out and place my hand on his chest. If for no other reason than to assure him this decision is best for both of us. I almost do.

Then suddenly, Oziel pulls back. "We aren't alone." He stares off into a wooded area. My body tenses, expecting another one of those monstrous creatures, but the man who steps into the clearing is one I recognize, and my body relaxes.

"Garvan, what information do you have?" Oziel moves in front of me. I have to peer around to see the gangly demon, dressed in a pristine black outfit.

"I don't mean to interrupt, my lord. But you said you wanted to be notified the moment I heard word from the kings." Garvan dusts off invisible lint from his shoulder.

"Go on," Oziel prompts.

"Alpha King Rip and King Allarick have responded. Both are willing to meet, though they've said nothing about including their queens. No word back from King Malix, but sources tell me his wife is with child, due any day now. I don't think we should count on his help."

"No matter. I only need one," Oziel says. "Set the

meeting up for three days from now. I must have time to prepare."

"Prepare, my lord?"

"Yes." Oziel turns to face me. The look on his face sends shivers down my spine—like I'm the shiny new toy he's been dying to get his hands on. It should piss me off, but my traitorous body gravitates toward him.

"Prepare the vow ceremony. We will wed at the witching hour." His smile turns positively feral before saying, "Oh, and Garvan? See to it that Miss Sinclair is properly prepared for the ceremony."

ISABELLE

Three female demons gaze upon my naked body, muttering to each other in a language I'm not privy to. If I were the modest type, there would be no way I could endure another bathing session with strangers around me. At least this time, no one is fucking. But that also means their attention is focused on me, and even as confident as I am in my body, this still feels intimidating as hell.

When Garvan found Oziel and me by River Hel and informed us of the correspondence from the other kings, Oziel immediately began to bark out orders. Most of them had to do with "prepping" me. I didn't like the way that sounded, but before I was able to protest, black smoke gathered around me and transported me away. I really hated that little ability of his. My stomach plummeted, the same feeling I get when I'm on a roller coaster going down a massive hill. Only there were no thrill seekers waiting for me once the smoke cleared in my room, but rather three demons with haughty, sour expressions.

The blue-skinned demon introduces herself as Greta. She seems to be the one in charge of the other two: a purple-haired demon named Lola and a short, stout demon named Paulina. Greta barks orders—or what I assume to be orders it's a language I don't know—to the others. Lola and Paulina usher me down the hall and into the bathing room. It must have been cleared out because it's empty, free of the orgies that took place earlier.

I don't protest when Lola and Paulina strip my clothes off, mostly because I'm still dazed from traveling via smoke and shadows. Greta perches on the edge of the tub in the center of the room, sprinkling in bundles of tightly bound lavender.

All three of them look over my very naked body, making plans for me I don't understand. "What's going on?" I ask, unable to continue standing here awkwardly while my whole pussy is on display.

Greta snaps her attention to me, her face pinched as if she just sucked on a sour lemon. Both Paulina and Lola look to her. "We are cleansing your body for your vow exchange, mistress," she explains as if it physically pains her to do so.

Mistress? Don't like that name one bit, but I highly doubt she would care if I made mention of it. "What does this cleansing entail?"

Instead of answering, Lola and Paulina take me by my arms and lead me into the milky-white water. The tub is grand and full to the brim. Water sloshes over the sides, landing at the demons' feet. None of them seem to mind or notice as they crouch down next to the tub. Paulina and Lola produce white washcloths out of seemingly nowhere and start to scrub my skin.

Greta reaches for my hair, murmuring something like a song crossed with chanting. Then cold water hits my head, followed by a soapy substance that stains the water red. Back in Grym Hollow, Greta would make a great—albeit grumpy—hair stylist. Her lithe fingers move easily between the strands of my hair, massaging my scalp. A sweet floral scent permeates the room, as if we aren't in a demonic washroom but rather a budding florist shop.

Lola and Paulina scrub *every* part of my body within an inch of my life. My skin is flushed red as if they scrubbed the first layer clean off. Paulina gestures for me to move closer, which I do, despite Greta tugging on my hair to stay in place. Once close enough, Paulina grabs a jar, unscrewing the top. She digs her hand in and comes out with a green lotion the color of seaweed. It's warm when she rubs it in, making my face feel tingly. She rubs the substance down my neck and to my chest.

"What is this?" I ask, even though I don't expect her to reply.

"Skin purification treatment, mistress," Paulina says in a low, sultry voice. "Enhanced with seduction enchantment."

"Seduction? Oh, that won't be necessary—"

"Hush, girl," Greta snaps. "This is the process. King Oziel expects us to uphold tradition. As his future wife and queen, these steps are necessary. We will not skip steps or deviate from tradition."

I bite my tongue, knowing I'd win no favors by speaking against Greta. She has a point, even if I hate to admit it. This ceremony has to be and feel real for me to help Oziel and his demons. That includes Greta with her rude ass. I might be a killer, but I'm not a senseless murderer, content to condemn people to their death simply because they have a bad attitude. Not sure if I can say the same about my future husband, though. He seems the type to kill for fun.

I should be more upset about that fact. It's a testament to how fucked-up I am that the thought of Oziel killing doesn't fill me with dread or anger.

After five minutes, Paulina wipes off the cream. My face feels smooth to the touch, soft like satin. Lola grabs my hands and pulls me to my feet. Water sloshes and drips down my body, and the slight chill in the air has me shivering. Every other place in this damn castle is a sauna—figures the one place you want to be warm isn't.

Instead of letting me out, the women pour three vials of oil on my body, rubbing it into my skin. I try not to shudder when Greta takes it upon herself to rub the oils between my thighs, gritting my teeth when Paulina massages the oil into my tits, paying extra attention to my nipples.

By the time they finish, I'm a slippery mess. It takes all three of them to help me out of the tub and keep me standing on the tile. One of them—I think Lola—wraps a towel around my body from behind before they escort me out of the washroom and down the hall to my room.

A dress that wasn't here this morning is sprawled across the bed. For the first time, the dress isn't black, though it's fairly close.

The dress is made up of dark purples and midnight-blue accents. Greta reaches for the bodice at the same time Paulina rips the towel away from me. Luckily, the fire roars brightly in the hearth, drying me quickly and warming me up.

The bodice is placed and tied first, accentuating my waist and pushing up my boobs in an obscene manner. They look damn good, I must admit. Greta takes her time lacing up the back. It's a little tighter than what I would prefer, but manageable.

Next comes the skirts. Lola hands me a skimpy pair of panties that I quickly shimmy on before stepping into the billowy skirts, which are layered with a mix of fabrics —velvet, leather, and chainmail. The layers cascade down in varying lengths, the longer sections trailing on the ground like a dark, royal train. If I'm not careful, I could easily get tangled up in the skirts and trip. Which, I presume, is a worry some brides face on their wedding day.

Wedding day.

What a weird thought. I never gave much thought to marriage. It was always an obscure concept that society pushed on people, especially young girls. From the hair to the makeup to the dress. It was a big spectacle of grandeur and a money pit. Too many marriages end in divorce, throwing away everything they promised and spent on their wedding day. And some even go on to have multiple weddings.

I never thought of getting married and have never been so in love with a person I wanted to commit to living the entirety of my life with. That sounds like a fairy tale. I doubt there is room for a murderer who likes to avoid people in anyone's fairy tale. Besides, those women marry a prince with a good heart. I've never read one who married a demon, the villain in many people's stories.

Paulina tugs at my hair, pulling it into an elaborate updo with random strands to surround my face. Greta and Lola work on applying a black paint to my cheeks and forehead in intricate designs. When I ask what they are, Greta says something about ancient ceremonial markings but fails to elaborate. I don't push her though. Already, I have used up my supply of social aptitude for the day, leaving me to run on fumes for my wedding.

At long last, Greta pulls back and barks orders at Paulina and Lola. They shuffle out of the room with a promise to be back in a few hours to retrieve me for the ceremony since the lotions and oils need to set into my skin, or some shit like that. Apparently, it's part of the process. The moment they file out of the room and close the door behind them, I sink into the leather upholstered chair, careful not to damage my dress.

Fatigue seeps deep into my bones. The events of the past week slowly start to pile up until I can't ignore them anymore. In a blink of an eye, my whole life has changed. The moment James came into my sister's life—and by extension, my own—was when I felt the change in me. The need for something that could only be satisfied with cold blood. That one decision landed me here, in a land full of magical creatures, fighting against a magical war I hold no part in.

Until I signed my life away.

I still don't regret it.

I didn't know what to expect upon my arrival, but Oziel isn't it. Yes, the king's power and strength are terrifying, and in the rare moments his guard slips, I catch glimpses of the evil lurking beneath. It doesn't scare me like it should. In fact, in some ways, it calls to me, playing on my deepest, darkest desires I have never given thought to. Because those things aren't normal. I shouldn't be tempted and yet...

I leave those thoughts where they simmer, not ready to look too closely at what that says about me. The day's events get the best of me, and I give in to bone-deep sleep, sprawled out on the stiffest chair known to man.

ROUGH HANDS on my shoulders shake me awake. Judging by the intensity of the shakes, she's been trying to wake me for a while. My body has slid down the chair, and my back is unnaturally hot due to the fire from the hearth and leather of the chair. My neck is twisted at an odd angle, forcing me to rotate my head side to side in hopes of getting the knots out.

Once my eyes and brain can focus, I see Greta has come back. "I thought you were dead." Her voice sounds disappointed. "Your presence is needed in the moonlight room. Come now. We don't want to keep the king waiting." She turns on her heels and makes her way out of the room, not looking back once to make sure I'm following.

"Time to get married, I guess," I murmur under my breath, awkwardly pushing myself out of the chair. I haven't seen my face, but I hope the markings Lola and Greta painted on aren't smeared. Greta would have said something if they were. Maybe?

I quickly catch up to the spirited demon, and we walk in silence through the castle. I haven't had much time to explore, but most of the hallways and rooms look the same. If someone were trying to escape the castle, they'd have a hard time navigating toward the exit, though I suspect that's the point.

Lola leads me to an archway with stairs ascending to a turret. There's a chill in the air here, as if the fires from the rest of the castle don't extend to this part. I see why the moment we make it to the top. There's no ceiling, but rather the circular room is open. The milky-white moon appears like a beacon in the sky, so close I feel like, if I reach out, I could touch it.

There's nothing in the turret except a single table with a chalice and golden rope. The cracks in the stone emit an eerie red light, resembling veins pulsing with molten energy, as if the turret itself is alive and breathing malevolence. Most of the castle feels alive with a powerful, malignant aura. Even the shadows pulse with a dark desire.

Two men stand in the middle of the room. Garvan wears long, dark robes with a crimson tunic underneath. His pale blond hair is slicked back, and his horns are bare, free of the rings and jewels he wore before. He stands over a table, paging through an inky-black book that seems to glow. At our arrival, he looks up briefly and smiles before going back to the book.

And then there's Oziel. My breath hitches in my throat when I see him. He wears tight black leather pants that accentuate his thigh muscles. It also does little to hide the indentation of his cock, which I tell myself I'm not interested in ogling again. He's shirtless. The same black markings on my face are present on his chest and torso. There are other markings too, in gold and silver, though those are fewer. His hair flows free of a band, hanging loose around his shoulders, matching his dark beard.

Something shiny catches my attention, and I notice the various rings decorating his horns. Gold, black, and red ones all placed precisely along the length to add a regal charm. A new energy surrounds him. One that nearly suffocates me with its strength, but I keep myself tall as I walk toward him, even though I want to tremble under his scrutiny.

Gold eyes darken and narrow into tiny slits. My skin heats as he drags his gaze over me. Wetness pools between my thighs, despite my attempts to keep myself at bay. His throat emits a deep, low sound, sending shivers down my back.

"Leave us."

I pause at his words, confused, until Lola says something and disappears without a trace, leaving me alone with the two male demons. Normally being left alone with men would make me on edge and ready to flee at a moment's notice. And even though I'm in a room with literal demons, I don't fear either of them.

There are still a few feet between Oziel and me, but like a magnet, I'm pulled the rest of the way toward the center. Toward him. Silence hangs between us. Even Garvan looks like he would rather be anywhere else but here. I don't think I've ever seen the demon so nervous.

At last, Oziel breaks the silence. "You are sin incarnate, Miss Sinclair." His words echo one of the first things he ever said to me: *"I smell sin on you."* From anyone else, it would be an insult. But from Oziel, it sounds like the highest of praises.

"You don't look hideous," I respond, earning an amused grunt.

"Your compliments are endearing, Kitten." He smirks, reaching for my hand. He pauses, waiting to see if I'll pull out of his grip. I think about it, but I'm not against him touching me. I nod stiffly before Oziel takes my hand in his.

"Before we begin, I need to tie your hands together," Garvan speaks up for the first time since I've arrived. The demon grabs the rope on the table, barely more than two feet long.

When Oziel nods, Garvan reaches for our clasped hands. Gently, he ties mine and Oziel's wrists together, making sure it is secure before pulling back. Garvan catches my eye and offers me a tight-lipped smile. If I didn't know any better, I would say there was something akin to sorrow in his eyes, which makes no sense. "You do look lovely, Miss Isabelle."

Next to me, Oziel growls. Garvan visibly pales and

stands up straight, grabbing the chalice. Red liquid sloshes over the top, spilling droplets onto the table. "Shall we begin?" he asks, making sure not to look at me out of fear of his king's wrath.

Oziel nods once to Garvan, and then to me, he winks. "Begin, Garvan. It is time I take my queen."

CHAPTER 15
OZIEL

Isabelle is the epitome of the queen of shadows. The moment she walked into the room, everything else faded away until there was nothing but her. This beautiful creature, clad in deep purple and midnight blue, wears the markings of my people. One would believe me to be a demon in my youth by the way my body reacts to her. A visceral need to be near her. It's an unfamiliar sensation, and yet I yearn to experience more.

I would do well to remember this marriage is nothing more than strategic. A political move to ensure my kingdom withstands our enemies. Anything else would be a distraction.

A weakness like my parents' marriage.

I'm many things, but weak? Never.

I harden my resolve the moment I take Isabelle's hand and Garvan ties the golden rope around our hands, symbolizing the bond we will create. At least for a little while, until I let her go.

Because that's how this will end. With Isabelle

leaving and making her own way in Mescos. She's either the bravest woman I know or the most foolish. I haven't yet decided.

Garvan clears his throat, thumbing through the demon grimoire until he finds the page he needs. He starts to chant, his voice low in tone, speaking in the ancient language of our people. I cast a glance at Isabelle, a frown on her face. She's clueless as to what he's saying, which is to be expected. No human outside our world would know the words. I take pity on her and translate.

"The ancient ones cast darkness upon us as we celebrate the joining of two entities," I say. Isabelle snaps her attention toward me, a furrow in her brow. "Today marks a new beginning, a new power, and a new era for demonkind. Darkness will reign, stronger than before, for two become one."

Garvan picks up the chalice full of crimson liquid. To an untrained eye, the contents appear as wine. This elixir is far older than wine, wielding power no other drink could. Concocted by demons, it has been used in every demon ceremony since the beginning of time. Every ancient history book has mentioned the elixir. Though the name has changed over the years, the ingredients haven't. These days it's called The Blood of Lucifer, one of the first demons in existence.

Garvan speaks again, and I translate verbatim. "The Blood of Lucifer will unite these two in sin and darkness. May it heighten every emotion and sensation of the body, mind, and soul. May it cast away doubt, sickness, and weakness. The Blood of Lucifer shall not be taken unwillingly. Do you accept this fate?" Garvan addresses me first.

"I accept this fate." My words echo around us, sounding both far away and near. My blood burns my body, preparing for the surge of power the bonding ceremony will provide us.

"And Miss Sinclair—"

"Isabelle, Garvan. Call me Isabelle," she chastises, and Garvan glances over at me for permission. Unfortunately for her, Isabelle isn't going to like my answer. I find myself eagerly awaiting her scorn.

"She is your queen, Garvan. You will honor her title."

Garvan bows in submission before offering Isabelle an apologetic smile. "My queen, do you accept the Blood of Lucifer willingly?"

"There's not much choice in the matter, is there?"

Normally I would enjoy her quick-witted tongue. May even push her for more, but for a ceremony of this importance, I don't take kindly to nonanswers. "You must answer him, Isabelle."

She scowls at me but otherwise doesn't argue. "Fine, yeah, whatever. I willingly accept...that." Her face scrunches up in disgust, and she gestures to the chalice.

"The betrothed will take a sip from the chalice. The ceremony will be complete once both parties have taken the Blood."

"This isn't literally blood, right?" Isabelle interrupts. "I'm not sure if you know this, but humans don't drink blood. At least not the sane ones."

"And what do you know of sanity, Kitten?" I ask despite myself.

I earn another reproachful glance from my bride. If she keeps looking at me like that, I may have to drag her to the bed and punish her. Or...better yet, she could punish me. That would be divine.

"Clearly nothing at all if I'm willing to marry the likes of you, even if this is only temporary." She attempts to keep the bitterness in her tone, but a sliver of lust shines through.

Perhaps I should tell her what the drink will do. Ultimately, I decide against it because it will be much more fun this way.

Garvan offers me the chalice first. I take it from his hands, pausing a second to look at the liquid. I steel my body, knowing the effects it will have on me. Without further hesitation, I bring the chalice to my lips and drink. The moment the Blood—which isn't actual blood, but rather a combination of magically enhanced herbs and alcohol—hits my lips, my body burns.

Garvan takes the chalice back just as heat erupts from my throat, expanding to the rest of my body. Every muscle and nerve are on high alert. The smallest of touches will produce a fire within, threatening an inferno.

Isabelle stands there, eyes wide and lips parted. Passion and lust ignite inside me, begging to be set free. It would be so easy to pull her in my arms and taste her. My cock hardens at the thought of the sounds she'd make. Would she moan? Whimper? Better yet, would she yell at me, voice laced with venom? I would devour her protest.

Oblivious to my internal struggle, Isabelle turns her

attention to Garvan. She studies the chalice as if it were some wild animal but then takes it from his hand. "Just one sip?"

"Just the one." Garvan's eyes dart to me. If I didn't know any better, I'd say my courtier is nervous. For what, I can't say. My brain isn't exactly working logically at the moment. It has one track, solely focused on the beautiful nightmare before me.

Isabelle takes her time grabbing the chalice and bringing it to her lips. Her eyelids droop as she takes a tentative sip, testing out the drink before committing. I know the moment the Blood takes effect. It's an instant change.

Isabelle's eyes snap open; her body stiffens. The chalice drops from her grasp, falling to the floor in a crimson mess. The metal echoes off the stone tile, and she draws near. Her pupils are blown wide with what can only be described as lust. Our bodies gravitate toward each other.

Her hand touches my cheek.

Fire blazes.

I burn.

And then we are one.

Isabelle's lips are on mine, and I completely lose the fight. I kiss her with raw need. Hard. Forceful. She matches me, not easily letting herself be dominated by my touch. When she parts for me, it's because she willed it.

My tongue finds hers in a forbidden dance. I taste her, drinking her in. She's not sweet. I doubt there's anything sweet about Isabelle. She doesn't taste like sugar or flowers. No, this woman tastes of spice. Cinnamon and cloves. She burns my tongue, and I enjoy every second of it.

Her curvy body presses hard against mine. In my pants, my cock strains firmly against her stomach. I feel her hard nipples through our layers, and I yearn to unlace her corset and take a bud into my mouth. I'm half tempted to do just that, but then two hands press against my chest and push me away.

Hard.

The force of the push isn't what moves me away from Isabelle as much as the surprise of it. She freed herself from the lust haze far quicker than I anticipated. I stumble back a step before regaining my balance. I don't go far since we are still tied together.

"What the fuck was that?" Isabelle's shrill voice fills the room. A storm of emotions crashes over her—anger, confusion, frustration, and maybe even a trace of heat she desperately wants to ignore.

I have no smug grin for her or taunting remarks. My hands float in the air. Had it been in her hair? On her back? For a moment, I allow myself to weaken. To fall back into the spell and imagine myself kissing Isabelle within an inch of her life. I'm not certain I would have had the strength to push her away.

Then, my mask returns. My lips curve into a slow, infuriating—to her—smirk. "Well," I purr, voice low and calm, "that was unexpected. Didn't realize you'd go from insults to kissing me so quickly. If I knew that's all it took, I'd have annoyed you sooner."

"Fuck off, Oziel." The words don't land as they

should because there's no real heat behind them. I've spooked her. Or she's spooked herself by giving in to me so quickly. Admittedly, I feel the same. The kiss rocked me out of control, and I desperately cling to what I can.

"The Blood of Lucifer heightens the emotion of the sin you feel most in the moment. Both of yours happened to be lust," Garvan explains, mostly for Isabelle's benefit. I forgot the demon was still in here. I wish he'd leave.

Garvan reaches out to untie us, and Isabelle instantly jerks her hand away from me. I would be lying if I said it didn't sting, no matter how much I wish that not to be so. "You are bonded. Congratulations."

Garvan says "congratulations" like someone would say "I'm sorry" at a funeral. This is the death of our freedom, so the demon isn't far off. Newfound power slithers inside me, and I feel stronger than I have in weeks. The color in Isabelle's cheeks suggests she may feel the same.

"So, is that it?" she asks, pretending not to be affected at all, even though I can still smell the lust on her. She wants me, even if she pretends not to.

"For today," I answer, my body buzzing. From our kiss or the new power inside me, I know not. Though, if I had to guess, I'd presume it was the former. "In the meantime, we will have a ball."

"A ball? Why the fuck would we do that? We have shit to do, or have you forgotten?"

"Ah, you have such an eloquent vocabulary, Kitten." My words earn me a slap to my shoulder. Isabelle notices her grave mistake the same time I do. This is the second one she's made in a short period of time. My queen would do well to learn manners.

No one strikes a king. Not if they wish to keep their head. Garvan sucks in a breath, and the pathetic fool takes a step back. With a single look, Garvan takes this as his sign to leave. Isabelle's gaze flicks between us before straightening her posture. The woman is brave; I'll give her that. But she's also foolish.

I move closer to her, and she takes a step back until she's caught between the table and myself. "You should know I won't hurt you, Isabelle. Not unless you ask me to."

"You're a dick, Oziel," she says breathlessly.

"I'm many things, Miss Sinclair," a slow smile curls my lips, "but that one happens to be my favorite." I wink, then lean in until only a breath separates us. Her heart beats like a war drum in my ears—fast, frantic. I can smell the sharp tang of fear mixed with something sweeter, something unmistakable. Desire.

She wants me. As much as she insists she hates me, her body betrays her. And it kills her to know it. I revel in it a moment too long before taking a step back.

"But to answer your original question, no, Kitten, I have not forgotten about the task at hand. This is precisely why we are having a ball. We can keep an eye out for people then. See who is there and make note of who isn't. See if we hear anything suspicious."

Isabelle takes a moment to mull this over. "Fine," she says at last, doing her best to compose herself. "Fine. We'll have a ball. But in the meantime, I think I should try talking to the Nephilim again."

"I agree. However, not until we speak with the other kings. Prolonged exposure to the Nephilim can't be good.

We must proceed with caution." There is still so much unknown about the creatures, and I'm not desperate enough to gamble lives for knowledge. Especially Isabelle's.

The other kings' wives, however...

"Oh, and, Wife?"

Isabelle tenses at my switch of tone and the intense, piercing gaze of my eyes. "If you strike me again, be prepared for me to show you what happens to bad girls who disrespect their kings."

"Literally fuck off." For the second time that day, Isabelle shoves me away from her, putting distance between us. It's like, if she allows me to get too close, she might realize she likes the proximity. "Fine. Whatever. Are we done here?"

"We are," I answer. Though many demons fuck the moment their ceremony is complete. Somehow, I don't think she'd take kindly to that. And as much as I would enjoy hate sex with my queen, it would be far more enjoyable if she wanted it as well. I'm not a monster. At least not to her.

"Good. Let me know when we meet with the kings. I don't wish to be bothered." With that, Isabelle turns on her heels and marches out of the room, leaving me with just the taste of her on my lips and the lingering smell of her lust.

CHAPTER 16
OZIEL

In the early hours of this dreadful morning, I'm summoned to the servants' quarters. A purple-haired demon had barged into my room, a frantic gleam in her red eyes. I recognize the maid as Lola, one of the demons I assigned to attend to Isabelle before our wedding ceremony three nights ago.

Even now I feel Isabelle's presence in her quarters, tossing and turning in her bed with unsettling dreams. Dreams are little more than secrets yet to be uncovered, and I yearn to uncover everything my wife hides. Starting with the reason she came here. Knowing what I know about Isabelle, she wouldn't have made this deal if the alternative wasn't unbearable.

My shadows surround Lola and me, transporting me to the part of the castle I rarely go to. The servants' quarters are located in the north wing of the castle, scarcely decorated with trinkets found by demons and frigid temps that seep deep into your bones. Some demons prefer the cold. I'm not one of them.

"Here, my lord." Lola quickly shuffles away, and I follow. We aren't alone. A few demons all wearing various expressions of concern greet me. Few remember protocol and bow deeply, almost reluctantly. Disgust and uncertainty radiate off them, proving to me that my people are growing agitated with me. Then there are ones that barely register my presence. I soon find out why.

Lola stops abruptly, an anguished wail erupting from her body before she drops to the floor weeping. Her display of emotion is foreign to me, casting unease around the room. I step around her to get a better look at what has this maid so distraught. Standing only a few feet in front of us is a blue stone statue of my head maid, Greta.

"Lucifer Rising," I curse under my breath. Greta's frozen expression is her usual sour self, showing no indication that she knew the curse was upon her. Like a thief in the night, it snuck upon her, robbing Greta of her physical being.

"When did this happen?" I growl, looking down at the sobbing demon on the floor.

Lola doesn't answer. Another demon walks up behind her, and I recognize her as Greta's shadow, Paulina. "Upon the hour. We came and got you as soon as it happened," she explains. "She was mid-sentence before the curse took effect."

"Were there signs?"

Paulina shakes her head. "None."

There had been warnings in the past. Each demon experienced a tightening sensation, fear or pain forever etched in their stone features. Greta is the first I've heard to not experience either of these sensations. Which means the curse is progressing, and I've nothing to show for it.

"Take her out with the others," I bark at the closest demons. They heed my order, pushing aside Lola and Paulina to carefully maneuver Greta into the courtyard. The courtyard was once a place of beauty, but now it holds nothing but reminders of my failure. I place the statues there to force myself to look upon them every day and never forget what I'm fighting for.

I storm out of the maids' quarters, caught up in my thoughts, and don't register Garvan until the man is only a foot away from me. "What?" It comes out more bitter than I intend, but Garvan shows no emotion. He's used to my mood swings at this point.

"King Rip and King Allarick have arrived, my lord," Garvan says, eyeing the commotion behind me. "Oh, dear. Another. This is very concerning."

It takes everything in me not to wring his neck for pointing out the obvious. It wouldn't kill him, but it would make me feel a lot better.

With the wedding ceremony and dealing with yet another cursed demon this morning, I forgot I requested the presence of the other kings. I note King Malix is absent, filing it away to use against him later, even though his wife is pregnant. Now isn't the most ideal time for a meeting with the kings, but I don't wish to put this off any longer. It's hard enough to get these bastards together.

"Get my wife," I command Garvan.

"I will go to her. What if she refuses to come?"

"Must I do everything on my own?" My face contorts in frustration. "I don't give a fuck if you need to drag her naked, screaming through the halls. Bring. Me. My. Wife."

With a tick to his jaw, Garvan lowers his head in submission. "As you wish, my lord. Miss Sinclair will be by your side soon."

TURNS out my wife didn't need to be dragged naked and screaming into the throne room. I was only mildly disappointed by that. I wouldn't have minded seeing her naked flesh on display, making the other kings squirm and stew in their discomfort. Instead, she wears a crimson-colored dress that fans out around her hips, looking like a waterfall of blood. She is a sight to behold. Even with her nose upturned in my direction and the permanent scowl she seems to reserve only for me.

It's quite romantic, really.

"Kitten, you are a beautiful nightmare," I say as she fluffs out her skirt, taking a seat next to me.

"I know." She sits back and crosses her arms. "Who are these kings we're meeting?"

"King Alpha Rip from the wolf kingdom and King Allarick from the sea kingdom," I say.

"Wolves and sea people. This place is strange," she murmurs to herself. Then, louder, she asks, "Are either of these men married to Erin Goodwin?"

"I suppose we'll find out." Though I know the answer to that. I make it my responsibility to learn the names of the humans the kings took. Names hold power, as does knowledge. I fear if I tell Isabelle that Allarick is married to Erin, the true purpose of our meeting will be forgotten in favor of Isabelle demanding a presence with the Kraken queen. "You will introduce yourself as my queen. These kings must see you as their equal."

I expect Isabelle to argue with me, but instead she nods. "Queen or not, I am their equal."

A satisfied smirk touches my lips. "That you are, Kitten. Don't forget that."

Her lips quirk up at the edges as she meets my gaze. Something passes between us. Understanding? Possibly. But there's more. A molten need to be close to her.

My gaze dips to her red lips, remembering the kiss we shared only days ago. It affected me more than I wish to admit. She made me *yearn*. Yearn for more of a taste of her. It's a feeling I'm not accustomed to, nor one I like. I'm used to taking what I want, but Isabelle is a closed book. She gives me glimpses of her pages yet hides her secrets.

But I hide mine too. Secrets have a way of breaking people.

Perhaps we can be broken together.

The door swings open, and I drag my gaze away from Isabelle. She goes to stand, but I place a hand on her shoulder, pushing her back in her chair. She shoots me a reproachful look, but I simply shake my head. "You do not stand for men. They stand for you."

Isabelle freezes, lips parted as if she wants to say

something but then thinks better of it. She nods once, sitting back in her chair and crossing one leg over the other.

King Alpha Rip walks in first. He's a large man and has to duck to get inside the doorframe. Next to him is a similar-sized Black male, scanning the room. I should have guessed Rip would bring his second.

King Allarick comes in next, his locs tied back neatly. Behind him, an older man with salt-and-pepper hair enters, sword at his hip. His age is deceiving, and I would bet he'd hold his own in a fight against younger warriors. Seems to me like these kings don't trust they're safe meeting with me without their lapdogs.

What I don't see is their wives.

"Oziel, it was a surprise to get word from you," Rip says in a way of greeting. His eyes flicker down to Isabelle, and something akin to jealousy and possessiveness flares to life within me. He doesn't linger on her long before his attention is back on me. "You don't reach out."

"Consider it your lucky day, Wolf." Rip huffs, causing me to chuckle. "May I introduce my wife? Queen Isabelle Sinclair."

Isabelle eyes the men warily. "Pleasure to meet you," she says, though her tone suggests the opposite. "Where are your wives?"

It's a question I'd love to hear the answer to as well. "Yes, Rip and Allarick, where are your wives? Or do you always make decisions without their consent and input?"

My words earn me a growl from Rip and a disapproving stare from Allarick. I don't fear the Kraken king here. There are no fish to do his bidding. Rip, on the other hand, would be a fun fight, but I didn't call them here for bloodshed. At least, not entirely.

"It's not every day we are summoned by the demon king. You'll understand why we're cautious," Allarick says.

"Enough of this. Oziel, tell us why we are here. What is it you need to discuss with us?" Rip, ever the impatient dog, barks.

I gesture at the seats in front of us. I only provide two, so their guards are forced to stand behind them. "I wish to speak with you both about our new problem. The Nephilim."

At the mention of the creatures, both kings stiffen.

"What curse befalls your kingdom?" Allarick asks.

"Ah, that's not why we're here." Though, if they entered through the courtyard, they probably have a good understanding of what my people are dealing with. "Have you trapped a Nephilim?"

The furrowed brows tell me everything I need to know, even before Rip shakes his head. "No. We were too busy killing them."

"We didn't deal with Nephilim. We had a Leviathan problem," Allarick admits.

I raise a brow, making a mental note to do research on Leviathan later.

"So, neither of you tried to communicate with them?" I ask.

"Communicate? Absolutely not. Why would we try to

communicate with them?" Rip asks, his temper getting the best of him. Such an emotional wolf.

"One spoke to me," Isabelle speaks up. Everyone in the room tenses and turns to her. To Isabelle's credit, she doesn't wither under their gaze. "We have an imprisoned Nephilim. It spoke to me and showed me things no one else could see."

"What did it show you?" Allarick leans forward, hanging on to her every word.

As Isabelle looks at me, smug satisfaction grows inside me. My queen looks to me when she's unsure, though I doubt she realizes she's doing it. She doesn't need my permission to speak, but I nod anyway. "It said war is coming. That all of this death is for *him*, but it didn't show me who *him* referred to. It might have, but—"

"It was manipulating Isabelle to walk closer. I pulled her back, and it cut off their link," I finish for her. Isabelle was not happy with me at the time. I couldn't—and still can't—bring myself to feel remorse for what I did. The Nephilim would have surely killed her the moment it got its hands on her. "Despite that, I assure you it was quite safe." Probably, that is.

"And is this the part where you ask us to willingly allow our wives to meet your captive Nephilim on the chance they could speak with it?" Rip's eyes flicker to black, his anger barely concealed.

"Precisely," I say. "If they can communicate and see in the minds of these creatures, we can learn their secrets. I don't need to tell you there's power in secrets."

"No," Rip says immediately. His answer isn't shocking, but it's still disappointing. "I won't allow Hettie to be put in danger. My stubborn wife would do so without any thought for her own safety. If there's a chance she could get hurt, I'm not willing to risk her."

"I don't like making decisions without my wife," Allarick says slowly. I brace myself for his rejection too. "However, Erin's safety is my top concern. She finally feels safe, and I don't want to put her in a place where she has to worry about her life."

"Did you say Erin? As in Erin Goodwin?" Isabelle speaks before I can respond. She uncrosses her legs and moves to the edge of the seat.

Allarick eyes her curiously before slowly, almost reluctantly, nodding. "Erin Goodwin is my wife."

"I need to speak with her."

"I just said I don't want her involved with the Nephilim—"

Isabelle waves off his concern. "I'm not talking about the Nephilim. *I* need to speak with her. It's very important."

"What is it you need to discuss with her?" the man behind Allarick asks. Delmare is his name, if I remember correctly.

"It's none of your business," she snaps.

Delmare hardens. "You'll learn Erin Goodwin is a beloved queen in our kingdom. None of us wish harm to fall upon her."

"If your protection means hiding her away, that's not protection at all. That's a prison, no matter how beautifully crafted," Isabelle seethes. In her anger, she reaches out to me, her hand on my knee. It's an interesting development, but one I find oddly comforting.

Delmare is taken aback by her words. "That's not—"

"My wife has a point," I interrupt. "Isolation isn't protection."

Neither Rip nor Allarick looks happy with me. In fact, they both look as if they would like to gut me where I sit. I'd like to see them try.

"You must understand, Queen Isabelle, my wife hasn't had the easiest of lives," Allarick said.

"You think I don't know that? I knew her before she came to Mescos. I'm quite familiar with what type of life she lived."

"So, you're her friend?" Allarick asks suspiciously.

Isabelle's hand on my knee tightens momentarily. I sense her change in demeanor and bring my shadows closer to strengthen her. After a moment, she shakes her head. "Not really. I don't think she knows who I am. But I know her. And I really need to speak with her. Could you at least ask her? It's very important."

The Kraken king takes his sweet time before answering. At last, he lets out a sigh. "I will speak with her."

Isabelle visibly relaxes next to me. "Thank you."

"But I don't change my position on her speaking with the Nephilim."

"Hettie won't speak with the creature either," Rip adds and then stands. "If that is all we need to discuss, Thorne and I will take our leave." Thorne nods, offering Isabelle a polite bow.

Allarick is next to stand. "I apologize we can't do more."

"You could," I say, voice cold. "What you mean to say is that you're sorry you aren't willing to do what needs to be done to win this war. My wife will take credit for that."

Allarick doesn't respond to my jest. I almost wish he would. Anger simmers low, but it's been a long time since I've let off so much power, and I'm itching to do just that.

Instead, the Kraken king addresses Isabelle. "I will speak to Erin and send word with her answer."

Isabelle nods once but otherwise doesn't respond. Allarick's tight-lipped smile fades as he gestures for Delmare to follow him out. I expected this meeting to be a difficult one, but did not anticipate an all-out refusal.

Despite my disappointment, a part of me can't fault Rip or Allarick for not wishing to risk their wives. Isabelle is capable of speaking to the Nephilim, but I had hoped she wouldn't have to do it alone—or at all, if I'm honest. However, it seems like we have no other choice. Isabelle will have to speak with the Nephilim again and soon.

I just fucking hate the idea.

CHAPTER 17
ISABELLE

Oziel simmers in quiet anger as the kings file out. The one with the locs turns back once more, but whatever he wishes to say is silenced by murmurs from his guard. A moment later, I'm left alone with my husband. I don't have to be a mind reader to know he doesn't like the outcome of today's meeting.

I don't know why I feel responsible for making him feel better either.

My hand is still on his knee. How long has it been there? I don't remember reaching out to him, and now that I know, I should pull away. Except I don't. I squeeze his knee.

Oziel raises his head, his golden eyes meeting my stare. He holds his tension in his jaw and shoulders. He's good at wearing a mask of indifference, but when you truly take the time to look, the cracks in his armor are apparent.

"You aren't satisfied with how it went." It's not a

question, but Oziel nods anyway. "What did you hope for?"

"That they wouldn't be blinded by love and do what needs to be done." His words sting, but I can't make sense of why. Our marriage is a contract with an end date. The other women may have found love, but it's not something I desire. I don't want to be caged like Anna.

"We don't need them," I say after a moment of silence. Oziel arches a brow, not fully convinced. "We don't. You have me. I can talk to the Nephilim, and you'll be there to pull me back if I get too close. We can do this, Oziel. You aren't going to let me get hurt."

I have nothing to back up my statement. Quite the opposite, actually. Everything about the demon king points at him either hurting or betraying me, and yet I don't believe any harm will come to me. Oziel needs me too much. As long as I'm useful, I'm safe.

"No, Kitten, you won't be harmed in my care. Unless I will it. But make no mistake. If I offer you pain, it will be because you want it." There's a seductive quality to his voice that has me pressing my thighs tightly together. I have no doubt Oziel is capable of causing me pain, and my body's instinct is to get turned on.

I'm fucking broken. Something in my head is wrong to get off on the idea of pain.

Ignoring his words for now, I push off the chair and let my hand drop from his knee. Before it falls to my side, Oziel's hand shoots out and takes my hand in his. He gives me a moment to pull away, but his touch interests me too much, so I let him.

"Take me to the Nephilim, Oziel. We won't get help from the others, so let me speak to it."

I'm prepared to fight his refusal, but his next words kill the protests on my lips. "Very well, Miss Sinclair. Let's go speak to our cursed friend, shall we?"

THE DUNGEON IS EERILY quiet by the time we reach the bottom step. Next to me, Oziel murmurs, "Lucifer Rising," and drops my hand, storming off toward something I can't see. It takes my eyes a moment longer to adjust to the dim light that roars to life in the room when we enter, and I see the reason Oziel is upset.

In the corner, next to the cell holding the Nephilim is a statue of a man. He's crouched with his sword drawn, frozen in a state of confusion. "Is that...?

"The guard assigned to the Nephilim, yes," Oziel finishes for me. "That's the second one today."

"Second? There was another?"

"Greta."

"Oh." The maid who helped prepare me for my wedding ceremony. Can't say I'm overly saddened by the news, but it's still terrifying to hear. She was fine just days ago, and now she's stone, which begs the question, is anyone safe?

No, not until the Nephilim are defeated and the curse is broken.

I approach the Nephilim's cell, but Oziel stops me from getting too close. My husband's fast. He was on the opposite side of the room a moment ago, and the next, he's near me, pulling me back against his chest. "Talk to it, but I won't allow you to get any closer to its cell."

"Fine," I huff with no true malice behind my words. I wait for him to let go of me, but Oziel's hold stays firm.

I don't have time to focus on his touch because a low growl fills the room, followed by movement from the cell. Fire roars to life on the floor to surround the cell, temporarily blinding me. When my vision comes to, I involuntarily gasp at the terrible creature before me. There's a low rumble like a purr, and it takes me a moment to realize the Nephilim is laughing at me.

"Pathetic humannn..."

Its voice is like many nails on multiple chalkboards. It's high in nature, but also deep like the lowest note on an untuned piano. My head starts to throb, starting behind my ears and working its way to the center of my forehead. This feels more intense than last time, lacking any of the build-up from before.

Oziel's arms tighten around me. I think he says something, but I can't make out the words because the Nephilim is speaking again. *"Warrr...cominggg..."*

The same words it said to me the first time, only now new images flash through my mind. I don't know if the Nephilim is somehow putting images into my brain, or if we've connected minds, but the world around me fades as I'm pulled into an old memory. The walls of the castle disappear, and I'm suddenly on a grassy field. But instead of green grass, the ground is painted in red.

Blood.

The crimson smell hits my senses, followed by the

putrid smell of death. Bile rises to my throat, and I retch. Chaos ensues.

Wolves and demons battle around me, taking down large creatures. More Nephilim. They stand tall in the sky, imposing creatures casting deadly blows down upon their enemies. Winged creatures fly in the sky, surrounding the Nephilim on all sides.

Dragons.

More creatures, some that look human and some that don't, are all engaged in combat against the enemy. One Nephilim stands out against all the rest. It's the only one not fighting, standing off in the distance. It towers a foot taller than its brethren, and although it appears just as monstrous as the others, there's a different aura around it. Something that makes it deadlier. Wiser in his bloodlust.

He's also not alone. At first, I confused the flying creature next to him with a dragon. The creature isn't a dragon and appears human but has wings. Large gray ones, flapping languidly in the wind to keep itself up. From here, the creature looks all gray, but they're so far away, it's hard to tell. Despite their distance, the power radiating off the creature makes my knees weak. My legs give out, and I sink to my knees, landing in plush grass.

An anguished wail rises above all the other noise. I jerk my head up in time to see another winged person above me. This one is female with the same gray coloring as the other. She wears black and mossy-green armor, silver bands decorating both her arms. She's bloodied and probably has multiple wounds. Her left wing seems damaged, as her right wing compensates to keep her up.

But it's the sheer devastation on her face that brings me to a standstill. The raw, soul-crushing anguish in her scream. Tears carve tracks through the blood on her cheeks, and for a moment, I can't breathe.

Her pain slams into me like a tidal wave, crashing through every defense I thought I had. I hear a scream—my own—and clutch my chest as if I can hold my heart together. But it's already breaking, shattering piece by piece right in front of me.

The physical pain is nothing compared to the betrayal slicing through me like a thousand blades, reopening wounds that never truly healed. Scars etched deep in places no one can see. And no matter how much time passes, they still bleed. It's not my pain. It's *hers*.

"Stop this! I beg of you! We fight for Mescos. We protect!" the woman screams at the other like her. I can't see the expression of the person she's speaking to, but I do notice when they turn their back to her. Another piercing scream rings out around us. Something snaps, breaking permanently.

The pain intensifies.

It's too much. Too hot. Too constricting.

Bright white light explodes within my head. My scream reverberates around me until all I know is pain.

Darkness creeps in, and for the first time, I'm afraid of the shadows. They claim me, pulling me down until I can no longer fight. I surrender, and everything goes black.

Then...nothing. Only silence.

CHAPTER 18
OZIEL

Blood pours from Isabelle's nose as her face drains of color. She lets out a piercing, bone-chilling scream that cuts through the air like a dagger. The Nephilim's cries join hers, a haunting symphony of terror that reverberates in my skull. The sound is unbearable. Standing becomes a struggle, and holding on to Isabelle feels impossible.

Then, she goes limp in my arms.

My heart pounds violently in my chest, as if there are steel hands gripping it, ready to tear it free from my body. Beads of cold sweat trickle down the back of my neck, chilling my usual warm body to icy cold. This emotion is foreign to me. Something I haven't experienced since...the roses. The day my parents died.

Isabelle grows cold to the touch. Any longer down here with the Nephilim will cause her body to shut down. It is just a guess, but not one I want to test. My queen is dead weight in my arms, but she feels as light as a feather. Shadows enclose us, far too slowly for my liking. Power flickers within me like candlelight, rapidly losing steam.

Finally, the shadows blanket us completely, silencing the cries of the Nephilim. When they part for me, we're no longer in the dungeon. Isabelle's room feels like a paradise. Adrenaline pulses through my veins, lighting a fire within me. With great care, I carry Isabelle to bed. The woman doesn't so much as stir as I lay her down. If it weren't for the slight rise and fall of her chest, I would mistake her as dead.

She's so pale. And her chest and bodice are soaked with her blood. Red stains her lips, painting them a menacing crimson color. I roar, shaking the very foundation of the castle. It's a call for any demon nearby. A distress call, one I have only given once before.

Garvan is first to Isabelle's room, followed by two other demons, one whom I recognize as a medic. Garvan assesses the room and takes one look at Isabelle before springing into action. He barks orders to the two demons in the room, and they fall in line, both coming to attend to Isabelle. I've never been more thankful for my courtier than this moment. The green-skinned demons attempt to move me out of the way, but I bare my teeth at them.

"My lord, Zain needs to assess the queen." Garvan takes a tentative step in my direction. He reaches out like he's going to touch Isabelle, but fury once again fills me, and my shadows circle his arm, forcing it back down at his side. And just like that, the feelings for my courtier diminish into something truly vile.

He stops approaching the bed, lips set in a grim line. "We can't help her if we don't go near her, my lord."

I know he's right. She needs the attention from the medic, but I'm unwilling to move. Distrust for my own people plagues me. In fact, distrust runs rampant throughout my kingdom, everyone always trying to point the finger at someone else. Anger demands an outlet. Someone has to be blamed. Do these demons blame me for not protecting our people? Will they hurt their queen in order to hurt me?

But if Isabelle doesn't receive help...that could also be a death sentence. One I have no one to blame for but myself.

The choice is simple, and yet I find stepping back the hardest thing I've ever had to force myself to do.

The demon—Zain—looks upon me with uncertainty but soon determines I won't attack them for touching Isabelle. Zain speaks to the other demon, one whose name I didn't catch, and together, they place their hands over Isabelle and chant. Garvan moves closer to me, but still keeps a sizable distance between us. Smart man. If I lash out, he would be the recipient of my wrath.

"What happened?" Garvan asks.

I answer him, though I don't look away from Isabelle. A sheer gray film radiates from Zain's hands as they trail across Isabelle's chest. "She spoke to the Nephilim."

Garvan's eyes widen. A flicker of unease flashes in his eyes. "Is that wise, my lord? With what little we know about the Nephilim, it seems dangerous to test the waters."

"And what would you have me do? Hmm?" I whirl on him, anger getting the best of me. "Isabelle is here to help this kingdom. Others may feel fine with locking their wives away in a fancy tower, but I will not be one of those husbands. She will not be caged here like a prized lamb."

Garvan backs up, holding his hands in front of him as a symbol of surrender. "I mean no offense, my lord. These are trying times. I know we are desperate to seek answers, but—"

"But nothing," I interrupt. His voice grates on my last nerves. "A king will do whatever it takes to save his people. As will his queen. The way you seek to lock us in the shadows and hope for the best further proves you aren't and will never be cut out to do my job."

The words cut deep as intended. Garvan flinches. Anger clouds his features, and his breathing speeds up. Part of me wants him to fight back. I would welcome an outlet for my emotions. But ever the proper courtier, he schools his expression into the loyal lap dog he is.

"Of course, my lord. This is why you are king. You know best, after all." Garvan's jaw clenches as he takes a step back. His heated gaze bores into me, even as I turn back around just in time to see Zain take her hands off my wife.

The demon turns her head in my direction and nods once. "The queen suffers from a mild case of vasovagal syncope."

"In plain language."

"It's common. Especially in humans. It causes the person to faint after the body has gone through severe emotional distress. She will wake soon, but she'll need to eat and drink plenty of fluids. She may also experience a headache or nausea." Zain digs for something in her coat, producing a vial of green liquid. "This will help the queen if she's experiencing intense headaches or fatigue."

I take the tonic from Zain's hand, pocketing it. "Very well. Have the kitchen prepare a meal and send up a pitcher of water."

Zain nods and takes her leave, along with the other demon assisting her. Garvan still lurks behind me but soon moves from his position. "Anything else you need, my lord? What should I tell the others who heard your call for aid?"

"Tell them their queen is healing. That she spoke with a monster today and survived. Oh, and Garvan?" I turn in time to see him take a step closer to the door. "If you ever question what I allow my wife to do again, there's a Nephilim downstairs that could use a cell mate."

His features don't change, but there's a sudden stiffness in the way he holds himself. He bows low before meeting my gaze again. "Of course, my lord." Garvan turns and leaves Isabelle's room.

Another time, I may reflect on wounding the pride of my closest courtier, but that isn't today. I drag a wooden chair next to Isabelle's bedside and perch myself upon it.

And then I wait.

For food.

For water.

For Isabelle to regain consciousness and throw insults in my direction. Then and only then will the heaviness in my chest disperse.

CHAPTER 19
ISABELLE

My body feels like it's been hit by a tractor and then backed over for good measure. I woke a few times, only for food and water to be pushed in front of me. A rather growly demon forced me to eat soup—which I hate—but then let me sleep after. And sleep I did. It was the type of dreamless sleep that makes you disoriented when you finally awaken from it.

I don't know how much time has passed, but when I open my eyes this time, moonlight filters through the black curtains. The window is cracked, but instead of the usual sounds of night critters, all I hear is the crackling of the fire. It's eerie. Like the entire kingdom is in a great slumber alongside me.

My body still aches, but it's no longer debilitating like it was before. I manage to awkwardly push myself into a sitting position, my back against the headboard. Despite the fire and mounds of woolen blankets, I still find myself cold. Shivering, I tug the blankets up to my shoulders.

"Need another one?"

I scream. My body jerks, and my head hits the headboard with a loud thud. "Fuck," I groan and fiercely rub the back of my head.

Soft laughter greets me, caressing my senses like a silky touch. I know that damn laugh.

When I turn my head slightly, Oziel's stupidly handsome face greets me. He's smirking because of course he is. Despite his teasing smile, there are dark circles under his eyes, and his clothes are unkempt. He's usually put together, but now he looks disgruntled and tired.

"Do you make it your job to scare me?" I frown.

"Scare you? Miss Sinclair, it's not my fault you don't check your surroundings when you wake up. It's not as if I hid in the shadows, waiting for you to wake."

The way he says it has me thinking that's exactly what he did. "How long have you been here?"

"Hmm, let's see. I was born here centuries ago—"

"No, you prick." Did he say centuries? Fucking centuries?! How old is this man, and why does he barely look a day over thirty? This is definitely a problem for later. Damn demons and their damn sexy features. "I mean how long have you been in my room?"

"Ah, that," he hums, eyes darkening. "You've been asleep for three days."

I wait for Oziel to continue, but the man has a knack for pissing me off with his nonanswer answers. It's like he gets a thrill from upsetting me. Perhaps he does and has some weird anger kink.

Nope, not thinking about kinks in relation to Oziel. Don't need to go down that road, no matter how hot it may be.

"Have you been here the entire time?" At my question, he meets my gaze. He doesn't speak, but his eyes give away his answer. "You have. Why?"

"The queen was hurt. I needed to make sure you didn't die." Then, as an afterthought, he adds, "The deal I made with Ender would be for naught."

"So, you stayed here for three days to make sure your contract wasn't voided?"

"Yes, Miss Sinclair. I stayed here for three days to make sure the contract wasn't voided. What other reason would there be?" Oziel speaks nonchalantly, as if we were commenting on the weather and not my mortality. I know a liar when I see one, though. I've been lied to too many times not to detect when someone is being disingenuous. Good liars can mask their face into a blank canvas. Great liars never make you question or doubt them. But no liar can hide the truth in their eyes.

Oziel was scared. For me.

A weird, foreign feeling stirs low in my belly. Before I can analyze it any further, Oziel leans forward. "What happened, Isabelle?"

Hearing my name on his lips momentarily stuns me. Since I've arrived, it's been Miss Sinclair or Kitten, but never Isabelle. I pretend like I don't like the sound of my name on his lips.

"I saw something..." My mind desperately tries conjuring up the memories the Nephilim shared with me. "It was like I was thrown into the middle of a great battle. I could smell the blood and rot of death. I heard screams of the dying. It was…" I shiver. "It felt so real, like I was really there."

To my surprise, he reaches out and takes my hand. It provides an odd sense of comfort. "It was real. Just not your reality. Go on."

I look down at our clasped hands, remembering the woman in the Nephilim's vision. "There was a woman. She looked human, but her coloring was different, and she had wings. She was crying, begging for someone to stop. I felt her pain, Oziel. Felt her utter devastation. Whoever she was begging to stop turned their back on her. That's when I felt the pain of betrayal, like a sword stabbing through my heart, and then…nothing."

I half expect Oziel to tell me I'm crazy. That I dreamed all this up. But he doesn't. His brow furrows, and he squeezes my hand. "Did you see the person she was speaking to? Anything you can tell me about them?"

"Not really," I admit, mentally kicking myself for not trying harder to see who it was. "I think it was a male? Though I could be mistaken. This person had wings too, but that's all I remember because his back was turned toward me. I don't think that helps much."

"On the contrary, Miss Sinclair, that helps a great deal." Oziel lets go of my hand and sits back in his chair. I instantly miss the warmth of his hand in mine. My husband drums his fingers against the armrest of his chair, deep in concentration. "A great deal, indeed," he murmurs more to himself than me, clearly lost in his own thoughts.

I want to ask him what he's thinking, but the intense

need to pee overtakes me. It feels like my bladder is close to bursting, so I not-so-graciously roll out of bed. "I'll be back," I say before half running, half walking to the restroom, clenching my entire body. If Oziel says anything, I don't hear as I shut the door behind me.

I manage to make it to the toilet without embarrassing myself. Pulling down my pants is the first time I realize I'm no longer wearing my dress. Someone changed me, and I feel my cheeks flame at the thought of Oziel changing my clothes. It's not like he hasn't seen me naked, thanks to the moment in the washroom, but that doesn't mean I'm comfortable with him seeing me naked while I'm unconscious. Then again, it could have been another demon whom he called upon to heal me.

I'm going with that version.

Once I'm finished peeing a damn river, I flush and wash my hands. I feel gross, hair matted to the back of my head, and there are still spots of dried blood on my face. The shower is calling me, but I don't think I have enough strength to bathe myself yet. And there's no way in hell I'm asking Oziel to help me. My pride can only take so much. Showering will simply have to wait until I get more energy.

When I walk back into my room, Oziel is no longer alone. Two other unfamiliar demons strip my bed. A whimper leaves my lips since I had planned on crawling back into it.

Oziel hears me and beckons, "Come," as he goes to a tall mural by the fire.

"Come where?" I ask, but my feet move on their own accord, gravitating toward him.

"My room."

"Your room?" I echo, sounding more like a parrot than a person.

Oziel doesn't answer. Instead, he steps forward and presses his palm to the mural. A soft click echoes through the corridor, and the mural shifts, swinging open like a door on silent hinges. A hidden passageway. I shouldn't be surprised. In a place like this, secret doors probably outnumber the regular ones.

Oziel reaches back for me, and I allow him to take my hand, leading me through the passageway. It's dark and hard to see, but Oziel doesn't appear to have the same problem. He leads me blindly, and when he stops abruptly, I run into his back with a grunt. He chuckles before another clicking noise sounds, and the other door swings open.

To another room. *His* room.

One similar to the one we just came from but slightly bigger. It's decorated in the same dark woods and crimson sheets. Instead of a single window on the far side of the room, there are two doors, pushed wide open, that lead to a balcony.

"You will stay here now," Oziel says.

"What was wrong with my old room?"

"It wasn't mine."

Oh. Part of me should be mad that Oziel assumes I will share a bed with him, but another part of me doesn't care if I sleep with ten other people, as long as I have a bed to lie down in.

"Fine, but just so you know, I will push you off the bed if you snore." I make my way to his bed. I don't know how it's possible, but Oziel's bed is even softer than mine. I slide easily into it, and if I died right here, right now...I think I'd be okay with that. Serenity washes over me.

Until Oziel speaks: "You snore."

I spring up, insulted. "I do not snore!"

"You do. It's cute though." He beams at my expense, and my cheeks redden at the thought of him thinking my snores are cute. "You even talk in your sleep."

Now that, I can believe. My sister always complained about me talking in my sleep when we shared a room as kids. I used to be so embarrassed by it, but it's not like I can do anything to change it. My mind, even in sleep, never truly quiets.

"What did I say?" In the past, it has mostly been nonsensical words. Or sometimes I ask for random things, at least according to my sister and parents.

"Names." Oziel stalks from his side of the room over to the bed. He perches on the end, near my feet. His next words feel like I'm being doused with cold water. "Three names actually: Anna, Erin, and James."

My heart nearly stops. I'm not even sure if I breathe.

"Isabelle?" Oziel says my name with concern I'm not accustomed to hearing from him. I meet his gaze, his intense stare boring into me. Into my soul.

I should expect his next question, but it still takes me by surprise.

"Isabelle," he says again. "Why do you want to speak with Erin?"

CHAPTER 20

ISABELLE

Oziel's eyes pierce through me. This is my chance to snap back. Tell him it's not any of his damn business. Part of me firmly believes Erin should be the first to know what I've done. But another part of me, one that nags me to my very core, just wants to tell *someone*. Make someone understand—that I did the only thing I could when no one else would.

I did something when the fucking police did nothing but defend an abusive asshole.

If anyone would understand where I'm coming from, it would be the demon king. After all, he told me what he does to creatures that break the law. I don't see a difference between his torturing and my killing. At least mine ended the suffering quickly...though I wish that bastard suffered for days. I wished he suffered in the same agonizing way my sister, and probably Erin, suffered. I would have loved to hear his cries and pleas, knowing no one would be there to save him.

Oziel sucks in a deep breath, as if he smells something delicious. He then lets out a soft hum. "You smell positively delightful, Kitten. Care to share what dark thoughts going through your mind?"

"I'm not a monster." The words tumble out before I can stop them, and they don't stop. "I did what I had to. What no one else would do. And yet, I'm the one they label a monster."

"In my experience, monsters don't care if you think they are monsters. You are far from it, Miss Sinclair."

"But I killed someone." I don't know why I say it. Maybe because I need him to see me for what I am. What I'm capable of doing when pushed to the extreme and have no other options at my disposal. "And I don't regret it. I don't seek redemption or forgiveness."

Oziel's expression doesn't change. He stares at me with a mixture of curiosity and interest. If I didn't know any better, I'd say there's also something akin to pride in his expression. "I see."

His response is lackluster, and my body deflates. "That's all? You have nothing else to say?" I'm not sure what I expected, maybe mild shock or horror, but definitely not acceptance.

Oziel shrugs. "Sounds like a normal Monday night, Kitten."

I frown. "I killed him in cold blood."

"I'm sure you had your reasons."

Despite myself, I laugh. Full belly laughs that leave me feeling breathless. Even Oziel smiles, a real genuine smile and not the damn smirk he usually wears. "Leave it to a demon to be okay with murder," I finally manage to choke out.

Oziel's eyes darken, but when I blink, it's gone, and he's back to smiling, making me think I just made up what I saw. "Some people deserve to be put to death. Others die too soon in life."

I wait for him to say more, but Oziel purses his lips. There's more he's not saying. How many people has Oziel had to kill? Has he lost anyone he loved? Those questions have to wait because we're talking about me now.

I find myself wanting to share. Erin would know soon enough, but there's no harm in Oziel hearing it too. Despite our tumultuous relationship, he's the only one who can see the sin and darkness in me and not shy away. I've never had that before. It's...refreshing.

Even though I've accepted that I'll tell Oziel the truth, I can't stop my heart from beating wildly in my chest, threatening to burst from its confinement. If Oziel hears it from his perch on the opposite side of the bed, he makes no comment. His eyes—black voids with golden embers smoldering in their depths—never waver from me.

"I had an older sister named Anna," I say, barely above a whisper. I haven't spoken about my sister in so long. She's a ghost that haunts me still—will probably forever haunt me. I might not cry myself to sleep every night, but it doesn't mean I've forgotten her or that I'm suddenly fine with her passing. The grief comes in unexpected waves.

"Anna was kind. Sweet. She liked to read and go to weird cafes for tea. She was the best big sister ever." I sniffle, holding back my emotions. "But she was kind to a fault. The type of good that people exploit. She had never really been in any long-term relationships, so when she told me she was dating James, a guy she met while working at a convenience store, I was a bit surprised by it.

"I didn't know anything about the man. He never came around much, and when he did, he never stayed long. He always had his arm around Anna, like she couldn't go anywhere without him."

Oziel makes a disapproving sound but doesn't interrupt.

"Anna started to change. It was small things at first. Getting scared when I approached her too fast. Spending hours in her room. Covering her face. We'd lost our parents, so admittedly, it took me longer to realize than it should have. I'm sure my mother would have picked up on it a lot sooner..." I mumble the last part. Our mother was always good at picking up when things were wrong. As a child, I thought it was annoying, but as an adult, I think it was her superpower.

"When I finally confronted Anna, she broke down and started crying. That's when she told me about the abuse. I saw the bruises on her, Oziel. They were all over her body. She also told me he was dating someone else and had been for a long time. Years, even. Anna only found out about it when she caught him at the bar with another woman. Her name was Erin."

"Ah," Oziel says at last, connecting the dots I've carefully crafted for him. "This is why you are interested in speaking to the Kraken queen."

"Kinda, but not for the reasons you think," I admit.

"My sister was devastated. She tried leaving him a few times, but it always ended badly. She felt trapped. Like nothing she could do would ever free her from him. I think James might have threatened to hurt me. It's the only thing I can think of as to why she would stay with him for as long as she did.

"Then one night, I got home late from work. Traffic was terrible because we were experiencing a massive rainstorm. Anna was usually in her room, so I didn't think it was weird that the house was quiet when I got home. I made myself dinner, watched TV, before finally going upstairs. I was tired, so tired from work, but I wanted to check on Anna—just to let her know I was home. But when I opened the door..."

The day is forever etched in my brain. The coldness of the house. The all too quiet silence. A heaviness clung to the house; one I didn't notice until it was too late. Maybe I could have saved her. Who's to say? I've beaten myself up over it for so long. I don't know how long she had been there. If I would have gone straight to her instead of eating and watching TV, then maybe...

"When I opened the door, I found Anna face down on her bed. Her room smelled heavily of vomit, and I ran to her, but she was so cold to the touch. Her skin had turned this awful blue color. That's when I noticed the pills—" A sob tears through my body at the same time Oziel reaches for my hand. It's a small, gentle touch. But it gives me something to focus on other than my own grief. It's an anchor in a rough sea of emotions.

"She took her own life," I finally manage to get out. "I think she felt it was the only way to free herself of James.

James may not have physically murdered my sister, but I blame him for her death. Her death is on his hands."

"He killed your sister." Oziel speaks the words with such conviction, I tip my head up. He's the only one who has ever believed me without question. He's resolute in his words, the tension in his jaw the only indicator of his fury. Funny how I can read these little signs after a short period with him.

"For months leading up to my sister's death, we went to the police to make reports of the physical abuse James put her through," I say. "The emotional abuse wasn't much better, but that didn't leave marks, so there was little we could do. They only cared about the physical marks, but even then, they always had a way of doubting the victim."

It was always the same story. *James is a good guy. Do you really want to hurt his reputation? How can we believe you didn't get those marks from someone else? Isn't he dating a woman named Erin?*

"And not a single cop did anything. This went on for months, until Anna died," I whisper.

"These are the people meant to protect humans?" Oziel asks, reminding me we come from different worlds. I nod, looking down at our clasped hands. Then Oziel places a finger under my chin, tipping up my head, so I'm forced to meet his gaze. "Tell me how you killed him, Kitten."

There's a wicked gleam in his eyes, like hearing this story is intoxicating to him. Maybe it is.

When he drops his hand from my chin, I'm instantly transported back to the day. "I drove myself to the corner store because I knew James stopped there every morning for beer. I arrived before him, but it didn't take long until I saw his mud-covered truck pull into an empty parking spot.

"I remember my hand tightened around the gun—"

"Gun?" he interrupted.

Again, our differences elude me until now. "It's a deadly weapon."

Oziel seems far too invested in a gun. I wouldn't be surprised if, by next month, he has designed his own version of one. But he nods for me to continue, falling silent so I can finish my confession.

"He had no clue I was there, holding a gun to his back. I wanted him to see my face when I pulled the trigger, so I called his name. When he turned and saw the gun, the bastard fucking laughed like it was some sort of joke. Like I was just some random girl he could easily manipulate into handing him over the gun."

"Seems like this pathetic excuse of flesh didn't realize he was facing the demon queen," Oziel interjects.

I feel my cheeks heat. "I wasn't the demon queen back then. I was just Isabelle."

"You've always been the demon queen." His words are unwavering, like they are some known fact etched into stone. He takes what I say as the truth—which it is —and instead of passing judgment, he simply listens. "Continue."

So I do. "I pulled the trigger. It was loud. My ears rang, and the world shifted to slow motion. The bullet hit James square in the chest, where his heart would be if he had one. Blood bloomed like a crimson flower around the entry point. Then our eyes connected. Just for a brief moment, but that was all it took for recognition to dawn on his face. He remembered me. Remembered my sister."

And the story is out. Every detail of the day will forever be painted on my memory. An echo of the past and the reminder that I'm capable of taking life. Despite not regretting what I've done, I need for him to understand why I did it. To understand I had no other option.

"I had to kill him," I whisper. The words feel heavy between us.

Silence.

My demon husband tilts his head slightly, his long fingers drumming lazily against my palm. "Say that again." His voice is velvet, dark and laced with intrigue.

I force myself to look at him, which isn't hard. I'm drawn to him, hypnotized by the demon in front of me. The attraction has been there since I arrived but has only heightened after our marriage. No matter how much I fight it, my body calls to him in a way it hasn't called to anyone before.

"The man who hurt my sister." My throat tightens, but I push through. "He's dead. I made sure of it. I killed him and watched his blood stain the concrete. Watched as the life went out of his eyes. I did it for my sister. Maybe even Erin too. That's why she needs to know what I did."

Still no anger. No horror. No disappointment. Only a slow, creeping smile curling his lips.

Seconds pass us by before Oziel rises from the bed with a languid grace, stepping toward me. Every movement, every breath of his presence is predatory, but not toward me. When he reaches me, he crouches down. The mighty demon king on his knees before me is a magnificent sight that spreads heat throughout my body.

Oziel reaches out, his claw-tipped fingers brushing against the inside of my wrist, where my pulse still pounds rapidly. Not only for what I just revealed, but for the very king before me.

"I wondered how long it would take you," he murmurs, reverence in his voice.

My breath stills. "You already knew?" Did Ender tell him? Did his abilities as king and a demon give him insight into my crimes?

His chuckle is low, rich with dark amusement. "Not the specifics, no, but I did know you harbored darkness inside you. I sensed it the moment I saw you. I've been waiting for you to embrace it, Kitten. Stop running from it. Command it."

My lips part, but no words come.

I smell sin on you.

He's known me, the real me, this whole time, and not once has he shied away. That has to mean something.

"You have done what weak men could not," he continues, hand sliding up to cup my jaw, tilting my face to his. I don't try to pull away or break contact. His eyes burn, filled with something almost tender. "You have protected your own. Taken what justice refused to give, and for that, you should be proud. This is what makes you a queen, Isabelle."

A shudder passes through me, not from fear but from the overwhelming relief that rushes through my veins. But also something else. Something that ignites my body, making me feel *things* toward my demon husband. Things I haven't felt in such a long time. It is terrifying.

He rises and presses a kiss to my forehead, his lips lingering against my skin, like it's the most natural thing in the fucking world. His words take my breath away. "You are more mine now than ever."

His.

I don't like being a possession. But the way Oziel said that makes me feel like an equal. I do the only thing I can...the only thing that will keep my sanity.

I push him away. I fucking hate that I do, but my ability to keep a wall between us is rapidly deteriorating, and I fear what will happen if I let it crumble completely.

Oziel doesn't fight me, simply steps back and puts some distance between us. There's a knock on the door, drawing his attention. "Food is here. I shall leave you to it, Kitten."

I don't get time to react because, in the next moment, Oziel is gone, swallowed up by shadows as his bedroom door opens and a demon rolls in a cart of food. She sets it in front of me and leaves just as silently as she came in.

I'm alone. After spilling my heart out to my husband. I can't bring myself to regret my decision to tell him. I needed someone to know. The only thing I regret is pushing him away. As I eat the food placed in front of me, his words replay over and over again in my mind.

You are more mine now than ever.

CHAPTER 21

ISABELLE

I don't see Oziel again that day, and when I wake up the following morning, he's not in his room either. Maybe I shouldn't have assumed he'd sleep in his own bed that night, but if he didn't sleep with me, what other bed did he occupy? Another's? White-hot anger simmers just below the surface at the thought of my husband warming another demon's bed.

I don't even love Oziel. Hell, I barely tolerate him. Or at least that is what I tell myself because the truth brewing at the back of my mind is not something I'm ready to deal with. But that doesn't stop my brain from wanting to kill the fucker who shares my husband's bed.

Now that I'm pissed, I kick off the heaps of blankets —all of which smell like Oziel—and push myself into a sitting position. None of my muscles scream in protest like they did yesterday, which I take as my sign to get a shower in finally. It's about time. I swear I'm starting to smell myself. Maybe it's a good thing Oziel didn't come back to bed last night.

My feet press against the warm stone floor, the heat seeping into my aching bones and soothing the stiffness in my limbs. Oziel's bed was like a cloud. Soft, enveloping, and far too easy to sink into, but after so many hours wrapped in its embrace, I'm desperate for some sort of movement.

I take another slow glance around the room, noting the luxurious furnishings and lingering traces of Oziel's presence before finally making my way toward the showers, eager to wash away the remnants of the last few days.

The bathing chamber is surprisingly empty when I walk inside. No rambunctious orgies or lustful moans echoing around the chamber. When I turn the knob, water spouts from the faucet shaped like a wolf's open mouth. Steam gathers in the stall as I neatly fold my towel and place it upon a bench.

The moment the hot water kisses my skin, I groan. All the collected dirt, blood, and grime from the last few days wash down the drain. I reach for the products lining the shelf. Lavender and honey fill my nostrils as I select a soap to use. It lathers easily, and I scrub my body until my skin flushes a faint pink.

There are more options for my hair. The shampoo holds more oils than I'm used to but leaves my hair smelling like a floral shop and silky to the touch. My poor, neglected hair all but sings out the praises for these homemade shampoos. There's even a gritty, textured paste I take for the demon's version soft sugar scrub, and rub it into my entire body until I'm slick and in danger of slipping around due to the excess oils.

Steam curls through the open shower chamber, thick and swirling. I stand beneath the cascade of hot water, eyes closed, letting it run over my bare skin, content to stay here all day if I could. I just might.

A distant creak of the door has my eyes snapping open, barely containing the urge to cover myself. I don't know if I'll ever be used to a communal shower. For a moment, nothing else follows the sound. Maybe I'm hearing things, or maybe someone saw the showers weren't empty and left. I tell myself it's nothing, just the shifting of the old iron hinges in the heat. But then, barely audible over the patter of water, comes another sound. Soft. Measured. A footstep on the smooth stone floor.

I turn my head slightly, listening as my muscles tighten. Part of me hopes to see Oziel, his full body on display for me. Would he join me? Would I let him? Yes, I think I would. Purely because I'm just a girl with fucking needs and no other reason.

Soon, a shadow wavers just beyond the steam.

My breath hitches. Someone's here. Watching.

Oziel? If it's my husband, he enjoys making my heart speed up. I don't speak, and neither does the imposing figure standing in the shadows. Something shimmers in the darkness, and my brain is slow to process the mystery figure wielding a dagger.

Definitely not Oziel.

A sense of foreboding washes over me, and I desperately look around for something to use as a weapon. I curse when I come up empty-handed.

The figure takes a step toward me.

My heart pounds rapidly in my chest. I can feel the presence now, far more sinister than Oziel's. Definitely not my husband then. Someone else. Someone who wants to hurt me.

There's only one way to enter and exit the bathing chambers. The door is on the opposite end, but in order to get to it, I have to run past the dagger-wielding shadow. I can be fast when I need to be, but I don't particularly want to chance running straight into his trap or slipping on the soapy ground.

"Get away from me," my voice quivers.

I'm greeted with a low chuckle that sends shivers down my spine. Not the confusing shivers Oziel gives me, but ones of terror.

The shadow crouches.

I brace myself, ready to fight my way through.

Time passes slowly, almost as if it has stopped completely. The only sounds are my labored breathing and water hitting the stone chamber.

Just as I think the shadow is about to attack, the door to the chamber opens, followed by the shrill giggles of two she-demons. The shadow retreats, slinking back into the darkness. The mystery person flees as quickly as they arrived, running past the newcomers and out the door. The two female demons don't seem to notice the dark shadows pass them, too preoccupied with each other.

My body unfreezes as the reality of the situation hits me. Someone tried to attack me, and I'm not stupid enough to wait around for them to come back. I hurry and grab my towel, wrapping it around my soaking wet body. The demon couple is too consumed with one another, their giggles slowly turning into moans as I race past them. Wet feet and stone flooring are the worst combination imaginable. My next step has my feet sliding out from under me, and I go down.

Hard.

My body hits the floor with a dull thud. I manage to keep one hand securing my towel while the other one braces my fall. I'll pay for that later. "Fuck, I hope no one saw that."

"Miss Sinclair, Lucifer Rising, are you okay, my queen?"

Fuck, someone saw that.

I turn just in time to see Garvan's lithe figure crouch down in front of me. His eyes wander over my body, but not in a sexual way—with the intensity of a concerned friend, trying to assess the damage. However, I'm still keenly aware that I'm sprawled on the floor with nothing but my towel on.

"I'm okay," I mumble, taking his offered hand.

Garvan stands and pulls me up. He then looks back at my water tracks. "Did something happen?"

My first instinct is to lie. For some reason, I don't want him to know that a crazy shadow demon wanted to hurt me, at least not until I can tell Oziel. "Yeah, just trying to get back to my room." The lie slips easily off my tongue. I hope that's the end of it, that Garvan will nod and go on his way.

But he doesn't do that. Instead, he says, "I'll escort you back, my queen." Before I have the time to refuse, Garvan starts walking toward my—Oziel's—room. I have no choice but to follow.

"Do you know where Oziel is?" I ask, doing my best not to sound too interested. Even though I am. Why hasn't he sought me out yet? Is my mystery attacker after him too?

"The king was called away this morning to the River Hel. There was word of a hooded figure acting suspiciously nearby."

"A hooded figure?" I echo, frowning.

Garvan stops right outside the door. As usual, the courtier is impeccably dressed in sapphire blue, with a silver tunic peeking through his overcoat. He nods once before reaching for the doorknob. "That's what the guards reported—" he cuts himself off, eyes widening. "My king," he says, almost imperceptibly.

With no decorum, I push past Garvan and peer inside. Oziel stands with his back to us near a table. There's a faint glow emitting from something behind him, but I can't make out what it is. Oziel turns, his usual golden eyes now midnight black. Much like Garvan, he's dressed like a royal. The only sign the king is tired is the dark circles under his eyes. Maybe he really didn't get any sleep last night. Oziel looks from me to Garvan, eyes narrowing to tiny slits.

"My king," Garvan says again. "I thought you'd be at the River Hel."

"I was," is all Oziel says, not offering any more information.

Garvan awkwardly clears his throat. "I was just escorting the queen back to your chambers. I found her on the floor—"

"I slipped while I was running," I cut Garvan off.

"Why were you running?" Oziel's question is for me, but his eyes never stray from Garvan. The temperature in the room seems to rise a few degrees.

"Because..." I hesitate. It's not that I don't trust Oziel, or Garvan, for that matter, but I'm still trying to figure out what I saw. Do all demons have the ability to move shadows, or is that an ability saved for the king?

Oziel finally moves, exposing the glowing object. In a glass dome is a bouquet of blood-red roses. Petals decorate the bottom, scattered all around. Has this always been there? I barely paid attention to the room since I've been in here, consumed with thoughts of the demon before me. Oziel's silence unnerves me.

"Check for updates with the guards, Garvan." His command is a clear dismissal.

Garvan nods once and leaves without another glance back. We listen to his retreating steps until I hear nothing but my own breathing.

Suddenly the door slams shut, startling me. "What the hell?" I ask just as Oziel whirls on me.

"Did you fuck Garvan?"

Out of everything he could have asked, this is not something I expected. My mouth opens and closes in stunned silence. Anger radiates off my husband in waves. I've never feared Oziel, even when I first met him, but now...I can see the terrifying demon king everyone else sees. The temper he barely keeps in check.

"What the actual fuck, Oziel?" My voice is a near shriek when I finally find it again, my anger mounting at his accusation.

"Answer me, *Wife*," he growls, closing the space

between us. Heat from his body kisses my skin; the sheer power of him is overwhelming. "Did you fuck Garvan?"

I laugh humorlessly. "Oh, you're a fucking bastard, you know that, right?" I jab a finger into his chest. "You're allowed to fuck any demon in this damn castle, but if I so much as walk with a man who's not you, then suddenly I'm a whore. How about you tell me whose bed you were in last night?"

For the first time since I arrived, Oziel's anger cracks, giving way to confusion. "No one. If I fuck another, you will know, Kitten. Because you'd be there with me."

My anger still simmers, but hearing his words makes my cheeks flush. Damn him. And fuck my body for liking that thought. "For your information, asshole, I was nearly attacked in the bathroom, and Garvan found me as I was running away."

In the blink of an eye, all residual anger drains from Oziel's face. A new fierceness I've never seen before takes over. He grabs my shoulders as if to keep himself upright. "You were attacked?"

"Nearly," I say, shoving him off. I need out of this damn towel, so I reach for the silk robe hanging off the chair. Oziel has already seen me naked, so I pretend that dropping my towel in front of him doesn't affect me at all. I don't miss the way his gaze heats as he looks over my naked body. I let him look his fill before abruptly closing and tying my robe.

"Do all demons have the power to manipulate shadows?"

"No," Oziel says immediately. "They shouldn't.

Though technically they could possess the power if they were stealing it."

"Stealing from what?"

"The River Hel," he explains.

I frown. Was my attacker the same person poisoning the river? But if so, why? Especially if they are benefiting from the power. "The attacker used the shadows and steam to hide himself. He had a dagger. I think...I think he meant to kill me."

"Lucifer Rising," Oziel growls in a way that tells me those are curse words here. "I've been dealing with the River Hel all morning. That's why I wasn't with you. Are you certain this person used shadows?"

I nod. "Yes. I should have been able to see him, but the shadows surrounded him like they do you. I couldn't make out any of his features. Hell, I'm not even certain it was a man."

Oziel curses again.

"Feel bad for accusing me of fucking another man?" I ask after a moment because, yeah, I'm still pissed about that.

Oziel has the decency to look ashamed. "My apologies, Kitten. I've been on edge all night. I'm not in my right mind. I saw Garvan with you and—"

"You thought I let him fuck me," I finish and roll my eyes. "No, dear husband, I was, in fact, trying not to die."

"Isabelle, I'm sorry." His apology sounds so sincere, and yet odd coming from him. Those words are likely not ones he says often. Maybe ever. What does a king have to be sorry for anyway? Still, part of me can understand where he was coming from. Doesn't make it right or justify it, but stress can do crazy things to people.

"Forgiven." I sink down into the chair. My shoulder accidentally bumps the table, causing the dome and roses to rock back and forth. On instinct, I reach out to steady it, but then strong arms wrap around my midsection and pull me away. The air leaves my lungs when I hit a solid chest.

"What the hell?" I watch as the roses and dome finally stop rocking, thankfully not falling over and crashing to the ground.

"Don't touch it," Oziel warns. "It's dark magic."

"Dark magic?" I furrow my brows. "What do you mean? It's just a bouquet." Then realization hits me. "Wait...is that...?"

Oziel's grip on me remains firm, yet not restraining. If I truly wanted to, I could pull away with ease, but I don't. A part of me refuses to dwell on what that might mean.

At last, he answers, his voice solemn with a heavy truth. "It is. This, Kitten," Oziel continues, his now golden eyes darkening with something unreadable, "is the curse upon my kingdom."

OZIEL

"What do you mean?" Isabelle turns, her wet body only inches from mine. This damn woman is under my skin. I don't like it.

Seeing her half naked and escorted by Garvan nearly sent me into a violent rage. Rage is no stranger to me, but I've never let it lead me before. Never let it control me. I control it. But when I looked at Garvan, all I wanted to do was tear him limb from limb until his cries echoed throughout the kingdom.

This growing need inside me slithers like a snake, ready to strike the moment I let my guard down.

Isabelle looks at me expectantly. Unlike most, there's no fear in her gaze in regards to me. Only a fierce determination I've come to associate with her. Together, I think we'd make a formidable pair. But unfortunately, this pairing has an expiration date.

My gaze flickers to the faint glow of the roses. Those damn roses, an omen and a curse wrapped up in one.

Isabelle takes my silence as reluctance to speak and continues to pry. "I know you said the roses are the curse, but why? Who would curse you with roses? Glowing ones at that."

This is the question I've dreaded. My hatred for roses is no secret to my people, but for Isabelle, who didn't grow up here, she has no idea what they symbolize for me. Memories I've shoved deep down resurface; the familiar pangs of sadness puncture through my barriers. It happened so long ago, and yet...it feels like it was just yesterday.

"Oziel," Isabelle speaks my name with reverence, like she's reciting a prayer. She reaches out, soft fingers dancing across my chest. "Talk to me."

Three simple words, and I feel myself yielding to my queen. She opened herself to me yesterday. It is only right I do the same. The words tumble out, each one feeling like a burden. "The Nephilim cursed me or, rather, my kingdom. They are known to use your weakness against you, and mine has always been roses. They were my mother's favorite. She used to weave them into her hair, into the tapestries of the palace. The gardens were filled with them. Blood-red roses stretching for miles, as if the land itself bled beneath our feet."

My jaw tightens, a muscle ticking as the memories resurface. "My father used to say they were a symbol of love. A promise that, even in darkness, beauty could thrive."

"Are you certain your parents were demons? They sound like hopeless romantics." Isabelle's question is a welcome distraction, lifting some of the heavy weight upon my chest.

"They were completely and disgustingly in love. A powerful duo with powerful enemies. Demon nature is chaos and discord. Love isn't something many of us experience. Lust?" I inhale Isabelle's spicy scent. It goes straight to my cock, making it twitch in interest.

She seems to notice the shift in me because her body tenses. My hands brush against her hips, and she lets out a soft gasp.

"Lust is more common amongst my kind."

Isabelle listens, silently urging me to go on. I narrow my eyes as my gaze flicks to the roses. "They died because of those damned flowers." My hand curls into a fist, claws pressing deeply into my palm. "An assassination. The kingdom was on the brink of civil war, and my parents made many enemies. Enemies who saw their love as weakness. Who believed their love would be the downfall of our kingdom. In a way, I suppose it was.

"Still, my father, ever the fool, believed peace was still possible. He invited the enemy, a man who fought him at every turn, to meet in our rose gardens in hopes of converting him to an ally." My voice turns bitter, the day playing out before my eyes. "He wanted the scent of roses to remind them of love instead of war. That peace was possible between all demons in our kingdom."

A hollow chuckle escapes my lips, humorless and cold. Much like how I've felt since their untimely deaths. "But the only thing the roses did was mask the scent of poisoned blades. By the time I arrived, the garden was redder than before. I found their bodies, along with their guards' bodies, among the petals, their blood soaking into the earth."

Isabelle reaches for me, fingers brushing against mine. She doesn't take my hand, nor do I take hers. Our fingers simply brush against one another, and that's enough. My shoulders tremble with a silent rage that has never truly faded. Something I'll keep with me for the rest of my days and well into the afterlife.

"The scent of roses has haunted me ever since." My gaze lingers on the bouquet in the dome. "To you, they are just flowers. To me, they are ghosts."

There's no pity in Isabelle's eyes when I turn back to her. Only understanding. Then, "How did you survive?" she asks, almost in a whisper. Her cheeks go red, and she shakes her head. "You don't have to answer—"

"I had the blood of the king and the rage of a thousand demons," I cut her off. "I let vengeance and my bloodlust fuel me. Killing the demons who killed my parents didn't ease the ache of losing them, but it helped me win over important court members. My ascent to the throne was easy. They finally got the bloodthirsty king they always wanted, one who wasn't distracted by love."

Isabelle stays silent. I wish I could hear what she's thinking, know the thoughts swirling around in her head right now. Her face gives nothing away. Soon her hand and body pull away from me, and she turns, slowly approaching the roses again. My body tenses, ready to pull her back if she gets too close, but Isabelle stops and runs her fingers over the glass dome. It does little to ease my worries. She's still too close.

"My sister loved roses." Her words catch me off guard. I'm desperate for any information about her life, even if it's about her sister. "They were her favorite flowers. She bought them every week, always decorating our kitchen table with them. I learned to love them, despite the many times the thorns made me bleed."

As if I needed another reason to hate roses, knowing Isabelle bled because of the thorns fuels that hatred. I may never understand their beauty, but I can appreciate that her connection to these flowers is vastly different than mine.

"Why are they glowing? Is that the curse?" She finally drops her hand from the glass.

I nod curtly. "I believe so. A petal stops glowing when it falls, signaling another has fallen to the curse."

"Hmm."

I raise a brow. "Something interesting?"

Isabelle shakes her head, tearing her gaze away from the roses. "Nothing, it's just that I can *feel* the power within it."

Before I have a chance to ask what she means, there's a knock on my door, and a raven-haired demon walks in. Her eyes glance toward me first before landing on Isabelle. Something akin to hunger crosses her features, pupils blown wide. This demon is interested in my wife.

My lips curve up, unable to hide my smirk. I don't know why it amuses me so much, especially since I was ready to rip Garvan's head off for simply escorting Isabelle back to my chambers. I suppose I'm in a better mood now.

"My lord and...lady," she purrs the last word, licking her lips. If Isabelle notices the not-so-subtle flirting, she doesn't show it. "The wine and food for your upcoming celebration have started to arrive. Would you like a sample?"

"Our upcoming celebration?" Isabelle's nose wrinkles in confusion. It's rather adorable. "What celebration?"

The demon laughs, though it sounds forced. Something she does to be noticed by her queen. "The celebration of your wedding, remember? The ball is a few days away. The kingdom anticipates quite the celebration. To welcome their new queen, of course." Again, the she-demon licks her lips as her predatory eyes roam over Isabelle's body, all but eye-fucking her in front of me.

This time Isabelle takes notice of the she-demon's obvious flirting and frowns, disinterested. My wife knows nothing of the lavish, debaucherous parties our kingdoms throw. Where the drinks never run dry, and the sex lasts well into the next day. Where rules don't exist, and our bodies do all the talking. It's not uncommon to wake up naked in between two strangers. Or more.

I still believe the ball is the best option to take note of who is in attendance and who isn't. It's a well-known fact that the kingdom will be enthralled with a celebration, giving whoever is poisoning the River Hel the perfect opportunity to sabotage it. Except this time, we'll be ready.

"You said there's wine?" Isabelle asks.

The she-demon smiles, showing off her white teeth. "Yes, my queen. I'll fetch some for you now."

She goes to leave, but my shadows slam the door closed, effectively stopping her. "Tell your queen what kind of wine it is." My voice is low, unassuming.

The she-demon freezes, not meeting my gaze as she turns around. "It's lust wine, my queen. Meant to put you in a haze of lust."

Isabelle's eyes widen, and she looks at me. "You'll be serving this to everyone at the party?"

"No," I say, and she relaxes her shoulders until I add, "*We'll* be serving it to everyone."

The look of horror on Isabelle's face is almost amusing, until she gets a wicked gleam in her eyes. "Bring the wine," she orders the she-demon. My curiosity piques.

The raven-haired demon looks in my direction cautiously. I dip my head, reining my shadows back in. The door opens with an audible click, and she scurries out quickly. Isabelle sits back on the velvet upholstered chair, an amused grin on her lips.

"When were you going to tell me about the kind of parties you throw here?" she asks, only mild curiosity in her tone.

I sit at the edge of the bed opposite her. "It's more fun to see you experience it. I couldn't do the party justice with my words."

"I'm sure," she hums. "I suppose after everything we've discussed, we both deserve a drink. Don't you think, Husband?"

This time, it's my turn to grin like a damned fool.

That's exactly what Isabelle makes me. A foolish demon playing a dangerous game. "Very much, Wife." Even if I have sworn off love, I'll happily indulge my wife in any way befitting a queen. Though, if I'm being honest, I want to ruin her.

CHAPTER 23

ISABELLE

The woman returns soon after with a dark bottle of wine and a tray of assorted foods. The latter is largely ignored as two glasses of wine are poured. The liquid is a deep red color, almost crimson, with swirling black flecks that sparkle when the light hits it. It's like no other wine I've ever seen before, more tantalizing in nature, as if its job is to seduce you to drink.

"Leave us," Oziel speaks, pulling my attention from the strange wine. I look up just in time to see the demon's face crumple in disappointment.

"My lord, I'm happy to assist—"

"I'm sure you are," Oziel says, though not unkindly. His tone lacks interest, and he pays her little mind, dismissing her with his body language. "But we don't require your assistance."

The woman sticks out her bottom lip before turning on her heels and walking out of the room with a haughty stride. The door closes behind her with a resounding thud, leaving me and Oziel alone. My body is keenly aware of him.

His hot gaze travels over me, not hiding his blatant perusal. "Why?" he asks after a moment.

"Why what?" I deflect, knowing what he's asking but needing more time to come to terms with my own answer.

"Knowing exactly what the lust wine will do, why would you still choose to drink it with me?" Oziel's voice is devoid of emotion, giving me no hint of the thoughts lurking behind the demon king's dark gaze. His finger traces the rim of his glass in slow, deliberate circles, a silent rhythm that feels almost hypnotic.

I train my eyes on the motion, looking anywhere but at my husband. "Because there's a lot of scary shit going on," I finally admit, not feeling compelled to hide my emotions any longer. At least not at this moment. I don't have the energy to. We both would do well with a little vulnerability. "Being the person who holds the fate of your entire kingdom in the palm of their hands is a burden I didn't fully comprehend until it looked me in the eyes. To say I'm stressed would be an under-statement."

Oziel remains silent, his gaze heavy on me—watch-ing, assessing, waiting for my next move. The weight of his scrutiny is nearly enough to make me falter and abandon this conversation entirely or pretend it never happened. But that isn't what I truly want. Conse-quences be damned.

This will change nothing.

It will change everything.

I ignore the voice, pushing on before my confidence leaves me. "For just a moment, I want to forget. I want to feel something that isn't impending doom. That one of your demons didn't just try to kill me, and the survival of your kingdom isn't on my shoulders." My gaze lifts, finally meeting his eyes. "I want you to make me forget. For just one day."

I don't wait for him to respond. I lift the glass to my lips and take a sip of the wine. The sugary sweetness erupts on my tongue. I'm normally not one for sweet wines, but this seems to be an exception. I take another long sip, and the wine heats my throat as it goes down.

The effects hit me instantly, similar to the wine we had at our wedding. My body—already attuned to Oziel's presence—ignites with a searing heat, a fire that spreads through my veins with devastating intensity. It's as if an invisible flame has been set ablaze inside me, and Oziel is the only thing that can quench it. My breath catches as I finally lift my gaze to meet his. His eyes are hooded, dark with something raw, something danger-ously close to need.

"You want me to be your distraction, Kitten?" he growls. I swear I hear disappointment in his tone, but disappointment for what?

"If you don't want to fuck me, then—"

"I didn't say that," he interrupts, hands tightening around his glass. I'm amazed he hasn't broken it into shards.

There is no use in holding back now. My lips are loos-ened, desperate to say anything for him to ease this ache. "You're my distraction, Oziel. That's all you'll ever be."

Oziel growls, lip curled back in anger at my harsh words. The last words are gas doused on a flame. We move as one, meeting in the middle, where we crash in a haze of lust and anger. Oziel's hand wraps through my hair before cradling the back of my head. His lips are on mine, kissing me as if I'm the very elixir to life and he's a dying man. It's not the kiss of a lover, gentle and full of promises. No, this kiss is rough. Dirty. Almost angry.

It's exactly what I need.

Oziel yanks my head back, pulling my hair. I cry out as the kiss breaks, panting heavily. "I will not be gentle with you."

"If I wanted gentle, I would fuck Garvan like you thought I did."

Oziel's eyes darken, flashing black as fury consumes him. Shadows surge around him, twisting and writhing before they descend upon me. It feels as though a hundred unseen hands are touching me at once, ghosting over my skin, tugging at the fabric of my robe. Then his lips crash against mine, demanding and all-consuming. I'm so lost in the heat of his kiss that I don't even register the moment my robe slips open and pools at my feet.

I'm naked before him.

It's not the first time, but it's different in every way.

I break the kiss to tug on his clothes, refusing to be the only naked one in the room. Oziel takes mercy upon me and calls his shadows back. In an instant, they disperse, and he stands naked before me. He's glorious. Beautiful. But also frightening. Every bit the demon king he is.

A few scars decorate his body. I don't know how he got them, but I want to trace them with my tongue. Every last one. My eyes trail down his body, mapping out every dip and curve. The way his muscles flex, hardening as they move. My gaze falls to his core, and his heavy cock stands at attention for me.

A hunger takes over. One that not even a Nephilim could pull me from. "This changes nothing. When my role here is over, I'm leaving. I get my freedom." I sink to my knees in front of him.

Oziel's nostrils flare. "Why would it change a thing?" He bunches my hair up, pulling it out of my face. Bitterness laces his tone, or perhaps I'm imagining it. Nothing matters. The only thing I can think about is taking his cock into my mouth.

His cock is long and thick, impossible for me to take all the way down my throat. That doesn't stop me from trying though. My tongue flicks out, licking his shaft from base to tip. A low, sexy groan leaves the demon's king parted lips. It's the most erotic thing I've ever heard. A deep throaty sound that goes straight to my core.

My tongue travels up to his mushroom tip, lapping at the bead of precum blossoming there. It's salty on my tongue, and I take great pride in the fact that the demon king is hard for me. Excited for me. It's a powerful position to be in, and I revel in it.

I slip his cock between my lips, breathing through my nose. I can only take half of his size into my mouth, but my hands are eager to please the parts that can't fit. I moan around his length, just as I feel another sharp tug on my hair.

Fuck, that feels good. I don't know if I like the sensation of pain, or if it's the wine, but I want more. Need more.

"I like that pretty mouth wrapped around my cock. For once not arguing with me." Oziel's breathy voice has me looking up; the heat in his eyes sends electricity straight to my clit. Still, his words make me growl.

"Bastard," I hiss, but with his cock in my mouth, it sounds like a whimper.

Oziel chuckles, but that sound soon turns into a moan when I start to bob my head, falling into a steady rhythm. The fire crackles behind us, the only other sound besides the low moans we make.

Before I can register what's happening, Oziel pulls away and picks me up off my knees. Effortlessly, he throws me on the bed as if I weigh nothing at all. I bounce on my ass once, trying to get my bearings before Oziel slithers over me. My disappointment from not tasting more of him or finishing him off is short-lived when Oziel trails kisses down my body. They aren't sweet. Even his kisses are dominating, demanding subservience. My body melts under his touch, desperate to give in.

But it's not in my nature to give in—not even in the bedroom, I like being in charge and being the one who's calling the shots. I determine my own pleasure, and by extension, my partner's. I'm tempted to kick Oziel off to finish what I started earlier, but my pussy has other plans. Damn her.

On their own accord, my legs part for him. Oziel teases my hips, kissing down to my inner thigh, but makes no move to kiss me where I really want his lips and tongue to be. I make a sound of impatience, arching closer to him.

"Eager thing, aren't you, Miss Sinclair?" Oziel ruins the moment with his damn voice. If he could just stay quiet, this would be so much better.

"Shut up and put your tongue to better use," I snarl, reaching down to grab his horns. Apparently, that's the wrong fucking thing to do, because Oziel growls, shadows surrounding him.

"Do that again," he hisses.

Or maybe it's the *exact* thing to do.

I'm not exactly sure what he means, but I pump my hands over his horns, like I would do to his cock. Oziel hisses, though I'm not sure if it's from pain or pleasure. Maybe a mixture of both. So, his horns are sensitive. That's good to know. I don't let up on the stroking, even though it feels a little awkward, and I'm not sure I'm doing it right. I don't like feeling inexperienced.

"Isabelle," he moans my name like a blessing—or a curse. Then he finally runs his tongue along my seam, giving me exactly what I've been craving. His tongue is hot, a little scratchy, but that only adds to the pleasure. He parts my folds, taking in a deep breath.

"So fucking wet, Kitten. And all for me." He laughs, but there's no denying it. I'm so fucking turned on. My body is primed for the taking. He drags his tongue through my folds before reaching my clit. The next swipe of his tongue has my back arching off the bed.

My heart beats a mile a minute as he dips his head, capturing my clit. A strangled gasp leaves my lips, and fireworks burst behind my eyes. Every nerve on my body feels extra-sensitive, and I'm wound up so tightly, I can't ever remember wanting to find release so bad. Is this from the wine? Or is this my own attraction to the demon between my legs? One thing is for certain: he has me under his spell.

His hand snakes between my legs, thumb replacing his tongue as he rubs small circles on my clit, eating me out in earnest. I whimper, gripping his horns tightly. "Fuck!" My hips buck up, grinding my pussy into his face. Oziel accepts it, letting me ride his face in a frenzy.

My moans only get louder, more desperate. Oziel is in control of my pleasure, and he knows it. The bastard smirks, looking all too smug about his power over me. When his thumb presses down on my clit, and his tongue spears me, I come undone. White-hot pleasure burns through me as my orgasm rips through my body with a ferocity I don't expect. I come all over Oziel's tongue and face, but the demon king doesn't seem to mind. He drinks me up like his own nectar, not stopping until he works me through my orgasm.

This should have quenched the fire raging inside me, but instead, it struck a spark, igniting me even more. Desperation surges through me as I summon every ounce of strength I have, driving my legs against Oziel's chest. He staggers backward. Not from my force, but from sheer surprise. If he wanted to, he could overpower me effortlessly. But right now, I don't want restraint.

A raw, primal hunger takes hold of me, and I bare my teeth in a growl. "More."

Oziel doesn't speak. He doesn't need to. The desire in

his gaze is answer enough. Dark shadows gather around my wrists. Like an invisible rope, they wrap around me, pulling me back on the bed. My arms lift above my head, anchoring me in place. I try to move them, but they are glued in place.

"What the fuck?" I scream, heat rushing to my core. "What is this?"

"Submission, Kitten. This is submission."

"Submission, my ass. I'll—" But I don't get to finish my sentence. Something wraps around my mouth, cutting off my ability to speak. My body flushes with a mixture of anger and desire. I hate that I fucking like this. I don't want to like this. But not even I can deny how hot this is.

Like a snake, Oziel slithers toward me. His body climbs over mine, kicking my legs apart until I'm completely exposed to him. My nipples harden into painful points, but Oziel doesn't miss a beat. He ducks his head and takes one of the sensitive nubs into his mouth. I cry out as his hand comes up to tease my other nipple. His heavy cock rests against my belly, so close to where I need it, but not close enough.

Oziel pulls back from my nipple, my arousal from earlier still shining on his lips. His dark gaze drinks me in, and despite the show he's putting on, I know he's barely holding it together. I don't want a carefully guarded Oziel. I want him to unleash on me. To consume me from the inside out.

Oziel didn't tie my legs, so I wrap them around his hips, my heels digging into his sculpted ass. His eyes flash, and the last bit of his restraint crumbles away. His lips are on me again, pressing punishing kisses to my neck. An embarrassingly loud moan leaves my lips before he bites down, easing the pain with his tongue. It's too fucking much.

The next second, he drives his cock inside of me. I scream out, moans muffled by the invisible gag. My pussy stretches around him, desperately trying to get used to his size. He's like no man I've ever had in my bed, and I've cycled through a lot of men. Probably because Oziel's not a man at all. Something much more sinister. His darkness calls to mine.

Oziel doesn't treat me like a glass doll. He doesn't fear he'll hurt me, because he knows I can take it. He starts to thrust inside me. In and out. In and out. It's hard. Fast. I can't catch my breath, but I think that's the point. The low moans from Oziel are fucking erotic, making me squeeze his cock harder.

"Lucifer Rising, Kitten. So fucking sinful," he says like a compliment. Watching the demon king come undone for me, even as he claims I'm the one submitting to him, is power. I find I quite like having this sort of power over Oziel.

Every muscle in Oziel's body flexes, and he roars my name. His orgasm overtakes him, and his hot cum pours into me. It was the last thing I needed, seeing Oziel break, to find my second orgasm. It rips through my body, more intense than my first one. The gag disappears, so my shouts of pleasure echo around us until the only noise is our heavy breathing and my rapid heartbeat.

"You bastard," I pant, no real malice behind my voice.

Give me an orgasm, and suddenly I feel much better. Who knew?

Without warning, the bindings around my wrists vanish, leaving behind the ghost of their pressure. A rush of relief floods my arms, the ache from their confinement slowly fading. My legs slip from around Oziel's waist, falling on either side of him. The demon king towers over me, his crimson eyes dark with something unreadable, sending a shiver down my spine. His gaze traps me in place, a predator assessing his prey.

He leans in, closing the space between us until his face is mere inches from mine. The heat radiating from his body is nearly suffocating, his presence overwhelming. My breath stutters, and my chest tightens under the weight of the moment. The sharp scent of smoke and something darker, something dangerously alluring, fills my lungs. I bite my lower lip, anticipation curling in my stomach like a coiled snake, bracing myself for whatever words will spill from his lips.

"This changes nothing," Oziel echoes my words from earlier, delivering them like a dagger to the gut. Those were the same words I said to him before this all started, and I meant them then. I *still* mean them. But hearing them from Oziel leaves me with an unexplainable ache in my chest.

He meets my lips once more, softer than the other kisses, but still just as dominating. When he pulls away, I feel his absence. "Enjoy the rest of your day, Miss Sinclair." Those are the last words Oziel says to me before he leaves our bed.

His shadows cloud him, and when they disperse, he's

clothed again. He doesn't so much as look back as he storms out of the room, leaving as quickly as the lust overtook us.

A strange, hollow sensation settles in my chest. Something eerily close to disappointment. I tear my gaze away from the door Oziel just disappeared through, as if looking any longer might somehow pull him back. The room feels emptier in his absence, the air still carrying the faint scent of him.

That's when my eyes catch on the small table beside me. Two glasses of wine sit upon it, the deep red liquid reflecting the dim light. My own glass is already halfway empty, the rich, velvety taste still lingering on my tongue. That would certainly explain the almost desperate hunger I felt for him and the heat in my veins, pulling me recklessly toward the demon king.

But when my gaze drifts to his glass, a flicker of confusion snakes through me. It remains completely untouched, the surface undisturbed, as if he never once considered drinking it. A slow realization creeps in, sending a chill down my spine.

Was this deliberate? Did he simply humor me, watching as I drank, letting the wine loosen my inhibitions while he remained perfectly in control? The thought unsettles me, a shiver dancing over my skin as I stare at the untouched glass, wondering why he didn't drink his wine.

CHAPTER 24
ISABELLE

I don't see Oziel for the rest of the day as I explore the castle, and I decide not to wait for him when I return to our room that evening. The sheets have been changed, and the bed is freshly made, all evidence of our morning together stripped away. If I didn't feel the delicious ache between my legs, I would think I dreamed up our time together.

The moment my head hits the pillow, exhaustion sets in. Free of wine lust and tired from the best sex I've had in my life, I fall into a dreamless sleep. I don't think I even move once throughout the night because, when I wake up the following morning—or what I assume to be morning since it's always like night here—I'm in the same position I fell asleep in: on my back with the covers pulled up to my chin.

Unlike last night, though, I'm not alone.

From the corner of my eye, I see Oziel lying on his back. I must have been exhausted because I never heard him come in last night or felt him slip into bed. I turn toward him, but he doesn't move. He's awake, his eyes wide open and fixed on the ceiling, unblinking. There's no way he hasn't noticed me, and yet he hasn't acknowledged me.

"Oziel?" My voice comes out rough, thick with sleep. "What's wrong?"

A heavy stillness clings to him, like a storm trapped beneath the surface, waiting to break. The dim light casts shadows under his eyes, deep, smudged bruises of exhaustion. He looks like he hasn't slept at all.

When he looks at me with his tortured expression, I'm reminded that he's an ancient being because exhaustion weighs heavily on him. "Four more demons turned to stone yesterday."

"Four?" I push myself up to a sitting position. My attention is drawn to the bouquet on the table in front of us. Another petal has fallen from the stem, floating to the table surface like an ominous warning.

We're running out of time.

And Oziel is losing his confidence.

I draw the covers away from me, getting out of bed. Oziel eyes me with curiosity. "Where are you going?"

"To get dressed. The ball is only a few days away, yes?" I search through my chest for something that doesn't cut off my oxygen. I find a simple black dress with no corset in sight and murmur a silent thank you to whatever demon supplied me with the garment.

"It is." Oziel gains back some of the ferocity in his voice that I've come to associate with him.

"Then we aren't without a plan," I remind him gently, tugging off my nightgown.

Oziel's eyes darken, drinking me in. Even without the lust wine from yesterday, I preen at his attention. But there's no time to act upon it. "We just need to figure out how to lure the demon poisoning River Hel out of hiding at the ball."

Oziel puts a hand up, silencing me. I'm almost offended until I hear a knock on the door. "Come in." He gives me a look to keep quiet.

The door swings open, and Garvan steps inside. The usually composed demon looks anything but. His hair is a tangled mess, strands falling over his sharp features, and his shirt hangs open, unbuttoned and wrinkled, exposing the pale expanse of his chest. He's lean, his body wiry and toned, but nowhere near as imposing as the man sitting on our bed.

Oziel, with his broad shoulders and raw, effortless strength, makes Garvan seem almost delicate in comparison. Yet there's something about Garvan's quiet intensity that demands attention despite his disheveled state.

"Any news?" Oziel continues a conversation I'm not privy to.

"The demons found early this morning were part of a morning watch, headed to patrol the eastern borders, toward Pixie Hollow," Garvan recites, earning a curse from Oziel.

"There have been reports of Nephilim activity near Pixie Cove. Which is...unsettling," Oziel murmurs.

"Why is that unsettling?" I'm unable to hold back my curiosity. I wish I knew more about the geography of Mescos. A whole kingdom of pixies? What other wonders exist here, hidden beyond my limited knowledge?

When I'm free, I'll explore every corner of it, uncovering its secrets for myself. The thought should fill me with excitement, the way it once did. But it doesn't. Not anymore. At least not alone. I push that uneasy feeling aside, refusing to acknowledge the weight it carries.

"Pixie Cove is the center of all magic in Mescos," he explains.

My brow furrows. "But I thought you got your magic from River Hel?"

Like a patient mother, Oziel nods. "Correct, Kitten. But the magic from Pixie Cove is the essence of all magic in Mescos. Without it, we would cease to exist in our current state. The River Hel would be nothing but a river. If the Nephilim seize that power, life as we know it is over."

"It will change everything if the Nephilim have access to that sort of power," Garvan interjects. His solemn expression shows he's worried about the news, just as worried as Oziel is.

"Then, using the ball to—"

"See to it that their bodies are brought out with the rest. Dispatch more demons to our eastern border and send word to the pixie king, Taivan, about the Nephilim activity," Oziel interrupts me, and I slightly seethe. This is twice he's spoken over me. I understand he's stressed, but I won't be the recipient of that stress.

Garvan lingers by the door, slow to acquiesce to Oziel's order. "Is it wise to send more men?" he asks after a pause. "We can't afford to lose more demons, my lord."

"I'm well aware of what we can and cannot afford to lose, Garvan." Oziel's voice is sharp as a blade. "Unless you have a better plan for scouting our borders, you'll do as you're told."

His tone is unyielding, pure authority, the kind that would make a lesser demon drop to their knees in submission. The air crackles with the weight of his command. Garvan stiffens, his muscles coiled with tension, but he doesn't lower his gaze. Instead, he holds firm, meeting Oziel's eyes head-on before offering a single curt nod.

"Then it shall be done." Garvan's gaze lands on me as he offers me the same respectful nod he gave Oziel. "Enjoy your morning, my queen." Effectively dismissed by his king, he turns on his heels and walks out of the room. The door closes behind him, leaving my husband and me alone.

I round on Oziel, just as the demon king stands up, placing his hands on my shoulder. It's a gentle touch, but it may as well be searing for how hot it makes my body. "I didn't mean to cut you off, Kitten," he whispers. It amazes me that this fierce demon, surrounded by darkness, can be so gentle when he chooses to be. It's very conflicting. "But as much as I want to trust my demons, I can't rule out anyone. Someone is betraying the kingdom. Betraying me. Until we figure out who, then all talk of finding the traitor stays between us."

The anger simmering inside me fades, replaced by a quiet understanding. He has to view everyone as a suspect until proven otherwise, which sounds like a relentless, exhausting way to exist. No wonder he looks like he hasn't slept in days, with shadows etched deep beneath his eyes.

I exhale, letting go of the last traces of frustration. "Then what's our plan?" My voice is softer now, laced with something closer to empathy.

"Normally, the celebration spans throughout the castle. This time, we will centralize it to one location. Much easier to keep an eye on everyone that way," he says. "We will celebrate as if nothing is amiss, but I'll make note of the demons who aren't in attendance."

"And what do I do?" Unlike Oziel, my knowledge of his people is minimal, but I don't wish for them to suffer. It would hurt Oziel too much, and despite my vow not to care for him, he's getting under my skin in more ways than one.

"You, Kitten, will dance, party, and mingle to get information."

I frown. "Have you forgotten that I'm queen? No demon will speak freely to me. Not if they know anything." The staff has seen my face, and demons talk. Those who haven't seen me yet still know I exist. It only takes one finger pointed in my direction for this whole plan to unravel.

Oziel appears unmoved by my problem. "Then you won't be the queen at the ball."

"Speak plainly," I grit through my teeth. "If you have a plan, share it."

"So impatient, Miss Sinclair. Yes, I'm quite aware that the demons won't speak openly with you if they think they are speaking to the queen. However, if they think they are just speaking to a pretty she-demon, their tongues may be looser." Oziel circles me. Predator assessing his prey. Except I'm not prey.

I whirl on him, grabbing his wrist. His eyes flash with emotion. Anger? Lust? Something else? I ignore it. "How will I disguise myself, then?"

"My power may not be as strong as normal, but I can shadow your appearance, making you appear different to anyone who looks at you. I can give you a few hours at most. As long as you stay within the ballroom, we shouldn't have a problem. You just need to play your part."

My part. How would a demon act at these parties? Considering what we are giving them to drink and everything else I've seen, it will require pretending to be drunk on lust. "So, you want me to flirt and fuck my way to an answer?"

There's no denying the anger written across his features this time. His golden eyes darken, body tensing. His hand curls around my hip, pulling me closer. "I said nothing about fucking, Kitten," he says in a low, gruff voice that would send weaker women to their knees before him.

I'm tempted to fall to my own knees, especially considering what I got to experience yesterday, but Oziel has made no mention of it, so neither will I.

"I will do what must be done to get answers," I argue.

"You don't need to fuck to get answers." His grip on my waist tightens, and he pulls me flush against his body. My breath hitches as he tilts my chin up, forcing me to look in his eyes. "Flirt if you must. Touch even. But under no circumstances will you fuck anyone."

"Anyone but you, that is." I wish my voice didn't sound so breathless, giving away my own lust. My mind conjures up pictures of last night. His throbbing cock in my mouth. His muscular body over mine, fucking me with abandon. Wetness and heat pool between my thighs.

As if in tune with my arousal, Oziel's nostrils flare, his tongue slowly and deliberately running across his lips. "Correct, Kitten. You fuck no one but me."

Mustering up my last bit of power against him, I tug on his pants, pulling his hips to mine. He stumbles forward with a grunt. "And you fuck no one but me either. If you so much as kiss another, I will retaliate. I've killed once. Don't think I'm afraid to do it again."

A sexy smirk crossed his lips. "Not even kissing? Why, Miss Sinclair, I gave you permission to kiss to get information."

"Yeah, you did. Dumb strategy on your part. I give you no such permission," I say, heat in my voice. There's no way I can stop him if he decides to play with another demon at the ball. I have no power against him. But I also won't watch my husband openly flirt with someone in my presence. When I'm gone, he can fuck through his whole kingdom. Until then, he's *mine.*

"Very well," he finally says after a brief silence, his voice smooth and rich, like velvet sliding over my skin. A slow warmth spreads through me at the sound, both alluring and dangerous. "I will stand by and watch my wife flirt with and kiss other demons in the name of gathering information while I keep my hands to myself. Hardly seems fair, but then again, I am nothing if not merciful."

"So, we have a plan."

"It seems we do," Oziel says. "And once this is over, Kitten, I would very much like to show you why you won't be satisfied fucking anyone else."

How could I possibly say no to that? Maybe I should. It wouldn't be wise to get too attached, and even though I try to ignore it, there's an undeniable pull. Unfortunately, I'm not strong enough to deny it.

CHAPTER 25
OZIEL

Over the next three days while my staff prepares for the ball, the kingdom is quiet. It's not the peaceful silence of a safe kingdom, though. The air is heavy with anticipation. Demons peer around every corner, expecting it to be their last moment before the stone curse takes them as well. The only distraction is preparing the ballroom for tonight's celebration. Despite the fear breeding through the castle, there's a hesitant excitement in the air for the upcoming ball.

My duty has torn me away from Isabelle, leaving an ache in my chest that refuses to fade. I crave her presence in a way I've never experienced before. An intense, all-consuming longing that tightens its grip with each passing moment. The time apart has made one thing painfully clear: I've enjoyed having her by my side far more than is wise.

My gaze drifts to the roses resting on the table, their delicate petals a stark contrast to the war waging within me. A reminder. An omen. Forming feelings for this human is a mistake. A weakness I cannot afford. Demons and love have never gone hand in hand. It makes great kings and queens vulnerable because it provides the enemy with our ultimate weakness.

Garvan's incessant tapping from his perch by the fireplace draws my attention away from preparing myself for tonight's ball. He's been by my side these last three days, only disappearing at night when I crawl in bed with Isabelle, tormented by her body next to mine. Neither one of us has made a move to continue what we started, though a fire simmers between us every night.

"Speak your mind, Garvan."

The demon's head pops up, meeting my gaze. He's the one demon who can handle being in the position of courtier. He doesn't shy away from tough conversations and providing his opinion. I don't always follow it, but he gives it nonetheless.

"I think you should reconsider the sacrifice tonight," he speaks plainly.

My brow cocks up. Every demon ball starts with a sacrifice of blood—not our own, but a criminal from another kingdom sent here for punishment. The ceremony is ancient, said to have started in the early ages of demons. This practice no longer serves the same purpose it once did, having slowly changed over the centuries, but traditions have a way of continuing on despite their ineffectiveness. We do it simply to remember our ancestors. And because the smell of blood and slaying a corrupt soul serves as an adrenaline rush.

"You don't think we should sacrifice the pixie? Fine. The fae will do—"

"No, my lord," Garvan cuts me off, shooting me an apologetic look for interrupting. "I think we should sacrifice the Nephilim."

It takes everything in me not to roll my eyes like a bored child. Garvan has taken upon himself to be unsatisfied with any other sacrifice but the Nephilim.

"You know how I feel. I will not risk the safety of the demons to slay a Nephilim in the open. It comes at much too high a price." Surely he understands the risks and uncertainties that come with harboring a Nephilim. Those are risks I'm willing to take with him locked in a secure prison. Bringing the Nephilim into the public would pose far too many risks without the safety protocols of the dungeon.

"It's because of that danger we should rid our kingdom of the creature," Garvan argues.

I see his point, but keeping the creature alive has other advantages too. The main one being Isabelle's ability to communicate with it in a way I cannot. Already she's provided valuable information—at the expense of her own safety, I might add—that has proven pivotal in understanding Nephilim and their origins.

"The Nephilim is too important and too risky to simply dispose of in a large, public setting." I push myself out of my chair, moving swiftly past Garvan. He falls in step behind me out of the room. I can't stay in my chambers any longer, not when the roses sit there, teasing and mocking me.

"My lord, just think about it. It would be a show of

strength. The king takes down a Nephilim, sacrificing him on the day of his celebration."

I take the stairs two at a time, as if that will carry me farther away from Garvan. Except my courtier is an incessant demon, not willing to back down easily. It's a trait I usually admire, just not today.

"It might stop the progression of the curse. Maybe the Nephilim being here is speeding up the process. It is their magic cursing us, after all," he says.

These things have all gone through my mind, making me question the Nephilim's captivity. The truth is, our people would fall to the curse regardless of whether the Nephilim is here or not. The roses and whoever is poisoning the River Hel are assuring that.

"My lord—"

When we reach the bottom of the stairs, I whirl on him. Garvan hesitates on the last step, fear flickering in his expression. He hides it well, but I've known this demon for decades. He's not hard to read.

"Enough. I know you mean well, but I won't entertain this idea any longer. The Nephilim stays in the prison until I say otherwise. We will sacrifice one of the pixie or fae prisoners—I don't fucking care which one—and I'll hear nothing more of it."

Garvan's expression tightens, his jaw clenching as a flicker of anger flares in his eyes. The emotion simmers beneath the surface, controlled but unmistakably present. He is no fool, so he swallows his frustration, burying it beneath a mask of composure. With a curt nod, so slight it's nearly imperceptible, he finally speaks, his voice measured and devoid of emotion. "As you wish, my lord."

Tension simmers around us, only broken up by the soft click of heels from above. We turn in unison just in time to see Isabelle stop at the top of the stairs. The shadows in the candlelit hall flicker as if bending toward her, drawn to the descending vision. She steals the very breath on my lips. A growing need burns bright within me. Even Garvan seems captivated by her beauty.

She's draped in midnight and gold. The gown clings to her torso like sin itself, the sweetheart neckline exposing the delicate lines of her collarbone before the fabric billows into a cascade of darkness. Gold embroidery embellishes the gown like enchanted fire, each delicate leaf and vine gleaming under the flickering sconces. The contrast is breathtaking—her mortal fragility wrapped in something fit for a queen of demons.

For the first time in centuries, something stirs in my chest. Not rage, nor hunger, but something dangerously close to reverence. My jaw clenches, clawed fingers tightening at my sides as I exhale slowly, getting my bearings.

She is ethereal. Untouchable. And yet, she is mine. At least at this moment.

A slow, dark smile curves my lips. "You're playing a dangerous game, little wife," I murmur. "Dressed like that, you'll have demons falling at your feet."

Crimson colors Isabelle's cheeks in an adorable blush. Her painted red lips part as she looks down at herself, almost as if she's also seeing for the first time. "It's a bit much."

"It's perfect," I say immediately.

"You look like the queen you are," Garvan adds, and I have the intense need to claw out his eyes. Though he isn't the only one who will look at Isabelle with affection and lust in their gaze. It would be unbecoming of me to blind an entire kingdom.

Doesn't mean I'm not tempted.

Like a mistress of the night, she steps onto the staircase, her gown cascading around her like liquid shadow. She lifts the voluminous skirts just enough to reveal golden heels that wrap around her ankles like delicate, gilded vines. Each step is deliberate, the soft click of her heels against the polished stone filling the expectant silence.

I move toward her. The black suit I wear is a masterpiece of dark elegance and tailored to perfection, the fabric absorbing the dim light like the void itself. Subtle gold embroidery traces along the cuffs and lapels, intricate and sharp, resembling the accents sewn into Isabelle's dress. A deep crimson pocket square peeks from my breast pocket.

We meet in the middle, the air between us charged. Isabelle's gaze flicks over me, her eyes dark with something unreadable. She hums, a sound both appreciative and teasing.

"I suppose you don't look completely hideous," she murmurs, though her voice is too breathy to make the insult convincing.

I, on the other hand, have no qualms about showing my interest in my wife. "This image of you will be seared into my mind. The only thing that could surpass your beauty in this moment is if your dress was lying at the foot of our bed, with you naked in my arms."

"Oziel," she hisses, the dark red hue of her cheeks deepening. She glances behind me at Garvan, embarrassment radiating off her. It's cute when she's flustered. I find I quite like it.

"Allow me to make sure preparations are going smoothly." Garvan bows, wisely taking his exit.

"And bring the pixie prisoner up for the sacrifice," I add.

Garvan stiffens at my requests, but nods once. He doesn't try to argue again, knowing it would be futile. Smart man.

"I will see you both at the ball," he says before making his way to the ballroom.

"What do you mean about sacrifice?" Isabelle asks.

"Another demon custom you will learn today." I can tell she has more questions, but I offer her my hand. She takes it without question, and I lead her down the stairs. "In fact, I think you should be the one to sacrifice the prisoner."

Isabelle's only reaction is a slight rise of her perfectly arched eyebrow. "Is that so?" There's no disgust or repulsion in her voice, just mild curiosity.

"Seems fitting for the new queen to have the honors."

"Even if this queen is temporary?"

I come to an abrupt stop, my gaze shifting toward her. The words hang in the air, more of a reminder than a statement, but whether it's meant for her or for me, I can't be sure.

Every fiber of my being loathes the thought of her

leaving. The very idea feels unnatural, like trying to sever something vital from my soul. And yet, I know all too well what love can do to a king. I've seen it unravel empires and turn sovereigns into martyrs. But the longer I'm around Isabelle, the less I care for all the reasons I shouldn't. Perhaps we could convince the kingdom that Isabelle and I together aren't a weakness.

However, I refuse to let my parents' fate be ours. I refuse to see us torn apart, slaughtered by the very people we are meant to rule. If there's any way to spare Isabelle from that destiny, I will find it. I will make certain of it.

"Even then," I say, walking again. Isabelle falls in line beside me.

"Is this pixie a bad person?"

"Would the answer matter?"

Isabelle nods. "Of course it matters. I won't kill an innocent."

"No one is innocent, Kitten."

"Maybe. But some people are inherently better than other people. I won't kill a person who is trying to do good."

But she has no problem putting to death a man who deserves it. Nor will she show any regret or remorse. It's the perfect quality in a queen—even a temporary one. So I tell her the truth. "This pixie is the worst of its kind. The worst of his crimes, though, are the crimes he committed against his family. He tortured his children for days until their bodies were broken beyond repair. He forced their mother to watch them die one by one, then tortured her mind and body more, before ending her too.

There's nothing but hatred in his heart, and he's far past redemption for what he did to his family. He deserves to die."

Isabelle's chin lifts, her eyes blazing with newfound resolve. There's no hesitation, no wavering, only the steady burn of determination settling deep within her gaze "Then I will do it," she declares, her voice clear and steady. She takes a step closer, shoulders squared, as if bracing for the weight of whatever is to come. "Show me what I need to do."

CHAPTER 26
ISABELLE

The grand ballroom stretches before us, a cavernous expanse of polished marble and flickering candlelight. The towering arched windows with their intricate latticework cast delicate shadows upon the gleaming floor. The soft light of the moon filters through, bathing the chamber in an ethereal glow.

It's both romantic and unsettling knowing what I must do tonight.

The demons spared no expense. Dark, gilded walls with swirling gold filigree hint of opulence and celebrations before. Chandeliers of elaborate crystal and wrought iron hang from the vaulted ceiling, their candlelit flames dancing in tune to the music.

Torches line the chamber illuminating the tables of food and wine. Glasses fill one table, stacked upon one another precariously—all full, swirling with glitter lust liquid. The most pivotal weapon in our arsenal tonight.

Just one slip-up, one pair of loose lips, is all we need to uncover the demon betraying us.

Demons begin to filter in. Some wear dark, glittering ball gowns, arriving on the arms of demons in full black or dark gray suits, perfectly tailored to their bodies. Then there are demons wearing clothing that does little to hide their assets, revealing the dips and curves of their bodies. Everyone looks as if they stepped off the cover of a fashion magazine, beautiful but deadly.

Tonight's plan is simple. Oziel and I will make our grand entrance soon and start the celebration with a sacrifice—still an odd choice to start a party, but if it rids the realm of another piss-poor excuse of flesh, then I'll sleep soundly tonight. After that, Oziel and I will go our separate ways, and he'll use his magic to hide my features, so no one knows they are speaking to the queen. He'll make an excuse as to why the queen is missing if anyone should ask.

This will work.

It has to work.

A warm hand presses to the small of my back. Oziel watches his people trickle in from the hidden balcony we stand upon. He's the picture of calm, at least on the surface. There are cracks in his armor, though. His clenched fist. The tension he's holding in his shoulders. The way his eyes dart around the room. All of it indicates his nervousness for tonight. In many ways, it feels like we have one shot to figure out who is sabotaging the River Hel. There won't be another opportunity like this.

I reach out and gently place my hand on Oziel's cheek. His skin is warm beneath my fingertips, tense with unspoken thoughts. For a moment, his gaze locks on the crowd gathering below, but then he turns to me. His golden eyes search mine, and though I can't be sure, I think he relaxes under my touch—just slightly, like a breath held too long finally released.

"We won't fail," I say, my voice steady with a conviction I have no right to claim. There's no logic behind it, no proof to lean on, only a feeling, deep and insistent, that something will be revealed tonight.

"We won't fail." He repeats the words like a prayer.

Oziel closes the distance between us and pulls my body flush against his. We move at the same time, our lips crashing together in a hungry kiss of lust and something else I can't consider. My brain tries to remind me that I'm walking a dangerous path. That once this is over, I'm leaving. But my heart seems to have other plans.

Would it be so bad to find love? Even with the demon king himself? I've seen how corrupt love can be with my sister, and his parents' own love got them killed. It can be deadly, leaving wounds that will never heal. There's a certain vulnerability in love that I'm not sure I'm ready for.

A loud chime pulls Oziel away from me. The moment his lips are gone, I can think clearly. What the fuck am I doing? Being a horny, stupid bitch, that's what I'm doing. I mentally shake myself before turning to see what the sound was.

The whole room has gone quiet, save for a few low murmurs as the entrance doors are cleared, forcing all the demons mingling close by to move back. "It's time,"

Oziel says just as the chime starts again. Two guards march side by side, wearing silver and black armor, deadly swords on their hips.

Shouts and screams soon rise above the conversation as another two guards walk out. This time, they both drag in a bound man. At least I think it's a man. Dirt and grime cover his entire body, like he hasn't seen a shower in years. His hair is shaved close to his scalp, bloody patches covering a few places. His clothes—if one can even call them that—are in tatters, held together by strings. There's also something on his back, shimmering and translucent. Some kind of magic?

As if reading my thoughts, Oziel says, "He's a pixie. The fading shimmers on his back are the remnants of his wings. They've been clipped."

Just then, the guards shove the pixie down onto his knees as they reach the center of the grand chamber. Heavy chains rattle as the guards secure them to the iron locks embedded in the floor, binding him in place. His shoulders slump, and for a moment, his delicate, wingless back rises and falls with a shuddering breath. Then he screams.

It's not of pain. There's so much malice behind his words, hurling insults like daggers. His words bleed together, making him hard to understand. The demons around him begin to laugh, clearly amused by the pixie's display. He's the entertainment for tonight.

White-hot anger sears my body as I remember the heinous acts this pathetic pixie committed. All my earlier hesitations are gone, and my heart aches for the family he never deserved. The lowest of bastards harms children, and I will take great pleasure in watching the life drain from him.

"Come, it's nearly our time." Oziel's voice is low but firm as he takes my hand, his grip both steady and unyielding. Without hesitation, he leads me toward the grand staircase, its marble steps worn smooth by centuries of passage.

Above the chaos, Garvan's voice rings out, cutting through the vexed screams of the dying man. He speaks our names with a practiced authority, commanding the attention of the gathered crowd.

Oziel's fingers tighten around mine for a brief moment, whether in reassurance or warning, I can't tell. Then, with synchronized steps, we descend, our movements deliberate, shadows flickering along the walls as all eyes turn toward us. Normally, I hate attention on me, eyes boring into me, silently judging me. But right now, I focus on the pixie, forgetting everything and everyone exists.

When we reach the bottom of the stairs, Garvan meets us. In his hand is an old box, opened to show a gold necklace. It's old and rusted, with a mysterious crimson stain on the pendant. "This necklace belongs to the pixie. It will help strengthen your power over him." Garvan hands me the box, and I hold it as if it were a lost artifact.

Then nervousness hits. "Power?" I whisper only loud enough for Garvan and Oziel to hear. "I have no power of my own."

"That is debatable," Oziel says. "But you will use my shadows. They are as much yours as they are mine now."

"Use your shadows, but how?"

Instead of answering, Oziel rests his hand on the small of my back and guides me away from Garvan, steering me toward the center of the room, toward the pixie. Bound and furious, the creature spits insults in our direction, his voice sharp with defiance.

As we pass, the guards lower their heads in deference. I hesitate, unsure if I'm expected to acknowledge them, but Oziel doesn't spare them a glance. Taking his lead, I keep my focus ahead, my steps steady despite the weight of watching eyes.

We move until we are standing directly in front of the pixie. The air is ripe with his stench, and I switch to breathing through my mouth to spare my senses.

Oziel stands behind me, his hands lingering on my hips. When he speaks, his hot breath tickles my neck. "Call upon the shadows," he murmurs.

"How? I don't know—"

"Yes, you do," he interrupts. "Close your eyes." He waits until I obey. "Think of wrapping this man in darkness. Shrouding him in nightmares. Think of the terror and pain his family felt. Make him feel the same level of fear and pain they did. Hold the necklace tightly, Kitten. You can do this."

I do as Oziel says. With my eyes closed, I think of the dark shadows that always linger wherever Oziel goes. I imagine those same shadows wrapping tightly around the pixie, suffocating him with his worst nightmares. Forcing him to relive the pain he caused his family, only worse. I think of the children he stole from this world, and the woman who had to watch her babies die. I do it for them, allowing my anger to fuel the shadows. It doesn't matter that I never met them; their pain is now my pain.

Muffled screams draw me out of my trance. My eyes pop open, taking a moment to adjust before I see it. A blanket of shadows obscures the creature. Blood-curdling screams and his begging are the only indicators the pixie is still among us. When I squeeze the necklace harder, the cries only grow louder. Then something is dangled in front of me. A dagger.

"Sacrifice him, Kitten. One dagger through the heart will rid Mescos of this vermin. It'll be a safer place because of you," he says.

I tentatively reach for the dagger. It's heavy in my hands, blade reflective in the light. The burden of killing him falls upon my shoulders, but instead of shying away from the task, I embrace it.

Just like I did with James. Making the world better by taking him out of it. Perhaps this is my purpose here. To have no one suffer like my sister did. To put an end to those who cause the greatest pain.

I tighten my grip around the dagger's hilt, wrapping both hands around the worn leather. My pulse pounds in my ears, drowning out everything else.

Slowly, I lift the blade above my head, the dim light catching on its sharp edge. Then, with all the force in my body, I strike. Swift. Unrelenting. The blade plunges into the darkness, slicing through flesh and sinew. The dagger buries itself to the hilt, refusing to go any deeper. My breath comes in ragged gasps, and my hands tremble as I hold my ground, feeling the tremors of life ebbing beneath my grip.

A wet, gurgling sound cuts through the silence as the shadows begin to retreat, peeling back to reveal the pixie. His wide eyes gleam with a mix of terror and disbelief, frozen in the moment between life and death.

Blood stains his lips, pooling in the corners of his mouth as he struggles to make a sound. A scream that never comes. The dagger has struck true, buried deep into his chest. Crimson spills in thick, pulsing waves, soaking into his tattered clothing and pooling beneath him.

He wheezes, a rattling, desperate breath that falters as his body weakens. I watch, transfixed, as the light in his eyes flickers... then fades, leaving them empty, hollow, and forever still. He's gone. Because of me.

I don't realize I'm shaking until Oziel pulls me to his chest, wrapping me in his embrace. "Good girl," he murmurs into my hair, sending heat straight to my core. I have to press my thighs together. Blood is literally and figuratively on my hands, and yet I grow hot with need for Oziel.

Maybe this is who I was always meant to be.

"The Queen has made our sacrifice to the Dark Gods!" Garvan's voice calls out. He's greeted by whistles and cheers, thundering around the ballroom. "Let the night's celebration begin. Pour the wine!"

At his proclamation, the true party begins, despite the dead pixie on the ground. His death has served its purpose.

The guards unchain the pixie from the floor. Two of

them pick up his lifeless body and drag him out of the ballroom, leaving a trail behind him. Somewhere, music starts to play again, low and seductive. It clashes with the gruesome scene from earlier. The evidence is still staining the floor.

"The party has begun, Kitten. Shall we mingle?" Oziel asks.

As much as I want to stay here with his arms around me and lips on my body, I know we have a job to complete. There's a lot weighing on this, which I have to remind myself as I pry myself out of my husband's arms.

"How will I know if my appearance is hidden?" I ask, not wanting to start prematurely and sabotage the plan. I have to do this in a way that doesn't cause suspicion.

"Get a drink, though only pretend you're enjoying the lust wine. Keep your head. In ten minutes, start making your rounds. No one will recognize you. They will simply see a pretty she-demon. They will all be far too drunk to think of you or me, but if anyone asks about the queen, I shall come up with a lie. I can give you an hour." Oziel says the last part almost apologetically. "I thought I could give you more time, but—"

"An hour it is then." I nod, strengthening my resolve. I allow myself one last glance at the demon king, handsome as sin and deadly beautiful, before I part from him. There's work to be done, and I can't get distracted by Oziel. It's time to figure out who's poisoning the River Hel.

"Oh, Kitten?"

Oziel's voice halts me before I can get too far. A shiver runs up my arm as shadows coil around it, slithering like living tendrils before pressing something cold and solid into my palm. Instinctively, my fingers close around it— a hilt, rough and familiar, just like the one I used moments ago. As the shadows disperse, a dagger remains in my grasp, its weight both reassuring and foreboding. How many daggers does this demon have? I don't think I want to know.

"You should have protection, just in case. Use it wisely," Oziel murmurs, his voice a ghost of a promise before he vanishes into the crowd.

I'm on my own now.

Carefully, I slide the dagger into the bodice of my gown, tucking it against my skin, wary of the blade's sharp edge. Taking a steadying breath, I step forward and disappear into the churning sea of demons, swallowed by the chaos of the night.

CHAPTER 27

ISABELLE

My body is still abuzz with the phantom touch of Oziel. The bastard has broken through so many of my barriers that I'm starting to wonder if I'll ever truly be free of him. If I *want* to be free of him. I was so close to giving in to my desires earlier and allowing myself to kiss him. Right here. In front of everyone.

And if I'm being honest, I wanted more.

The task at hand is the anchor keeping me grounded. A demon carrying a tray of sparkling wine walks by, and I reach for a glass. Oziel's words replay in my mind. I have an hour. An hour to pretend I'm drunk on lust wine—hence the prop drink in my hand—and find out any information I can from the partygoers. I know the moment Oziel's magic is working because my skin heats, feeling the caress of his magic over me, hiding my features.

To anyone else, I'm just another demon. Not their queen.

Bodies upon bodies dance in a sea of demons. A few eager couples and groups have wasted no time throwing themselves at one another, getting right to the point. A man sits on a chair while another demon straddles his lap, moving their hips in a suggestive manner. Behind them, another demon kisses his neck.

I never thought I would be one for voyeurism, but my body grows hot at the scene. I can't help but wonder if Oziel ever participated in these activities publicly? My nostrils flare with jealousy at the thought of anyone else touching or fucking my husband. Another part of me wonders if Oziel would ever want to *play* in public together like the couples around me.

Scarier still, I don't think I would be opposed.

Something is seriously fucked up with me. My horny vagina shouldn't be trusted to make decisions. Ever. It'll lead me down a path I won't know how to come back from.

The atmosphere of the room intensifies as demons grow more frenzied. Getting anyone to talk will be a challenge, as they all get drunk with lust. This room will quickly turn into one big orgy, and no matter how fun that sounds, I have a job to do and only one chance to do it.

Loud giggles echo beside me, and I turn just in time to see a group of demons walk by, discussing something about the party. I quickly blend in, joining the group by snuggling up to a woman in the back. She grins at me, clearly not realizing who I am, which means the shadows are doing their job. The demon strokes my hair, a preda-tory nature in her touch, and I'm the wide-eyed prey.

"Pretty little thing," she purrs.

Acting drunk—especially around a bunch of drunk people—isn't hard. I giggle too loudly and lean against her, straining my ears to listen to the conversation happening in front of me.

"...Did you see what she was wearing?" a feminine voice asks, laughing haughtily. "You would think she made it from scraps."

"Perhaps she did. It's just going to come off anyway," the masculine voice responds, taking another sip of wine. "Except her little boy toy isn't here."

My ears perk up at this.

"Oh, he's here alright. He's just otherwise occupied getting his ass fucked by her brother," the male demon says, earning a round of cruel chuckles from the others. My shoulders sag, realizing this is going to be a lot harder than I originally thought.

I drift away from the group, finding others to mingle with. It's easy to infiltrate groups of demons—I'm another warm body they can potentially fuck. I play my role well, all but throwing myself at the demons who give me attention, trying to get them to speak.

"Who do you think the king will fuck tonight?" A conversation from a group of three demons stops me in my tracks. I pretend to take a sip of wine, craning my neck to listen.

"That human queen, I figure," a feminine voice says, sounding disinterested.

"Ah, yes. The queen who is supposed to save us because our king is too weak or too much of a coward to do it himself," a familiar voice says.

My head snaps to the side, and my eyes widen as I take in who spoke.

Lola. The servant who helped me get ready before my wedding with Greta and Paulina. She's not wearing a maid uniform now, but rather a skin-tight black dress with heavy makeup. There's no humor in her expression, just seething hate. It makes sense because Greta, her boss and maybe friend, turned to stone. She seems to be taking the loss of her friend hard.

"Don't speak ill of King Oziel," the woman next to her says. Pride swells inside me at having someone defend Oziel—until she speaks again. "It will hurt my chances of getting him to fuck me if he hears us talking."

I decide I hate her.

Lola just mumbles something under her breath, breaking away from the others. I note her displeasure with Oziel, but is it enough to betray him? How long has she felt this way? Despite her contempt for my husband, I don't think she's the one poisoning the lake, but it doesn't completely clear her either. I make a mental note before continuing my rounds to speak with other demons.

They speak a lot. About fucking. Who they wish to fuck. Who they wish to never fuck again. But they never speak of anyone missing or enemies of the king. It was a far-fetched plan to begin with, but I had hoped this would provide me some insight. Yet I'm no further than I was at the start of this, other than the new information about Lola.

Defeat tastes bitter on my tongue. My hour slips away, and the partygoers are long gone in their lust, all engaged in sex. The room fills with lewd sounds of skin smacking against skin, moans and cries of pleasure, and the heady scent of sex. I don't even have the chance to enjoy the sight before me, knowing I've come away with nothing of substance.

I can't make out Oziel, or even Garvan, for that matter, amongst the crowd. My brain begins to conjure up images of Oziel with another, naked and sweaty, moaning as he slips inside her or him. They would scream out for him because I know how good his cock feels buried deep inside me. Anger slowly boils within me at the scene playing out, no matter how many times I tell myself it's not real. He wouldn't betray me that way after he promised me he would behave.

Before I can work myself into a raging fit, something catches my attention. I turn just in time to see a hooded figure leaving through the courtyard. My body tenses, and for half a second, I contemplate finding Oziel or Garvan to accompany me, but by the time I find them, this mystery figure could be long gone.

No, this is my chance, and I can't risk missing it.

Sidestepping the writhing bodies on the ground, I make my way out the doors leading to the courtyard, taking note that no guards are stationed here. Oziel surely had guards stationed at each door? Now that I think about it, I haven't seen guards since the ritual.

The warm breeze hits my bare arms the moment I get to the courtyard. My eyes dart to the tree line just in time to see the hooded figure disappear through the thickets of evergreens. I start to run but only get so far before my feet scream in protest.

"Fuck," I growl, leaning down to unclasp my heels and quickly discard them before starting my chase.

The hooded figure stops in his tracks, and I quickly roll behind a tree, flattening myself against it to blend in with the scenery. For a few tense moments, the figure doesn't move, and I think for sure they've seen me. That this entire operation is over because they're going to kill me. But just as I'm mentally writing my will, they turn their back to me and start walking at a faster pace deeper into the forest.

In the direction of the River Hel.

My heart pounds loudly in my chest, drowning out all the other sounds in the forest. The dagger's cool blade against my chest reminds me I'm not without protection, and I reach for the only weapon I have, clutching it tightly in one fist.

I keep my footsteps light, doing my best to not step on anything that would cause the hooded figure to turn back and spot me. I feel every rock and piece of sharp earth against my bare feet but ignore the pain. For five minutes, we walk, me a short distance behind him until the smell of the river infiltrates the air.

The River Hel is in poor shape, even worse than last time. It's almost completely black in color and smells of rot and decay. The putrid smell nearly makes me vomit up the remnants of breakfast this morning. Does Oziel know just how bad the river has gotten? What does this mean for his magic?

The hooded figure crouches alongside the river, pulling something small out of his pocket. Shiny black liquid gleams in the vial, sparkling like a captured miniature galaxy. There's a presence to the liquid, one that makes every part of my body rebel, telling me something isn't right. This is wrong. All wrong.

It's the poison.

The only thought going through my mind is ridding the hooded figure of the vial. They're so preoccupied with its contents, they don't hear me approaching. The weight of the dagger doesn't seem like a burden any longer, but a necessity. A necessity to kill and protect what is mine. Because, for as long as I'm married to Oziel, this kingdom is mine to protect. I will go to any lengths necessary to protect those I deem important, and Oziel is important to me, no matter how much I wish to deny it.

The dagger rises above my head as I come within a few feet of the hooded figure. Then, just as I prepare to strike, the hooded figure spins around with supernatural speed, their face obstructed by shadows. I see nothing but their deep red orbs shining with malevolence, a true evil I've not yet experienced. Not even with James. There's nothing remotely human about this thing in front of me. And yet, I can't help but feel a familiarity, like I've seen them before.

"Foolish human," it screeches, voice unrecognizable. They say "human." Not "demon." My disguise must no longer be in effect. The little protection I once had is now gone, leaving me vulnerable.

The stranger brings their hand up, blasting me with a red smoke. It hits my chest, stealing the breath from my lungs as I stumble back. Something snags my foot, causing me to lose my balance and flail as I fall. Pain erupts within me the moment I hit the ground. Small rocks and hard dirt do nothing to cushion my fall. My chest burns from where the red smoke hit me.

I don't have time to gather myself because the hooded figure is on top of me. Fear surges within me, and I scream, kick, and wildly swing the dagger, hoping to cut something. I've never had formal training with any weapon—Grym Hollow isn't exactly known for producing warriors, but I know how to survive. Pure stubbornness has kept me alive this long, and it will help me now.

I manage to get one of my legs free from under their weight and use all my strength to bring it up between their legs. Male or female anatomy, a knee to the groin is going to hurt. My attacker grunts, loosening their hold on me. With quick precision, I slash the dagger across their arms and face, drawing blood. It isn't a killing blow. Hell, it won't even hold them back for long, but it is enough for me to wiggle free from underneath them.

Scrambling to pick myself off the ground, I round on my attacker. Despite the clear pain they're in, they haven't dropped the shadows from obscuring their face. "Show yourself, you coward!"

Low, mocking laughter greets me in response, but it's still impossible to tell if the attacker is a man or woman. Their mockery sends chills down my spine, reminding me I'm alone. A human in a world of monsters. I don't have Oziel or his powers on my side, even if Oziel says I have my own power. I don't even have Garvan to run to for protection, assuming the advisor would help. He seems nice enough, but is he a fighter?

"Fools. All of you," my attacker speaks again, stalking toward me like a predator in the night. I'm the cornered prey, looking for my escape route. I'm too far away to scream for help; someone should have heard me already. Besides, they are all too busy fucking to decipher the difference between a scream of pleasure and a scream for help. I'm completely alone and at the mercy of the stranger before me.

Keep them talking. Find a way to get out of this.

"Why are you doing this? You're putting your people in danger." My back hits a tree, and I silently curse. I grip the dagger like a life force, wishing it was a gun. Guns seem much more effective. Daggers? This is some medieval bullshit I'm not accustomed to.

"Only temporarily. I'm the only one assuring our survival. Your precious king is growing weaker by the day, occupied with you, his new human queen. It's only a matter of time before he falls, along with anyone else who tries to stop me."

"So, what, you want to be king? Is that it?" I think back to Oziel's story of his parents. How his own people betrayed them. Is the past repeating itself now? Do enemies blend in so easily that we overlook them? Clearly.

"I deserve to rule!" they hiss. "And I will do more to bring down the Nephilim than a weak king who can't save his people. The king is far too prideful to see past his own nose. His reign will end us all if we allow it, and I won't."

Anger blooms in my chest. Anger for Oziel, but I can't fly off the handle. Any sudden movement will alert them to my attack. There's only one way out of this, and it's to fight.

My opportunity to strike comes a moment later when rustling in the bushes followed by a demon giggling with another pulls my attacker's attention away from me and into the forest. I don't think; I just act.

The hilt of the dagger is heavy in my hands as I rush the attacker. I pushed a dagger through one person today; I can do it again.

Their chest is exposed to me, providing a perfect target. I grip the dagger tightly, channeling every last ounce of my strength as I raise it high, ready to deliver a fatal blow. But just as I thrust downward, the demon attacker twists away with inhuman speed. My blade misses its mark, sinking instead into the thick muscle of their thigh.

A guttural howl erupts from my attacker—a monstrous sound laced with both agony and fury. Their crimson eyes burn like bright embers in the darkness, radiating pure malice. My body freezes, terror taking over.

"You'll pay for that—" they start, but they're eclipsed by dozens of screams coming from the direction of the ball. Terrified voices grow closer as demons escape into the forest for safety.

What is happening? And where is Oziel? New fear I've never experienced before takes hold of me. Part of me knows I should stay with this attacker because it might be our one chance at figuring out who is betraying us. Yet every fiber in my body calls out to Oziel. He needs me, and I need to make sure he's okay. He *has* to be okay.

But my decision is made for me when I turn back to the attacker. Darkness and shadows surround them, covering their entire body. "I will see you and the king dead soon enough," they speak. When the shadows clear a moment later, the attacker is gone.

There's no time to mourn losing the attacker, though the missed chance to uncover their identity is infuriating. I can dwell on that later. Right now, I gather up my dress, muttering curses at the cumbersome—albeit beautiful—ballgown, before breaking into a sprint, racing toward the ballroom. Toward the danger.

Toward Oziel.

CHAPTER 28
OZIEL

Hearty laughs give way to lustful moans as the evening goes on. A few demons attempt to get my attention, but I pay them little mind, scanning the bodies in the ballroom. I lost track of Isabelle half an hour ago, and my body has been on edge ever since.

The power I used to disguise her has worn off—I was unable to hold it any longer. If the River Hel was still at full power, my small display of magic would cost me nothing. Now, though, I feel drained. A glimmer of magic resides in me on reserve, so we're not completely power- less. Though my defenses are waning quickly.

I wrap my hands around the iron banister, perched up on the dais. My throne sits empty, a harrowing reminder of everything I can lose. Normally I'd be sitting upon my throne, overlooking the frenzied fucking taking place in my kingdom, but the thought of sitting still fills me with dread. My body itches to move, and a sense of foreboding keeps me on edge.

I can't shake the feeling something is terribly wrong.

Where the fuck is Isabelle? I need to get Garvan and have him help me search for her.

This human woman has shaken up my entire world in a matter of weeks. My reason for bringing the human to my kingdom was to save it, not to fill an empty void inside me I've kept locked and hidden away since the death of my parents. The years have hardened me, making me the demon king I am today. But Isabelle reminds me of the one thing I've always secretly wanted but will never allow myself to have.

The human is my weakness.

Even though I should be conserving my powers, I send my shadows out to locate Isabelle within the castle. But there's no sign of Isabelle. A foreign feeling takes up residence within my chest, tightening my muscles and churning my stomach. Knowing she's not within the castle, I call my shadows back, but not before they pick up on something. An unknown presence stalking the halls.

There's no need to investigate because, the next moment, the ballroom breaks out into screams. Demons flee in terror, pushing and shoving others in their way to escape the room. The chaos erupting has me running from the dais, conjuring my sword made of deadly shadows. Adrenaline and fear from my people fuel me, giving me a boost of strength I need. Then a terrible high-pitched scream reverberates around the room, making my blood run cold.

The Nephilim.

Specifically, the one who should be tied up in my

dungeon right now. No one escapes. Never. There are too many security measures in place to prevent this. Even if this Nephilim was somehow able to break through his chains and his cell, the moment his foot touched the stairs, it should have been eviscerated on the spot due to the spells placed on it, alerting me to the security breach.

A demon must have let him free, knowing we'd be distracted today. And only a demon who is stealing shadow magic could override all the safety nets placed upon the dungeon.

When I find them, no amount of torture will be enough. I will show them the extent of my wrath.

But where the fuck is Isabelle?

The Nephilim brings his fist down, cracking the flooring and sending the demons within a ten-foot perimeter flying backwards. Some hit the wall with a sickening crunch, while others knock into those trying to flee. Guards rush the scene, weapons drawn. I note they all come from the same direction, making me wonder if any of them had been at their post.

"Get everyone out!" I command, making sure my voice is heard above the rest.

My guards immediately follow my command, swiftly spreading out to herd everyone toward the exits. The Nephilim's sharp gaze flicks toward the demons as they flee, and its expression hardens in contempt. Raising its hand, it conjures a swirling sphere of gray energy, dark magic coiling around its fingers like living smoke. With a hiss, it hurls the orb into the panicked crowd.

The impact is instantaneous. If I hadn't seen it with my own eyes, I wouldn't have believed it. Magic erupts in a violent burst, sending a shockwave rippling through the air. Those caught in its radius don't even have time to scream before their bodies stiffen, their skin hardening into lifeless stone, frozen in place with wide-eyed terror and mouths open in silent cries, forever etched into their petrified forms.

The room reeks of dark magic, smelling of rotten eggs. This is no longer a curse, but deadly magic being used to take my kingdom down. There's only one Nephilim, and yet it has the room in shambles despite enduring weeks of torture. A whole fleet of healthy Nephilim? Despite my best efforts, I shudder.

The Nephilim forms another orb, staring at a group of demons still recovering from being thrown across the room. Before it has a chance to hurl dark magic at my demons, I act, concealing myself in shadows. My sword extends, bright red flames bursting along the dark metal, dancing in a deadly fashion. The Nephilim doesn't see me, providing me with the element of surprise.

I leap, using my shadows to get me airborne. My sword slices through the air, murderous and formidable, and cuts through its hand like paper. The Nephilim screams as blood spurts from its wound. Its limp hand, no longer holding the magic orb, falls limply to the floor. Its attention is on me, which is precisely what I want. The injured demons are able to scramble free, fleeing to safety.

"Not my people. Not my kingdom," I snarl, my voice laced with fury as I drop from the air, landing with a resounding thud. The impact fractures the tiled floor beneath me, jagged cracks splintering outward like a web. The uneven flooring pushes me closer to the Nephilim before me.

I don't hesitate, immediately moving, forcing the creature to turn as I circle it, my muscles coiled, ready to strike. The Nephilim reacts, free hand crackling with energy as it hurls a bolt of magic in my direction. I pivot sharply, the air humming as the blast narrowly misses me.

That was close. Too fucking close. But I don't dare glance back to see where it landed. Not even to check if any of my people were caught in the crossfire. I can't afford the distraction. Not now.

The reason this Nephilim is here in the first place is because I wanted it. It was a plus that Isabelle was able to communicate with the creature, but that wasn't the initial reason I imprisoned it. No, this was my own vanity speaking. My need to have the creature as a trophy. Even Garvan tried to warn me. Well, in the end, it has cost me my people.

But it ends now.

I summon magic from the River Hel, the last bit I can squeeze out. My body burns hot—too hot—as the magic flares to life inside me. Blue flames erupt around me, licking my skin, eager to be let loose. I burn brightly. Burn hot. Burn with the thoughts of Isabelle and the strength she provides me but doesn't know it yet. Burn with the fear of my people.

And then I let go.

Fire bursts from my body, and the sudden loss of power forces me to my knees. Blue flames hit their mark, engulfing the Nephilim in an inferno hotter and more potent than normal flames. Another perk to wielding shadow magic.

The putrid stench of burned flesh fills the air as it melts from its body, exposing bone underneath. Its terrible cries of distress do little to quell my anger and frustration. Anger at myself for harboring a dangerous creature. Frustration for not being able to find my fucking wife.

All of a sudden, the screaming stops. The Nephilim teeters from side to side until it succumbs to its injuries. Its large body drops, falling to the floor in a bloody, fiery mess. For just one second, the Nephilim's eyes meet mine. Defeat registers in its gaze, then the light flickers out and leaves it completely dead. At my hand.

Silence follows. It's as if the whole room is holding its breath, waiting for my next move. I've exhausted all my magic and power. Fatigue threatens to overwhelm me, but there's still one person on my mind. One person I have yet to see and need now more than ever.

With shaky legs, I rise from the fire and ash. The room is nearly empty, save for the frozen statues of those who tried to flee but couldn't, and a few of my guards waiting for their instructions.

But I ignore them. Ignore the fallout I must deal with. My voice roars into the silence, one name reverberating around me over and over again.

Isabelle.

Isabelle.

Isabelle.

ISABELLE

"Let me through! I need to get inside!" Trying to shove the demon is as effective as shoving a brick wall. It doesn't help that my body already feels drained from my fight with the hooded attacker. Making my way this far into the castle was no easy task, especially since every demon is running in the opposite direction. But not me. I'm running toward the danger.

Toward Oziel.

Only to be stopped by his fucking guards. Guards who were not here earlier. Had they been called away? Was that why the attacker easily slipped through? I file away that thought for later, focused on getting to Oziel right now.

"We can't let you in. King's orders." The demon places his hands on my shoulders to push me back. "Please, ma'am—"

"I'm your fucking queen," I snap, smacking his hands away. This time they fall to the guard's sides, his beady black eyes boring into me. The guard takes me in, maybe for the first time, and recognition flickers across his features before it is replaced with unease.

The demon bows. "My queen, I apologize," he says hastily. When he straightens back up, I'm prepared for him to move aside. But he doesn't move. If anything, he stays firm in his position. "The king would want you safe. You must go."

A scream rings out, followed by loud cracking that jostles the foundation. It provides me enough of a distraction to sprint past the first guard, but my victory is short-lived. Hands grab my wrist, nearly yanking my arm out of its socket, pulling me back into a hard chest.

"No! Let me fucking go!" I thrash, kicking out wildly and trying to free my hands. The iron grip on me only tightens.

"My queen, you must stop!" an unfamiliar female voice shouts. A demon guard stands only a few feet away from us, something akin to pity coloring his features. If demons could be remorseful, I imagine they'd look like him.

He takes a step forward, brows drawn together. "Melisanda, perhaps we should—"

"No!" snaps the female—Melisanda—holding me. "We were given orders, Borzon, and no one can defy the king."

"But she's the queen," Borzon argues.

The hands around me loosen slightly, though not enough for me to break free of Melisanda's iron grip. The demon pauses, clearly weighing her options. I may be their queen, but I'm not truly one of them. I bruise easier.

Break faster. But I'm still the queen; hopefully my voice carries the same weight as Oziel's.

"She's human, Borzon. She can't defend herself. Oziel wouldn't want her in there. She'll only be a distraction," Melisanda barks, confirming the fears swirling around in my head.

Before either Borzon or I can say more, another loud scream comes from the ballroom, followed by the sound of a large body hitting the floor. Then...silence. Deadly quiet that speeds up my heart, spreading unease.

Then comes a roar—deep, ferocious, and raw—that nearly drives me to my knees and sends me spiraling.

"ISABELLE!"

My name explodes through the air, a thunderclap that shakes the very walls. The sheer force of Oziel's voice sends a shiver down my spine, the desperation in it cutting through the chaos like a blade. Melisanda's grip falters. Just for a second. But it's enough. I rip free, lungs burning as I bolt toward the ballroom. I don't dare hesitate.

I have to find Oziel.

The ballroom is free of partygoers. Tables of food and wine are turned over. Food and shattered glass litter the floor. A burning blaze catches my attention. Blue flames burn brightly. Upon first look, the flames seem to be coming from charred wood. But a slight twitch to the body tells me it's not wood at all.

A Nephilim is burning. How the hell did the Nephilim get here?

And right in front of it, on his knees with his back toward me, is Oziel.

Oziel's body is on fire too; blue flames lick at his skin. Unlike the Nephilim, Oziel isn't burning. No, his flames cling to him, waiting for their next move, as if he is their master. I suppose he is. I've seen many facets of my husband, but never have I seen him look so...like a demon.

Perhaps I should be scared. My pulse races, but not out of fear. Out of a carnal need residing deep in my soul.

"Oziel."

My voice is the hammer that shatters the glass. Oziel's flames leave him, replaced by his familiar shadows. He stands, turning slowly. His once pristine suit is slightly charred and untucked. What are normally gold eyes are a bright, crimson red. His body is pulled to mine. It's not so much a walk as it is a glide.

"Isabelle," he purrs, his voice not entirely his own because he doesn't seem to be in control of himself. Too gruff and deep, a sound that goes straight to my clit.

I'm enjoying this far too much. Probably not the reaction I should have to my husband just single-handedly taking down a Nephilim—and I still don't know how it got in here.

"I'm here. I'm safe. You're safe." I speak the words to know they are true.

Oziel closes the space between us, reaching for me, his hand going around my neck in a tight grip and pulling me to his chest. I don't argue, just let myself be pulled. Maybe he needs to feel me just as much as I need to feel him.

"Oziel, I—" My words are swallowed by his lips.

Harsh, punishing lips claim my mouth. I've no other option but to submit.

The moment my lips part, Oziel's tongue possesses my mouth. I moan, or he does. I'm not certain anymore. I kiss him back with just as much frenzy, realizing for the first time just how truly fearful I was of losing him. I never wanted to get this hung up on some guy.

But Oziel has proven himself not to be *some* guy.

He's a demon king. He's crude, rough and frequently infuriating. But he's also passionate, loyal, and gentle when he wants to be. He knows my darkness, but instead of running away from it, he embraces it. Lets *me* embrace it. I've never been a conventional woman, always attracted to the wrong thing, but Oziel doesn't feel wrong.

He feels right.

"I want you, Wife." His deep purr makes me shiver.

My body is already hot with need for him. Oziel still isn't himself. He's dirty and bloody. More demon than I have ever seen him, and yet I've never wanted him more. I think he needs me to feel grounded and to gain back his self-control. There's still so much pent-up energy within him, begging to be let out. Begging for an outlet.

"Take me." My voice is breathy, far needier than I intend. That seems to please Oziel. The corners of his lips pull into a sinister smile, and I know this man is about to ruin me. He squeezes my neck, and I gasp, arching into his touch.

"Beautiful," he murmurs, leaning down and licking a line from my ear to my neck. It shouldn't feel as good as it does, but wetness pools between my thighs. With his head still close to my neck, he shouts for the guards behind us, the ones I nearly forgot were here. "Dispose of the body." His demand is met with affirmatives from his guards.

Oziel pays them little mind. His shadows wrap around us, caressing my skin like silk. The world around us fades away, and everything goes quiet. A moment later, the shadows disperse, leaving us completely, and Oziel stumbles, clearly using up the last of his reserve power. We're no longer in the ballroom, but rather the shower chambers. No one else is in here, which is good because, while Oziel may be fine with public sex, I'm not certain I'm there yet.

"Such a fucking beautiful dress," he says before flicking his hand and removing my dress without touching me. Perhaps he had a little more shadow magic left in him.

"Nice trick," I say breathlessly.

Oziel does the same to himself, and soon he stands before me in all his naked glory. His body tightens, and my gaze lowers to his hard cock pressing against his stomach. His eyes drink me in, and he circles me like a lion stalking a little lamb. A shiver goes down my spine because Oziel's monster is out. And his focus is on one thing and one thing only:

Me.

CHAPTER 30

ISABELLE

The next moment, my back hits the wall, knocking the breath out of me. Pain shoots down my spine from the force of it, but I barely register it because Oziel's lips are on mine. He's claiming me from the inside out, searing his presence into my body, as if every minute not kissing me is torturous for him.

A low hum from the shower heads above is the only warning before warm water douses us, heating my body to an almost uncomfortable level. Oziel wraps my hair around his hand, tugging me back. The pull is the perfect amount of pain and pleasure I crave, and the bastard knows it. How this demon knows what my body needs after such a short amount of time, I'll never know. It was as if he was made for my pleasure and I his.

"I thought I lost you." His voice is gruff and not entirely his own. He's far more demon than he is man, still not in control of his body. If I were a smart woman, I'd do anything in my power to push him away. But my fucking horny body can't stand the thought of leaving him right now.

"You didn't lose me, Oziel. I'm right here." My hand reaches up to caress his cheek, and the other one moves to stroke his horn. A lustful sigh leaves his lips, eyes closing as he leans into my touch. This is dangerous territory. We both know how this is going to end. With me leaving him once my role here is done. It's what I want…

Wanted?

Fuck, I don't know anymore. I can't make decisions when my heart and brain are at odds with each other. I don't need to decide now, but I do need this demon more than I need the air in my lungs.

We move as one, being pulled together by strong, invisible magnets. Oziel's hands reach around to grab the back of my thighs and lift me up. My legs wrap around him, supported by the tiled wall behind me. Both of his hands come to rest on my ass, and mine slide up to grab his horns. Oziel hisses a curse, bucking up against me, his hard cock teasing me relentlessly.

"You scared me, Kitten," he hisses, lifting my ass higher as he positions me over his cock. My pussy is so wet for him, desperate to be filled. I'm a wanton woman, trying to shimmy out of his grasp to sink down on his cock, but his hold is too strong. Fucking demons. "That wasn't very kind of you."

My instinct is to yell, reminding him I was only doing what we planned. It wasn't my fault the damn Nephilim got out. Just as I open my mouth to tell him off, he drops me down on his cock, filling me up in one fell swoop. I scream at the sudden intrusion, gripping his horns like life support. "Oh fuck!"

I've had good dick and pussy before, but Oziel is different. Everything about him exudes sex, made from every wet dream and dark fantasy. It could be my imagination, but his cock feels as if it's buzzing inside me, sending waves of pleasure through my body.

"Now you get to make it up to me, naughty girl," he purrs.

"I didn't fucking do anything," I hiss, my voice sounding too breathy to be convincing. Damn him and his cock.

Oziel bucks once, making my eyes roll back in my head. "You did, though. You came into my fucking kingdom and wormed your way under my skin. Every waking breath, I think of you. You are the first person I think of when I wake up and the last I see when I fall asleep. You plague my mind like a sickness. You, Isabelle, are responsible for this desire burning inside me."

For once in my life, I'm stunned speechless. What do you even say when the king of demons professes his burning desire for you? The need isn't one-sided, clearly. My body craves him on a level that's honestly frightening. But I don't have the words to tell him any of this. My thoughts are fragmented and broken. How can I tell him how I'm feeling when I don't even understand it myself?

So I take the coward's way out of it.

I kiss him. Maybe my lips can say what my words cannot. Words I'm too scared to admit, even to myself. Oziel doesn't protest. He kisses me back just as fiercely, tongue sweeping out to part my lips. When I open for him, he dominates my mouth, drinking me like a fine wine.

I can't stay still. My hips begin to move, pussy squeezing his throbbing cock. Then my husband begins to fuck me in earnest. It's like a switch goes off within him. One moment he's barely containing himself, and the next, he unleashes upon me. His hips snap up, and my body jerks in response.

"Oziel!" His name is the only word I know. He guides me up and down on his cock, pulling nearly all the way out of me, to the point my pussy is weeping and begging for more, before thrusting all the way to the hilt. He hits deep inside of me, mounting my pleasure quickly.

I ride his cock with wild abandon, body arching toward him. His hands squeeze my ass, one moving close to my back hole. I shudder as his finger rims me. Oziel breaks the kiss to lean forward and take a nipple into his mouth, sucking and licking. Damn this man and his sinful tongue.

"Oziel…"

"What, Kitten?" he hums, tongue lapping at my hard nub.

"Don't stop…please, don't stop."

"Wasn't planning on it." If anything, Oziel's thrusting grows more rapid and frenzied. He abuses my pussy in the best way possible, and all I can do is take it. My body heats; my eyes close. Fireworks burst across my lids, and I scream out for him again.

My orgasm hits me hard, coursing through my entire body. Every nerve sense is heightened. Oziel lets out a strangled grunt and comes deep inside of me. It's just another way for him to claim me, but I'm not mad at it.

"I'm not done with you, Wife," Oziel says, hunger still gleaming in his eyes. Despite him fucking me like an animal against the wall, he barely looks satiated. Are all demons like this? If so, mating a demon has an amazing perk.

Oziel pulls out of me, his release dripping down my thighs. It's messy and crude, but so fucking hot. "You're going to let me lick that pretty little pussy clean, aren't you, Kitten?"

Fuck yes I am. All I can do is nod, but Oziel isn't satisfied with that. "Tell me you want it."

I narrow my eyes at him. "I want it."

"You want what?"

"You're such a dick," I hiss, and because I'm pretty sure my vagina would revolt and walk out on me if I deny him, I say, "I want you to lick my pussy."

There. Dick.

The smirk Oziel gives me is wolfish, pure masculine energy. He sets me back down on the floor. I sway on my feet, but he doesn't let me go. In fact, he reaches for one of my legs and lifts it up on a raised bench. He then turns my hips slightly until I'm completely bared to him. Then, the demon king sinks to his knees.

"Mine." The word is murmured, soft like a promise. But that's the only thing soft about Oziel. In the next moment, his tongue licks me from my ass to my clit. My body jolts when he takes my clit into his mouth, sucking on the bundle of nerves. Desperately, I reach out, resting one hand against the wall to keep me up. My other snakes down, landing on his horn to keep him in place.

A soft chuckle vibrates my kiss. This smug bastard knows exactly how much he's affecting me. His name leaves my lips, whispered in reverence, "Oziel."

He spreads my folds with his fingers, and his tongue laps at me. My cheeks flush because he's truly lapping up the mess he made in me. It's so erotic, I can't help but move one hand to my chest, squeezing my tit and plucking my nipple between my thumb and pointer finger.

Already, I can feel my pleasure growing, my orgasm close to the surface. Another perk about demons is they definitely make you finish quickly. I'm a needy woman, riding my husband's face, desperate for another release. It's almost enough to make me forget about everything that happened tonight. We're going to have to talk about it eventually, but that can wait.

All it takes is another swipe of his tongue along my clit for my legs to buckle and vision to go fuzzy. My orgasm is even stronger than before as Oziel works me through it. He doesn't stop until I'm blissed out, barely able to keep myself upright.

And for just a moment, I imagine a life with Oziel. What it could be like. What we could achieve together. In that moment, I realize just how deep into his web he's spun me. Now I fear there might not be an escape for me.

But I'm not certain I mind.

CHAPTER 31
OZIEL

The taste of Isabelle coats my tongue in sweet and tangy bliss. The fog clouding my judgment slowly starts to disperse, allowing me to regain a semblance of control. I was a lost man, using all the darkness I could summon to defeat the Nephilim. She gave me strength, and in my time of need, I called out for her.

And she came.

A mistress of darkness, coming out of the shadows.

At that moment, I needed her. The pull was strong, taking over my whole body. Never in my life had I felt more demon than I did in that moment, transporting us out of the ballroom and into the shower chambers. My body moved on its own accord, knowing one thing and one thing only.

Isabelle.

Being inside her felt like victory after a tumultuous war. Nothing could have kept me from her in that moment, not even a horde of Nephilim. I was truly and completely under my human wife's spell.

Even now, after both my tongue and cock have been inside her, I still feel like a starved demon. Isabelle sways on her feet, a satisfied smirk on her face. Her chest rises and falls in rapid succession, still coming down from her second orgasm. I'm tempted to pull another one out of her before dealing with the reality of our situation, when the door to the chamber cracks open, followed by a familiar voice.

"My king, are you in here?" Garvan's voice breaks the lust-induced spell Isabelle had over me.

Anger, another familiar emotion, overtakes me, and I stand. The modicum of power still residing in me burns through me as shadows press against the door, keeping it closed. Garvan is a good advisor, but I'm feeling particularly violent and don't want to gouge Garvan's eye out upon seeing Isabelle thoroughly fucked. Some things are for my eyes only, and this is one of them.

"Report, Garvan," I project my voice to be heard through the sound of falling water on the thick concrete walls.

There is an intake of breath on the other side before Garvan's voice filters in. "The Nephilim's body has been burned to ash. Guards are discarding the ashes as we speak. There were no fatalities, but," he pauses, as if preparing himself to give the message, "we lost more people to the curse. Ten, to be exact. Tonight's events must have triggered something in the curse to speed up the effects."

Isabelle lets out a soft gasp from behind me. My gaze

moves back toward her, watching as she bites her lip. I get the distinct impression she knows something by the way her body freezes. It's something to discuss with her once Garvan is gone.

"Shall I put the statues with the others?" Garvan asks when I don't respond, voice bordering on cautious. I wouldn't take the full force of my anger out on those loyal to me, but I also don't reassure him.

"Yes." More failures to add to my ever-growing collection. "Is there anything else?"

"Not at the moment, my king."

"Good. Then leave us. I'll speak to you soon." There are things I need to discuss with Garvan, like safety protocols for the dungeon and what our next moves will look like, but that can wait until I'm done speaking to my wife.

Garvan's soft footfalls move down the hall once he's dismissed. I wait until I sense he's far away, presumably carrying out my orders, before I turn back to my wife. "Where were you before the Nephilim attack?" This is the question I should have asked her the moment I saw her, but I wasn't in control of my body then. The lust and need are still there, simmering just below the surface. It's easy to ignore now.

However, with my wife's body on full display, flushed and thoroughly used, concentration is a dangerous game.

Isabelle sucks in a deep breath before pushing past me. Disappointment sours my tongue when she reaches for a fluffy towel to wrap around herself, hiding her body from me. "I saw a hooded figure," she finally says.

I tense, slow to process her words. "What do you mean you saw a hooded figure?"

"I mean," she paces a path in front of me as if she's unable to stay in one place to tell the story, "I did as we discussed, blended in and tried to talk to people. That didn't give me any leads, though Lola seems upset with you. I think she's just upset about her friend though, so I don't think she's our person. Anyway, I was close to giving up when I happened to see a hooded figure through the glass window, running out into the forest."

"And you didn't think to come and get me?"

Isabelle stops pacing to scowl at me. It would be adorable if I wasn't pissed at her for endangering herself. "I tried to find you. Hell, I even tried looking around for Garvan, but I didn't see either of you. I wasn't going to just let this person get away. So, yeah, I followed them."

"You could have died, Isabelle," I hiss, my body heating up in anger.

"Well, I didn't, so don't fucking get growly with me. Do you want to know what happened, or do you want to stand there pissed?" She narrows her eyes, her hands resting on her slim hips, chastising me as if I were a child. For anyone else, I would burn them where they stand for speaking to me like that. But because this is Isabelle? It's practically foreplay.

The corners of my lips turn up into an amused smile. Isabelle notices my change, and heat rushes to her cheeks. "I followed the attacker out to the River Hel. They were poisoning the water, and I tried to stop them."

"You were going to stop a demon, Kitten?"

Isabelle's nostrils flare as her cheeks stain a deeper

crimson. "I wasn't thinking about that. I was thinking about capturing the demon. I managed to injure them, but they escaped when I was distracted by the Nephilim chaos."

"You drew blood?" Both pride and an unfamiliar sensation swell my chest. This human amazes me around every corner.

"Yes, I did," she says rather smugly.

"Do you have the knife on you?"

Isabelle's cocky smile falters. "Erm, no. I think I dropped it back at the river. Was it important to you?"

The dagger itself isn't. Just another dagger from my weaponry. But what could potentially be on that dagger is important. "Tomorrow, we will go and scout out the area. If there's blood to be found, I can use it to identify the traitor."

Isabelle's eyes widen at that. She looks ready to bolt for the door. Her words only confirm my suspicion. "Then we should go now. Before it's too late—"

My hand snakes out and wraps around her wrist, silencing her. Whether from my touch or her own confusion, I don't know. Though, I'd like to think the former. Perhaps I've grown soft in my wife's presence, but my body is tired. I pulled deep into the well of magic, scraping every last drop to take down the Nephilim. Then I used the last of my adrenaline to fuck my wife.

My bed is calling. I need rest after the display of magic I used earlier.

The River Hel can wait a few hours. "Sleep first," I say, but Isabelle opens her mouth, ready to argue with me. I quickly add, "We both need rest. Neither of us will be of use tired. We can attend to the area first thing in the morning."

At first, I think Isabelle is going to argue with me regardless. The truth is that my body craves sleep. This weakness frightens me above all else. Not only am I not the strong king my people need, but it further proves our magic is almost gone. We will be completely exposed and vulnerable to our enemies.

However, Isabelle sags, a deep sigh leaving her pink lips. "Fine. Sleep and then we scout the River Hel." With that, she turns her back on me and heads out of the shower chambers. I find myself following her, and I can't help but wonder how much longer I'll have her in my bed.

Our time is fading quickly.

CHAPTER 32
ISABELLE

As much as I was against sleep, it came easily the moment my head hit the pillow. It didn't occur to me that I was running on pure adrenaline from fighting the hooded attacker, worrying about Oziel, and fucking him. My body fell into the bed, and I slept until soft hands gently nudged me awake the following morning.

For a demon, Oziel's touch can be gentle. Soothing even. I doubt many others get to feel their king caressing them like this. My eyes flutter open, the flames from the fire burning in the hearth dancing across Oziel's face. Despite having slept, dark circles underline his eyes. The usual teasing smirk dims to a soft smile. Maybe it's my sleep-riddled brain, but he appears gaunt and paler than usual.

"Get dressed, Kitten. Garvan is going to meet us by the River Hel to assist in our search this morning. Are you hungry?" His knuckles run across my cheek in an intimate gesture.

I shiver, my body betraying how much I enjoy the touch. It feels different than normal.

My stomach churns, but not with hunger. Nerves fill the void, and I'm too worked up for breakfast. Answers first, food second.

"I'll eat later," I decide, pushing myself up. Oziel is dressed, making me wonder just how long the demon king's been awake. After throwing back the covers, I get out of bed to search for clothes, Oziel's hot stare boring into my naked body.

Maybe I bend down a little more than I need to when selecting my clothes. I'm rewarded with a growl and a swift ass spanking. My body heats, already primed for him, despite just having him hours ago. *Fucking focus.*

The dress I pull out is black—of course—with a fitted bodice and flowing skirt. I don't bother with panties, which earns me another satisfying growl, and pull the dress over my head. I quickly fix the top, making sure my tits aren't spilling out, before slipping on sandals. "I'm ready."

"That you are." Even his voice lacks its usual playful humor. Yesterday must have taken more out of him than he's willing to share. Before I have a chance to pry, Oziel takes my hand. I'm prepared to walk to the River Hel, but his shadows wrap around us.

"Oziel, no—" But my protests go unheard as the familiar feeling of being swept away overtakes me.

A moment later, the shadows retract, slithering back to Oziel. He sways precariously, and I reach out to grab him. "You shouldn't have done that," I chastise.

"And yet, it's done." Oziel's words aren't unkind, but

they are dismissive. He pulls out of my grip to get a better look at the river behind me. The inky river is a foreboding reminder of all we have lost and will continue to lose if we don't repair the damage that has been done. How do we save something that looks beyond our help?

Oziel's jaw clenches, his entire form shrouded in seething darkness, visible in the dim light. Fury radiates from him, a storm barely contained beneath the surface. He is livid, mourning what has been taken and sharing the same fears I have. Is it too late? The very air crackles with his rage, nearly suffocating me with unspoken threats.

"We are almost out of time," he growls, his voice a razor-edged warning. The weight of his words sends a shiver down my spine. Even though I know them to be true, it makes hearing them out loud no easier than before.

"What can I do?" Feeling useless, I go to his side. On instinct, I reach out for him, taking his hand. At first, Oziel doesn't respond, but then his warm hand squeezes mine, and he sighs.

"Show me where you were attacked," he says.

My brain tries to conjure up the scene from yesterday. Running through the woods in hopes of catching the demon traitor left very little time to map my surroundings. Still, I try to remember my steps from last night.

My hand slips from Oziel's, and the absence of his warmth is immediate; I find myself missing it. Memories of last night crash over me—the struggle against my attacker, the sharp pain as my back slammed into a tree, the frantic search for the castle when demons began to flee in fear.

My feet move on instinct, carrying me across the clearing toward the spot where I think the fight happened. My gaze sweeps over the area, searching for anything familiar. Then, something catches the light. Just a faint glimmer. My head snaps toward it.

A blade.

"There." I point in the direction of the knife, quickly running to it. My dagger lies in the grass, untouched, with dried, dark stains on the blade. Blood. My attacker's blood.

"There's still blood on it," I tell Oziel as he approaches my side. My husband crouches, examining the dagger. When he doesn't speak, worry seizes me. "Is it not enough?"

How much blood does he need to identify the attacker? Is dried blood as potent as fresh blood? After my failure yesterday, I want some success to come from today. I had the traitor so close, but I wasn't powerful enough to stop him. It wasn't for lack of trying, but rather the fact I'm human. Here, I'm not as powerful as Oziel or his demons. Yet, it is I who must save the kingdom? Ender had to be mistaken.

Oziel grabs the handle, bringing the blade up to inspect it. I hold my breath, as if waiting for a doctor to tell me grave news about my health.

Then Oziel tilts his head up and smiles. A true Oziel smile that he lacked this morning. "You cut him good, Kitten."

Pride swells in my chest. "Yes, I did."

"This is enough blood." Oziel stands up, careful with the dagger in his hand.

A rustle has me turning my head just in time to see Garvan partially shrouded by trees. Much like Oziel, the demon looks tired. He manages to offer me a smile, bowing his head slightly. His gait is slightly stiff, and his face is flushed.

"My apologies for my tardiness," Garvan says. "I just received word from King Allarick and his wife, Queen Erin."

My body tenses. Out of the whirlwind this past few weeks have been, I've completely forgotten about my request to speak with Erin. "What did she say?"

"Allarick said Erin will see you, though I have not been given a date yet."

The weight I've carried for far too long has finally begun to lift. Not entirely. It won't be gone until I speak with Erin, but the crushing heaviness has eased, just enough for me to breathe a little easier. My shoulders slump, the tension unwinding from my body like a frayed rope finally loosening. A shaky exhale leaves me.

"Thank you," I whisper, the words laced with quiet relief. Oziel's hand comes to rest on the small of my back. He knows what this moment means to me and how important it is for me to speak with Erin.

"Of course, my queen. When I hear back about a proposed date, I'll inform you at once," he promises before his eyes drop to the dagger in his king's hand. For a brief moment, his eyes widen in shock. "You found it?"

"Isabelle did." Oziel's praise warms something deep within me. "The blood of the traitor is still on it. We can track them, Garvan. Finally, we can find the one who has betrayed their own and punish him with the full extent of my command."

I fully believe the traitor will wish for death, beg for it even. Oziel will show no mercy.

"We must go now." Oziel takes my hand.

I start to follow him, but then something makes me stop. Call it a pull or a feeling, but I can't shake the sense that something is here that we missed. Something I need to find.

"I want to stay here a little longer," I tell him. Oziel's brow furrows, confusion in his gaze. Unasked questions linger in his eyes, which I'm quick to answer. "I just want to look around a little longer. See if we missed anything. If I find anything, I'll let you know at once."

Oziel purses his lips, debating on letting me go. In the end, he lets my hand drop. "Fine. But don't be too long. I want you there when I find the traitor. I can send guards to stay with you."

"I won't be long," I assure, not wanting to wait on guards. "And I want to be there, but I just need another look."

"Very well." He nods once and then turns to Garvan. "Come, old friend. I will need your assistance with this." He's allowing Garvan to help, but still keeps him at arm's length until we find out who is betraying us.

Garvan doesn't argue, appearing resigned to helping. Not eager, which I note as strange, but he's been dealing with this a lot longer than I have. I'm sure he's ready to see it over just like Oziel is. If all demons take strength from River Hel, it makes sense why Garvan looks tired and walks as if each step takes great effort.

"I'll be in my study when you need me." Oziel leans in, pressing a soft, fleeting kiss to my lips. I return it instinctively, but before I can fully savor the warmth, he pulls away.

He produces another dagger from his hip, handing it over to me. "I trust you'll use this if necessary." With a final glance, he turns, his dark silhouette retreating toward the castle. Garvan follows close behind, their figures soon swallowed by the distance, leaving me alone with my own thoughts.

Silence settles around me, but it's not empty. It hums with possibility. A lingering sensation stirs in my chest, a quiet certainty that the answers I seek are here, waiting to be uncovered.

I simply need to figure out what those are.

CHAPTER 33

OZIEL

Leaving Isabelle behind feels fundamentally wrong, like I've abandoned a vital part of my soul and left it exposed and vulnerable. She's still within the bounds of the property, close enough that I can sense her presence. Unlike yesterday, when I didn't know her exact location, and my mind was occupied with all the potential dangers. That awareness gives me some comfort. If she were in danger, I'd know instantly. But knowing isn't the same as being able to protect her, and I hate this distance between us.

Still, my headstrong human insisted on staying behind, determined to uncover answers I'm not convinced exist. I've been wrong before—admittedly, not often—but I'm hoping this is one of those rare occasions. I want her to find whatever truth she's looking for. And if I'd tried to stop her? Isabelle would've stood her ground and argued until I was too drained to continue. Frankly, I don't have the strength for that battle today. If she's gone for longer than a few minutes, I will send guards to her for peace of mind.

Garvan follows me, silent and obedient, like a shadow. He says nothing when I enter my study, going straight to my desk. The door closes softly behind him, and he hesitates slightly before making his way over to me.

"This traitor needs to answer for his crimes. Do you not agree?" As I ask, I reach for the mortar sitting atop the desk, surrounded by various herbs and dried flowers. It's been a long time since I've had to perform a blood tracking spell, but the ingredients come back to me as if they are permanently seared into my brain.

"You've always been swift to deliver punishment, my lord," Garvan says, his gaze flickering to the dried blood on the blade. "But perhaps we should consider speaking with this demon first and hear their reasoning. Knowledge is power, and if they possess insights we lack, this could be our chance to uncover valuable information."

My fist comes down on the table hard; capped jars of ingredients fall over from the force. Eyes flashing, Garvan wisely takes a step back, never once looking away from my ire. Anger rolls off me in waves, suffocating me with its intensity.

"The time for speaking is over, *courtier*." I hiss his title like a vulgar insult. Garvan's fists tighten at his side, jaw clenched. "We will do this my way. Death will be a mercy compared to what I have planned."

This demon will find no mercy. Time and time again, they have endangered our kingdom, leaving us vulnerable so our enemies could strike when we were at our weakest. There is no redemption for such treachery, no path back from the destruction they have willingly invited. And I will not grant mercy, especially not to a demon who has stood by as their own kind fell to the curse.

Garvan doesn't push again, stepping back out of the light. It filters onto my desk, illuminating my work area. With great caution, I scrape the dried blood from the dagger into the mortar. This spell doesn't require much blood—a simple drop will do—so I have more than enough to find my traitor. Crushed-up cardamon and dried thyme are placed in next. The last two ingredients aren't easily found. Blood of an elder dragon and tears of a pixie priestess. There's just enough to complete this spell, but I'll have to pay someone a great sum of money to obtain more.

A problem for another day.

Gripping the pestle tightly, I press it into the mixture, grinding the ingredients together with steady, deliberate force. As I work, I channel the last remnants of shadow magic I possess, willing it into the spell. At first, nothing happens, only the sharp, earthy scent of thyme rising into the air around us.

Then, ever so slowly, a change takes hold. The mixture stirs with an unnatural energy, a faint red glow flickering to life within the bowl. It pulses, weak at first, but with each passing moment, the light deepens, intensifying until the entire concoction is engulfed in a rich, crimson hue, pulsing like a heartbeat.

The mixture is strong, taking on a life of its own. A flash of bright red light nearly blinds me before a thin wiry line, like a strand of yarn, branches off. This is it. The moment I come face to face with the demon that has put themself above those in my kingdom. The glowing red line glides around the room, as an invisible tether pulls me along. The light moves to the window, flickers once, and goes out.

It happens again.

And again.

"What the fuck?" I snarl, my voice sharp with frustration. This isn't how it's supposed to work. The glowing light should have surged forward, hunting down the traitor with precision. Instead, it falters and dies at the window, flickering as though some unseen force is caging it in, refusing to let it escape.

I clench my fists, my pulse pounding in my ears. I did everything right. Every ingredient measured perfectly. I spilled enough blood to ensure the spell took hold, enough that failure should have been impossible.

And yet...

The light won't move beyond this room.

A slow, creeping realization slithers down my spine, cold as a blade's edge. The sweltering-hot room chills to an uncomfortable cold. There's only one explanation.

The traitor isn't out there.

They're in here.

Just as the thought crosses my mind, I spin around, but it's too late. He's once again one step ahead of me. A sudden, invisible force seizes me, locking my body in place. My limbs stiffen, frozen mid-motion, as if time itself has conspired against me.

Then, like stone, my body hardens. And everything fades to black.

CHAPTER 34

ISABELLE

Ever since I was a little girl, I have been obsessed with mysteries and true crime. That should have clued me in to the fact I would be a star in my own true crime video, but I digress. What I loved most about them is trying to find what others missed. The answer is always there, looking you straight in the eyes; you just have to be able to see past your own nose.

I know the answer to reversing the curse is here, just waiting for me to find it. Now that I'm by myself, I no longer have the distraction of my husband. The air around me is crisp with the pungent odor of death. It seems to linger over the entire kingdom, eclipsing the castle in ominous shadows. I can't help but feel a pull to the castle, a feeling of being home and desperately wanting to rid my space of the dark entities.

Which is laughable, since my husband is the darkest entity of them all.

Still, something unnatural lingers here. It's like a call, one of desperation, telling me I'm on the precipice of...

something. Slowly, I gravitate toward the poisoned river, perching upon the rocky soil, just a few feet shy of the water. I'm tempted to touch it—in the same way I was tempted to touch the roses in Oziel's room. Well, our room now.

Everything I've learned and been told about the curse floods my brain. The attack on the demons and turning them into stone. Oziel believes a cure can come from the River Hel, but not in its current state. It seems likely his theory is correct, or why would someone go to so much trouble to poison the river? More importantly, why would someone want to do damage to something that affects them as well?

Unless it's not hurting them, and this person has kept their power this entire time. But then that also begs the question...why? What is their goal?

I shake my head, getting ahead of myself. One thing at a time. According to Oziel, the curse started the day a bouquet of flowers was left on his doorstep. I know very little about the Nephilim, but having spoken to one, it doesn't seem likely they would send flowers as nothing more than a symbol of Oziel's weakness.

There's magic in those flowers; that much is for certain. I remember being pulled forward, tethered by an invisible thread, as magic hummed in the air around them. The energy was impossible to ignore. It's the same pull I feel from the river—a deep, aching need, as if it's calling to me. Like two halves of a whole, the roses and the river are bound together, connected by something older than Mescos itself.

Maybe even older than time.

The river isn't just in danger; it's sick. Dying. The once-healthy waters clouded, the magic's hum all but silent now. A plea to anyone who will listen. I'm here, trying to listen. Trying to figure out what they need, but my mind keeps coming back to one thing: those damn roses.

The roses aren't just beautiful; they're powerful. The more I think about them, the more certain I am that they hold the key to restoring the river's strength. Not just a symbolic offering, but a true cure, pulsing with the same ancient magic that flows through the water. The petals glow with a promise I don't yet understand, but plan to soon. There's no explaining it or shaking this feeling taking form inside me.

A thought has blossomed and is growing strong. I have no proof of this newfound idea—nothing to back up this claim. But I know, deep in my bones, these flowers aren't just meant to be a reminder of the curse. Perhaps their magic can heal too. The pull toward them is too strong to ignore.

I need to touch them.

I jump up at the realization, the words filling me with newfound determination I haven't felt in a long time. Apprehension clouds my excitement though, because when I propose my idea to Oziel, I don't think my husband will take kindly to it. There is a chance I'm wrong, and the moment I touch the roses, I'll turn to stone like the other demons. I would be lying if that possibility doesn't scare me, but I also know something much more terrible could happen if I don't do it.

There's really no choice. Steeling my resolve, I head

back to the castle. Oziel mentioned he'd be in his study, but I'm not sure how much time has passed since he left. Maybe an hour? He could be on his way to find the traitor, but I don't think he'd search without me.

The castle is quiet when I enter. Only a few guards stand at their post, silent except for the occasional whisper. A few acknowledge me as I pass, and I return their bows with a tight smile. I really need to learn the proper way to greet people here, but considering my focus is keeping the demon kingdom alive, that falls low on the list.

The hallway leading to Oziel's study is quiet, which isn't surprising. He prefers solitude and little distraction when he's working. The door to the study is closed when I reach it, and I place a hand on the wood. Normally, the door would open without me having to do it myself. My husband is in tune with the castle, from what I gathered, but specifically everything I do in the castle, and my arrival shouldn't be a surprise for him. Though, I imagine he's too busy trying to figure out the demon who is betraying him to open a silly door for me.

Grabbing the handle, I push the door open. The room is dark—darker than other parts of the castle. No fire burns brightly in the hearth, nor are sconces lighting the way. Faint light flickers in through the window, but something dark is blocking it.

"Oziel?" My voice echoes around a seemingly empty room. "If you're working in the dark, this is a bit much. Even for you." I try to keep my voice light, even as my heart speeds up.

As I step into the room, an unnatural chill seeps into

my bones, spreading like ice through my limbs and making them ache. The air feels thick, weighted with something unseen, pressing against my skin.

"Oziel?" I call out again, my voice barely more than a whisper. But the only response is the hollow echo of my own words, bouncing off the unseen corners of the space.

My eyes struggle to adjust to the darkness as I venture deeper inside. Shadows stretch and shift, playing tricks on my vision, and an unsettling feeling crawls over me, like I'm being watched. The sensation clings to me, prickling the back of my neck, as if unseen eyes are lurking in the darkness, observing, waiting for whatever is about to unfold.

My body connects with something hard, stealing the breath from my lips. "What the fuck?" I mumble, rubbing the shoulder that smashed into the object by the window. "What the fuck are you keeping in here, Oziel?" I murmur to no one in particular as I reach out...

...and feel cold stone against my fingers.

My body locks up, every muscle tensing as my mind scrambles for a rational explanation—anything other than the truth I can already feel sinking into my bones. A flicker of light from outside spills into the room, casting shadows over the figure before me. As the dim glow spreads, more of its form is revealed. Solid, unmoving, utterly lifeless.

The sheer size of it is staggering, towering over me by at least a foot. Its shape is unmistakably demon, yet it is no longer flesh and blood. Every inch is carved from cold, unyielding stone. My breath stutters as I take it in, and my heart threatens to pound out of my chest. I don't want to believe it, don't want to think about what this means, but there's no denying the truth.

This isn't just any statue.

This is my husband. Oziel.

"No..." The word leaves my lips as a strangled cry. My legs give out, and I fall to the floor, crumpling at my cursed husband's feet.

Anger is frozen into his expression, as if he saw the curse coming before it took him over. This wasn't supposed to happen, not to Oziel. He was supposed to be my partner, my husband who stood by my side as we faced this evil together. I didn't want to care for this damn demon, but he slithered his way into my heart and planted himself there. He's part of me, just like I know I'm part of him.

And now that he's gone, I don't feel whole. Part of me feels as if it turned to stone too. Tears flood my eyes, running down my cheeks. He wouldn't want me to cry or give up. Oziel would want me to keep going, but how do I do that when the man I love is nothing but a memory in stone?

Consumed by my own grief, I don't hear the footsteps behind me until a familiar voice whispers, "Queen Isabelle."

I whip my head up to see Garvan standing by the doorway—with the encased bouquet of roses in his hands.

CHAPTER 35

ISABELLE

"Garvan," I choke out, my voice a strangled cry. "Oziel, he's...he's..." I can't bring myself to say it. Speaking those words out loud will make them true, and I desperately want to wake up from this nightmare. I want to see Oziel's teasing face above me and smell his heated scent that reminds me of bonfires and roasting marshmallows late into the night.

"He's cursed." Garvan's voice shatters my delusions like a knife straight to the gut, tearing me apart. It isn't supposed to hurt this much. It's not meant to be this way. I never wanted to give a damn about my husband, and yet here I am, crumpled in a heap on the ground, crying over a demon that feels so out of reach.

My legs tremble as I push myself up from the ground, each movement slow and unsteady, as though I am lifting the weight of the world. It definitely feels that way because so much is upon my shoulders now. *I will fix this, Oziel. I will fix you.*

A sharp ache radiates through my limbs, and for a

moment, I fear they won't hold me. But somehow, I manage to stand. My breath is uneven, shuddering in my chest, and hot tears continue to blur my vision, stinging my already burning eyes. I blink rapidly, struggling to clear my sight.

Through the blur, I can just make out Garvan's silhouette. He stands, rigid and unmoving, his posture eerily still. He does not rush forward or avert his gaze in deference. He doesn't even so much as acknowledge his king. Instead, his eyes remain locked on me, unreadable and void of their usual flicker of warmth.

He has never been an overly friendly man, nor one who has shown a full display of emotions, but this...this is different. There is a chill in his stare I have never felt before, a deliberate, glacial distance. It tightens something in my chest, making it difficult to breathe.

Then Garvan takes a step forward, out of the shadows.

My breathing stops.

Those eyes. Soulless and full of malice. I've seen those eyes before. Once during the attack in the shower and again by River Hel. There's also a scar across his cheek, one I missed before. He favors one side over the other, because of course he does. I stabbed him in the thigh, so putting weight on it must be painful.

"It was you," I whisper, barely audible, but for how quiet it is in here, it may as well have been a shout.

The corner of Garvan's lips twitches up into a smile, the only indicator of the validity of my statement. It's enough though.

"This whole time it's been you." My voice is louder

now. How did we miss the signs? Oziel trusted Garvan as his closest confidant. He worked beside Oziel as he prepared to defend his people from the Nephilim. And yet, the very person who betrayed the demons was standing right in front of us the whole time.

"In the shower...that was you. And by the River Hel—"

"I imagine this is quite the shock for you, *my queen*," he sneers at my title, like the name personally offends him. Knowing what I know now, it probably does. "You may not believe this, but I didn't want it to be this way."

"Fucking classic villain line." I laugh, but it holds no humor. Only anger that threatens to overtake me. "What are you going to say next? That you tried to make Oziel see your way? That you never wanted to hurt me?"

A crimson glow flares in his normally gray eyes, the unmistakable spark of rage searing through them. My breath catches, and a shiver races down my spine as fear coils tight in my chest, turning my blood to ice. Every instinct screams at me to step back, to retreat from the storm brewing before me. But I don't. I force my feet to stay rooted, my body rigid with tension, refusing to show weakness. Refusing to move away from Oziel, even if he's lost to me at the moment.

Garvan takes another deliberate step forward, his presence looming, and the air between us grows thick with unspoken threats. He is close now—too close—but still, I don't move. I meet his glare head-on, my heart hammering wildly against my ribs, sounding loud in an otherwise silent room.

His voice is low, almost a growl, and laced with frustration. "I tried to make Oziel understand. Tried to get him to see reason, to open his damn eyes. But he's so fucking stubborn, so blinded by his own pride, he refuses to listen to anyone." He exhales sharply, his fists clenched at his sides. Then, his gaze darkens, sharpening as it fixes on me. "No one... until you showed up."

Something slithers around my legs, and I tear my gaze away from the demon before me, only to see the tendrils of darkness wrap around my ankles, snaking their way up my body. I'm frozen to the spot, helpless to do anything other than watch the shadows overtake me. This magic reminds me so much of Oziel that, for a second, I forget my husband is stone, that this isn't his gentle shadows pulling me to him.

No, these shadows feel different. Evil. Poisoned. Garvan is the one who has been stealing the shadow magic from the river. The shadows bind me in place until I no longer have control over my body.

"You are the greatest threat to our kind, whether Oziel sees it or not," he says, his voice edged with certainty. "In time, he will. He'll understand why I've done what I've done when I wake them all up in the new world. Mescos has changed. The time of the six rulers is gone. The Nephilim have risen up, and unlike you, I refuse to watch my kingdom burn because Oziel's pride stands in the way. The demons deserve a chance to rule alongside the Nephilim!"

As the words leave his lips, Garvan moves with deliberate ease, his attention shifting to the glass dome that encases the roses. With a slow, measured motion, he lifts the cover, allowing the air to rush in around the enchanted flowers. He doesn't hesitate as he reaches down and plucks a rose from its stem.

A pulse of magic hums through the delicate petals, a vibration so subtle yet potent that I feel it in my bones. The magic didn't take on a dark tone until Garvan touched it. Just as I suspected, these flowers are infused with power. Power that might just save us if I can get it away from Garvan.

The magic should have affected him, but does nothing. He remains unmoved, as though the magic does not even register against his touch.

"Unfortunately, you won't be around to enjoy the new age of Mescos. But I assure you, my people will be in good hands."

With that, he closes his fists around the flower, crumpling it. He then opens his hand and blows the crushed-up petals toward me. My body remains frozen to the spot. I don't even have the ability to grab my dagger. I half expect to turn into stone, but I'm still very much myself and able to think and feel. However, I can't move my body.

A satisfied chuckle leaves Garvan's lips as he steps away, blending into the shadows until I can no longer see him. A few moments later, he returns, only this time, he's dragging a large trunk, the size of a coffee table, and stops right in front of me again. The trunk opens, exposing its emptiness. True terror finally takes over as I realize what he's planning to do.

I can't move. Can't speak. Can't scream. I can do nothing as he takes the dagger from my body, letting it drop to the ground, and then he lifts me as if I weigh nothing at all. He tosses me into the trunk with no care about hurting me. I hit my head, and pain explodes, causing my vision to blacken around the edges.

The last thing I see is Garvan's smiling face as he shuts the lid of the trunk and leaves me in total darkness.

CHAPTER 36

ISABELLE

Darkness is all I know. It surrounds me, pulling me deeper and deeper under its web. I scream, or at least I try to, but no sound leaves my mouth. It's as if the darkness swallows it. My body is jostled from side to side, hitting my head against the hard interior walls. My breaths come in short gasps as the beginning of a panic attack sets in.

It's so dark.

The room is closing in on me.

My heart pounds rapidly in my chest. Is this a heartache? A heart attack?

Invisible hands wrap around my throat, and I'm choking. If this is how my life ends, in a cramped dark box, then let my last thoughts be of Oziel. How I wish I had more time with him. How I wish I told him how I felt before it was too late. Two creatures that should have never been capable of love found it in each other. Because I'm pretty sure he loves me in his own way.

Sadly, I won't ever get the chance to experience that life with him now.

I wait for the sweet release of death, wondering how I'll meet it. I don't know how Garvan plans on killing me, but I hope it's quick. Selfishly, I don't want to feel any pain. If there was any chance of fighting back, I would. But I'm weaponless, my husband is stone, I can't move, and Garvan possesses magic. My odds don't look good.

The impending sense of doom takes over my body, my stomach lurching as the sensation of falling through the air consumes me. It only lasts for a moment before the bottom of the trunk hits the hard ground with an unforgiving thud that sends pain throughout my body. Muffled footsteps come from outside, and then nothing at all.

Silence scares me more than anything.

A surge of anticipation coils inside me. What the fuck is he doing? Panic tightens its grip as my mind races through the worst possible scenarios.

Then, suddenly, the lid of the chest bursts open, flooding my vision with the harsh glare of the outside lights. The brightness stings my eyes, forcing me to blink rapidly—once, then twice—before my vision clears.

Garvan looms over me, his face contorted in a mask of deranged rage. There's little left of the courtier I thought I knew. No, this is the face of a man who is willing to risk everything.

Garvan reaches for me, grabbing the front of my dress and hauling me out of the chest as if I weigh nothing at all. My body is still tightly bound, and whatever magic he used from the roses has me unable to feel certain parts of it. The flowers in question are set next to the chest, untouched but buzzing with unused potential. I get a moment to check out my surroundings and find he has taken me back to where I attacked him near the River Hel.

Garvan tosses me to the ground, and I crash onto my hip. Pain detonates through me as jagged rocks bite into my skin, a fresh wave of agony layering over the bruises I've already collected today. At this rate, my body will be covered in them. Though, if I don't make it out of this alive, I suppose it won't matter.

Two polished black leather boots step into my line of sight, stopping just inches away. A cruel chuckle follows. "You don't look well, my queen." Garvan almost sounds genuinely concerned.

Rage ignites inside me, burning brighter than the pain because he doesn't get to pretend to care but also want to kill me and Oziel. I have never wanted to kill anyone more, and that includes James. Fuck, his death seems like a lifetime ago. So much has changed since I stepped through the portal and into Mescos.

"Fuck you, Garvan," I spit, finding my words, even if my voice comes out hoarse.

My comment only makes him frown. "You know, I'm actually sad, believe it or not, my queen. Admittedly, I didn't want you in Mescos, but once you were here, I deluded myself that you would be good for Oziel. I even encouraged him to make you fall in love with him." His last words drop an octave, like he hates he's even admitting that.

"But I miscalculated the weakness you'd bring our

king, and by extension our kingdom. Just like his bloody parents. It was then I knew I made the right choice to align myself with the Nephilim fully." The bindings around my body disappear, but the effects of the roses still linger, and I feel heavy. Like each movement takes a great amount of effort and concentration.

"The Nephilim won't spare you," I growl, thinking back to the visions I shared with the captive Nephilim. How a woman begged them to stop. They wouldn't until they reached their end goal. Which is...? Power? To take hold of Mescos? Whatever it is, Garvan is a fool if he believes he can trust those creatures. I felt the pain and loss the woman in the vision felt. I know from her just how deadly the Nephilim are.

"They will. We might be weaker, but we won't be eradicated like the other kingdoms," he says, voice teetering on madness. Garvan is too far gone to talk any sense into. "I just have to destroy the river. That's the sacrifice they demand to reverse the curse. I'll do it. The demons will understand. I'll make them understand. Right after I poison the River Hel for the last time and destroy the roses. Oh, and kill you too, human queen."

Destroy the roses?

"Why would you need to destroy the roses?" I demand, but my question goes unanswered. Garvan doesn't acknowledge me—whether he's ignoring me or simply no longer sees the need to speak to me, I don't know.

My gaze shifts to the delicate roses resting unprotected just a few feet away. A sense of urgency grips me. More than ever, I'm convinced they hold the key to the kingdom's salvation. If only I could get my damn body to move. My hand twitches, but even that feels like a monumental task.

Garvan pays no attention to me, clearly not deeming me a threat. All my focus is getting my body to move. Slowly, I manage to scoot myself forward, inching like a worm. It's infuriatingly slow, but at least I'm no longer stagnant.

Despite my better judgment, my gaze wanders back to Garvan just in time to see him take a vial of inky black liquid from his coat pocket and pop open the lid. It's the same bottle he had the other night when I caught him poisoning the river during the ball.

Every movement is agony, my battered body screaming in protest with each desperate pull forward. Pain radiates, sharp and unrelenting, but I grit my teeth and push through it, refusing to give in. Tears blur my vision, yet I don't stop. I can't stop no matter what.

The roses lie just ahead. The petals sway gently, mocking me with their nearness. So close. *Just a little more.*

I sink my nails into the damp earth, clawing at the grass and dirt, summoning every last ounce of strength to drag myself forward. My fingers stretch out, trembling, the very tips just inches from the bouquet.

Then a sound cuts through the silence. A rustling in the woods behind me.

My breath catches. Garvan's head whips around, and his eyes land on me and my proximity to the roses. Then he jerks his head up, staring at something behind me. The subtle widening of his eyes has me on alert.

I strain my neck to look behind me at whomever has made Garvan tense. Part of me hopes, though it's impossible, that I'll see Oziel. Even knowing I wouldn't see my husband, I still feel a wave of devastation.

And then confusion.

A man stands in the shadows of the forest. His features are familiar, but my brain is slow to process him. His skin is dark, the color of the tree bark around him. His locs are neatly pulled back; a few specks of gold hit the light when he moves.

But I don't stare for long because a new figure steps out from behind him. Slender. Tall. Skin only a few shades lighter than the man's. But, unlike the man, this woman I know well, even if she has no idea who I am. My breath catches in my throat.

Then Erin Goodwin steps into the clearing and looks directly at me.

CHAPTER 37

ISABELLE

I feel like I'm seeing a ghost. After so long of knowing someone from the sidelines and making up their mannerisms in my head, seeing them stand before you is like watching someone walk out of the grave. Besides, this woman looks nothing like the woman I saw in Grym Hollow. No, that Erin was meek and kept her head down, always dressing in clothes that hid her entire body from the world. Even in the midst of summer when temperatures hit well above one hundred degrees Fahrenheit, Erin always wore pants and long sleeves if she was out in public.

The woman standing before me is no longer the timid, fragile soul she once was. Her posture is poised, head held high with a quiet confidence she never possessed before. There's a newfound strength in her presence. Steady, unshaken, and undeniable.

Her bare arms, once marred by bruises and the ghosts of past wounds, are now smooth and unblemished, a testament to her newfound freedom in Mescos.

295

Even her face, which she used to hide behind a curtain of hair, is fully visible, radiant and untouched by the remnants of James's wrath. She doesn't just *look* different. She *is* different. She looks like a queen.

Erin attempts to take another step forward, but the man behind her reaches out, grabbing her wrist before she can make it too far. His name finally reemerges in my memories. Allarick. Erin's new husband. He says something I can't hear because they are too far away. Erin's brow furrows, but she nods once and stays by his side.

"The king of the sea," Garvan hisses from behind me. His hot breath hits the side of my cheek. In my awestruck state, the demon behind me moved closer.

Garvan violently yanks me up by my hair, pain blooming in my skull. I scream as he pulls me back against his hard chest. Something sharp presses against my neck, the undeniable touch of a blade. My fucking dagger. The one Oziel gave me.

"You aren't supposed to be here, Kraken King."

Garvan is fully gone. Hysteria laces each word, and his body trembles as he holds me in an iron grip against him. I no longer recognize the courtier; he's been replaced with this unhinged demon.

"Seems to me my husband and I came at the right time," Erin says, voice unwavering.

I blink, still astonished by this woman before me. Strong. Fierce. Determined. Erin eyes me—not like she recognizes me, but more like she understands I'm not a demon. I'm human, like her.

"Garvan, you hold Oziel's queen against her will.

Only a cowardly man would use a woman as a shield." Allarick's deep baritone voice reverberates around us.

Garvan presses the blade harder against me. It's so fucking sharp, already digging into my skin. Despite myself, I whimper.

"Please," I beg, though I don't know what I'm begging for. To let me go? To kill me and end all of this? The last few years of my life have been hell. Every day was a fight for justice, but never have I felt so powerless. Oziel's absence has ripped my heart in two, leaving me feeling empty and lost without my husband's strength next to me.

He wouldn't want me to give up. But fuck, it's so tempting. I'm so fucking tired of fighting.

"You don't want to do this, Garvan. Allarick and I have been through this. We can—"

"You can't help!" Garvan's voice roars above Erin's. "You know nothing of what I'm going through. What is at stake for our kingdom. No one does! I'm the only one willing to do what needs to be done."

"You're wrong! Oziel would have saved us all. Would have saved you!" Fire ignites in my blood again, the words pouring out of me before I can stop them.

"He would have gotten us all killed! That reckless fool would have led us straight to our doom." Garvan's voice is eerily calm, yet the quiet fury simmering beneath his words sends a chill down my spine. His restrained anger is far more terrifying than his outbursts. "I am the only one willing to do what is necessary to save the demons." His words aren't just a declaration; they are a promise, a warning, and a threat all at once.

"This is not the way it works, Garvan. The Nephilim will not spare you because you bowed to their whims. You are doing nothing for your people but sending them to an early grave." Allarick takes a step forward, keeping Erin behind him, but his face is determined, locked on Garvan's every move.

Fear settles low in my belly, and I silently thank the higher powers that Allarick is on my side...I think. I don't want this man as an enemy.

"Don't get any closer!" Garvan screams.

This time, the blade at my neck cuts deep, drawing my blood. I can't see it, but I smell it and feel warm liquid sliding down my neck. I barely feel a thing though; my adrenaline is far too high.

Allarick doesn't listen. He takes another step closer. "I'm afraid I can't do that, Courtier. You see, this is my fight too. The Nephilim are the most dangerous enemies to my people. My battle may be over, but my war is not. I can't let you aid them."

"And we won't let you hurt her." Erin steps up next to her husband. Allarick shifts slightly so his body is angled in front of her.

Even with Allarick and Erin here, they're too far away to reach me in time. If Garvan decides to slit my throat, nothing can stop him. Not even a kraken king and his queen. But once I'm gone, there will be nothing standing in their way. They'll take him down without hesitation.

Maybe this is why Ender brought me here—to die so the kingdom might live. A necessary sacrifice to prevent its downfall.

Oziel would have to rule alone, but that was his original plan before I ever arrived. He might grieve me, might carry the weight of my absence, but in the end, he would be the king his demons needed. Strong and unshaken.

My death will bring salvation for him and his kingdom.

Something akin to acceptance passes through me. It is true what they say about death; once you accept it, a sense of peace overtakes you. I only have one regret. And that's not telling Oziel how I feel about him.

"The queen's blood will be on your hands!" Garvan yells.

And this is it. The world seems to slow down; the noises around me fade away. My eyes close, preparing for the end. For Garvan to slice the dagger through my neck, and for my blood to stain my body until death claims me. I wait...

And wait...

Then a shocked gasp pulls me back to the present. Garvan's hold on me loosens, his dagger dropping to the ground, and I take this as my chance to pull free from him. There's no resistance on his part, and his arms fall away from me. I manage to get a few feet away before I look back.

Garvan sways from side to side, face drained of all color. It takes me a moment to realize what I'm seeing, but sticking out of the side of his neck is a dagger. Then I notice the excessive amount of blood staining his shirt.

I think it's done. It should be done. But then he lunges for me with his last bit of strength. I hear someone yell my name, but they are too far away.

Garvan is a dying man, but he's not willing to leave

without taking me with him. His body collides with mine, and we tumble to the ground in a bloody mess. His hands tighten around my neck, cutting off my oxygen, even while he chokes on his own blood.

He doesn't want to die without taking me with him. He's about to be thoroughly disappointed.

I thrash, doing everything I can to push him off. He's far stronger than he appears, and heavier too. Even halfway to the grave. I manage to get my arms out from under me and grab the knife at his neck, twisting it roughly. His eyes widen, and his hands on my neck loosen enough for me to break free. I push him off me with all the strength I possess, and he stumbles back.

Garvan opens his mouth once.

Nothing but blood comes out.

He takes one step closer before falling to his knees. I'm frozen to the spot, watching this play out with morbid curiosity. For a moment, our eyes lock. There's a flicker of sorrow in his expression before the light goes out completely. Garvan tumbles forward, dead before his body hits the ground with a final thud.

"Good work, Delmare," Allarick's voice comes from behind me, steady and approving. "And you too, Isabelle. Are you okay?"

I nod. Maybe. Truthfully, I'm too frazzled to know if I'm truly fine. Nothing feels okay. Garvan's dead. My husband is a statue. My body hurts.

The sound of boots crunching against the earth pulls my attention behind Garvan's lifeless body. I lift my gaze just in time to see a tall, older man step out from behind the tree. His salt-and-pepper hair is tousled, streaks of silver standing out against the darker strands. He's bare-chested, his toned physique on display, and clad only in dark pants that blend into the shadows. A sword hangs at his hip, its hilt well-worn, and several daggers are strapped to his belt, their metal edges catching the light.

His gaze lands on me, and he bows slowly. "Queen Isabelle, a pleasure to see you again." The strange man knows my name. It should unnerve me, but then I remember he accompanied Allarick to the meeting with Oziel. A hand rests against my shoulder, but because I'm on edge and not paying attention to my surroundings, I nearly jump out of my skin.

"I'm sorry!" a feminine voice answers. I turn just in time to see Erin take a hesitant step back. "I didn't mean to frighten you. I thought you knew I was behind you."

"Why are you here?" My question comes out harshly. Angry. I don't mean for it to be. Shame instantly heats my face. "I'm sorry. I'm just..."

"There's no need to apologize, Isabelle," Allarick says, coming up behind Erin. She leans into him at the same time he puts an arm around her waist. Not in ownership, but rather as if every moment not touching her is agony. Their love is evident and effortless. A pang of jealousy darkens my mood.

"We were already on our way to meet you. You requested to speak to my wife, and she was eager to meet you." He smiles at Erin, and she returns it. They share a whole conversation with no words. "We tried to get into contact with Garvan, but he stopped responding to my messengers. I feared something might have happened, so

I came here myself. Where I go, so does Erin. Where Erin goes, Delmare goes."

"For the most part. Sometimes we actually do spend time apart." Erin laughs good-naturedly.

Delmare crouches down next to Garvan's lifeless body. He reaches for his dagger, lodged deep into his throat. "I told you Queen Hettie's axe-throwing classes would come in handy, my king."

"So you did," Allarick says, amused. "Good work, old friend. However, I still don't believe you'll be able to beat my sister in darts."

Delmare sighs, as if agreeing with his assessment. "Then I shall practice some more," he says before pulling out the dagger and wiping the blood off on Garvan's clothes.

I stare down at the fallen courtier, searching for even the faintest trace of sympathy or remorse. But there's nothing, only a hollow indifference. He doesn't deserve my pity. Not after what he did to our people. To Oziel.

His betrayal was calculated, ruthless, and nearly successful. And, despite his death, the curse still lingers. If I can't find a way to cleanse the River Hel and save the demons, his treachery may claim its victory after all. Nephilim could overtake demon territory if I fail.

No fucking pressure.

"Now that we're here, we want to help you," Erin says, and both Allarick and Delmare nod in agreement.

"We can't have even a single kingdom fall to the Nephilim," Allarick says gravely, a tense silence settling over us. After a moment, he continues, "You are queen, Isabelle. I'm guessing something has happened to your husband, for I know he would have never let Garvan capture you. At the moment, you're the only ruler of this kingdom, so you must decide our next move."

Once again, no fucking pressure.

My time of giving up has passed. Allarick's words ring true. Without Oziel here, I'm the only ruler of this kingdom. I won't let it fall simply because giving up would be easier. It's not what Oziel would want. Hell, it's not what *I* want.

But the question remains—what is our next move?

As the thought takes hold, my eyes land on the roses scattered across the ground where Garvan dropped them. Their petals seem to pulse with an unseen energy. An inexplicable pull tugs at me, silent yet insistent, drawing me toward them. I don't understand it, but resisting feels impossible. The magic calls to me. Not malicious or dark like it was for Garvan, but, rather, it carries a healing quality to it.

I inhale sharply, steeling myself. Whatever this force is, whatever it means, I know one thing: I have to follow it.

Lifting my gaze, I meet the eyes of my three new allies, a newfound determination settling over me. "I have a plan," I say, my voice firm. "But I can't promise it will work."

CHAPTER 38

ISABELLE

Delmare leaves to round up guards back at the castle. Everyone seems concerned by the fact I don't have a fleet of guards following me wherever I go. That seems dreadfully suffocating, though I admit it would have helped out when Garvan kidnapped me and tossed me into a chest as if I were nothing but an old blanket to be discarded at will.

"I'm usually with Oziel or Garvan. Even when I walked the castle, Oziel usually knew where I was. He has a freaky connection to the castle," I explain.

Erin seemed to understand, but Allarick didn't look convinced that was the best choice, which is why he sent Delmare to bring back a fleet. I wonder if he fears there will be more attacks. If the River Hel isn't cured, what will become of our new reality?

As we wait for their guard to return, I take the opportunity to fill Allarick and Erin in about the roses and the start of the curse in the kingdom. But keeping my gaze on Erin for too long is nearly impossible, weighed down by the crushing secret I'm keeping from her.

Every fiber of my being screams to confess—to spill the truth about what I've done, but I force myself to stay silent. The warmth in her eyes only intensifies the turmoil twisting inside me, making it even harder to hold my composure.

Now isn't the time to lose focus. We're not safe yet.

And Oziel... Oziel is lost to me.

"So, you said everyone who has touched the roses has turned to stone?" Erin asks slowly, as if she's still wrapping her head around everything. I don't blame her. It's a lot, even for me. "And when a petal falls, they also turn to stone?"

"I haven't actually seen it, but yeah. That's what Oziel said. Garvan made comments about it too, though he was able to touch them," I explain.

"Because he was the harbinger of the curse, which probably explains why poisoning the river didn't seem to have any negative effect on him. The Nephilim seek out those with the most malice in their heart and those easy to corrupt to do their bidding," Allarick murmurs, seemingly lost in thought. His arms are crossed over his chest, and his fingers gently strum against his biceps absentmindedly. After a moment, he finally says, "I'm not sure it's wise to risk you touching the roses."

My face flushes with anger. "I'm not asking for permission," I snap, the stress and events of the day boiling over. "I can't just sit here and do nothing. Ender wouldn't have chosen me if he didn't think I could help."

"And if you're wrong, your kingdom will be more

vulnerable than ever before. No leaders will breed chaos. That's exactly what the Nephilim thrive on," Allarick argues.

"And my kingdom will be vulnerable if I do nothing!" My words sit between us, heavy and tense. Allarick's nostrils flare, his body tensing as if bracing for a fight.

Before he can reply, though, Erin reaches out and gently places a hand on his arm. Almost instantly, Allarick's shoulders relax, and his face softens as he turns toward her. "Yes, Sweet Girl?"

I can't see his eyes, but I bet they look similar to those cartoon heart eyes. There is so much love in the way he looks at her, I feel like I'm intruding on an intimate moment. Still, I can't look away.

"Isabelle is right. Ender brought us all here for a reason. If there's one thing I know for certain, it's to trust your heart. That's what led me back to you, knowing you needed me, even when you thought the best thing for me was to be far away. If Isabelle believes this is what she must do, then we can't stand in her way. Instead, we have to assist in any way we can," Erin says.

I wait for Allarick to lash out. To tell Erin she doesn't know what she's talking about. And for her to cower before him. Perhaps I'm still thinking of the lost and beaten girl James turned her into.

Allarick's hand reaches up, and I flinch, ready to attack the kraken king if he thinks he can hit Erin in front of me. But instead of hard, fast hands, he reaches out and caresses her cheek affectionately. "How did you become so wise, Sweet Girl?"

"I married a sweet and gentle kraken who gave me

the opportunity to grow and heal at my own pace." She smiles.

Now I know for certain I'm intruding on something.

Rustling behind Erin and Allarick signals Delmare's arrival. He's flanked by four other guards, all demons I've seen around the castle, but I don't know their names. Definitely something I need to change after this.

As one, the four demons bow to me. When they straighten and take in my surroundings—including a very dead Garvan—I can see the unasked questions on their faces.

"Garvan betrayed our kingdom," I announce, making sure my words are heard, and no one can mistake them. "He was the traitor poisoning River Hel, and he died a traitor. King Oziel..." My voice breaks on my husband's name. I was doing so damn well until this moment. The severity of the situation truly settles in, along with the new responsibilities thrust upon me. It's...a lot. Too much.

"King Oziel," I try again, managing to keep the tremor out of my voice, "has fallen victim to the curse."

At that proclamation, the guards' eyes widen. Clearly, nobody has discovered his body. He's alone, in his office, a man of stone. My heart aches for him.

"We stand with you, my queen," a feminine voice speaks, followed by the grunts of the other guards.

My body sags in relief. Part of me was afraid they wouldn't stand with a human queen. I didn't realize how much I needed to hear their belief in me.

"Stay with your queen," Delmare barks. The older guard isn't fazed by the cold looks the demons are giving him, but none of them look keen on arguing with him either.

"What do you need from us?" Erin pulls my attention back to her.

"If this doesn't work—"

"It's going to work," Erin interrupts me.

"But if it doesn't, I need to make sure my kingdom is protected."

"Done," Allarick says easily, like he'd have it no other way. "If one kingdom falls, we all fall. Your fight is our fight."

"Thank you." Tears sting my eyes, threatening to fall. I can't fall apart now, not when I'm needed the most.

As Erin said, I need to trust my heart. Right now, it's telling me to follow my plan. Even if it sounds crazy. It is, but that doesn't mean it won't work. With my mind made up, I turn my back to everyone, training my eyes on the bouquet lying on the ground, calling to me like a flame to a moth.

The first step is the hardest. My entire body aches. The initial rush of adrenaline is now fading, leaving behind a trail of soreness from today's events. Every movement sends a sharp reminder of what I endured, but I force myself to push past the discomfort.

I move forward, drawn toward the soft glow of the roses. Kneeling before them, I hesitate, my hand hovering just above the delicate petals. Fear tightens around my chest, whispering doubts and urging me to reconsider. What if I'm wrong? What if I can't save the demons' kingdom?

For a moment, I nearly pull away, my fear too strong.

But then, from somewhere deep within, a quiet strength surfaces. It overpowers the fear, steadying my resolve. My fingers move again, closing the final distance between me and the bundle of roses.

My breath hitches. I brace myself for the impossible—for my body to stiffen, my skin to harden into lifeless stone.

But the transformation never comes.

There's no pain or loss of consciousness, even as my fingers touch the delicate petals. An audible gasp sounds behind me, followed by, "Impossible."

But it's not impossible. The magic of the flowers has no effect on me since it's no longer in the hands of a monster looking to destroy us. Because that's what it is. Living, breathing magic. Not a curse. A solution. One that taunted the demons, but a solution nonetheless.

I stand tall and move to the edge of the river. Gently, I pluck the roses from their thorny stems, setting them down next to me. I can't help but think of my sister and her love of roses. They were never a curse for her, not like Oziel viewed them. They always brought her happiness.

Perhaps the true magic depends on who wields the roses and their intentions. I want to heal this land. Save my husband. There's no future without Oziel—I see this now.

The five buds in my hand hardly seem enough to heal an entire river, but I don't let the doubts overcome me a second time. One by one, I crush each flower between my hands, until the petals all separate, and drop them into the river. I do this five times until nothing remains in my hand.

Bright pink petals float in the black water. Oziel once told me the river ran red, and the hum of power could be felt all throughout the kingdom. I want to see that for myself, experience River Hel in all its glory.

At first, when the petals do little more than float, a trickle of doubt creeps back into my mind. Before I can spiral, one at a time, each petal dissolves into the river, making a sizzling and crackling sound as they disappear before my eyes. The wind picks up, my hair blowing behind my shoulders as the ground begins to shake as if reacting to the magic, gently at first, and then harder until it feels more like an earthquake.

"Cover the queen!" someone yells before I'm dragged away from the river's edge, shoved between demons as the world feels like it's about to split in two. The sheer force has me stumbling and grabbing on to the nearest guard. Delmare and Allarick both shield Erin, her eyes wide with fear.

What did I do? I messed with magic I had no business messing with. This doesn't feel like I've saved my kingdom. No, this feels like I've damned them all over again.

As abruptly as it began, the shaking ceases, leaving me dizzy and unsteady. A strange lightness fills my limbs, as if the ground has momentarily vanished beneath me.

"Look!" exclaims the demon I'm still clinging to, his voice edged with urgency. He points at something behind me, eyes wide with shock.

I take a steadying breath, forcing myself to find my balance before turning to see what has captured their attention. As my gaze lands on the river, a jolt of disbelief shoots through me. My expression mirrors the astonishment of those around me.

I'm no longer looking at a black, poisoned river. Instead, I look upon a river where the water runs as red as roses, buzzing with energy I have never felt before. The color is breathtaking, but the power it emits also leaves me breathless. It feels like a living entity—powerful, determined, resilient. The surface glitters as if thanking me for restoring it.

"You did it," Erin says from somewhere behind me. "Isabelle, you did it!"

"I—"

My words are cut off by a loud splash and the sound of someone gasping for breath. No, not just someone... two someones. They emerge from the river, arms stretched up to the sky as if they were trying to get out for a long time. I've seen these demons before, back when Oziel first explained the curse upon the kingdom. He had shown me two stone statues at the bottom of the river.

Well, they certainly aren't statues anymore.

"Go to them!" I shout at the guards surrounding me, and they quickly spring into action, running to help the two demons out of the water. Oziel thought the River Hel would cure the demons, and he was right. The two gasping for breath a few feet in front of me are proof.

It's like a fire is lit beneath me as I desperately look around for something to capture the water in. As if sensing what I'm looking for, Erin reaches into her pocket and pulls out a small vial of what looks like perfume.

"I started carrying this with me a while back when I surfaced after someone made a comment about a fishy smell. Here, take it. Fill it up and take it to Oziel. We'll be right behind you," she promises.

A truly selfless queen would shake her head and declare that her people must always come first. And while I won't forget them, because I fully intend to help them, I can't pretend to be that kind of ruler. Because I am selfish.

Oziel comes first.

And he always will.

"Thank you." I snatch the bottle from her, quickly open it and spill the contents onto the ground before running to the water. I don't even think about the consequences of touching the river as I dunk my hand in to fill up the vial. Luckily, there are none other than chilly water. It doesn't take long, and, once full, I inspect the bottle. It's not much, but I hope it's enough to bring Oziel back to me.

With water from River Hel in my hands, I turn back toward my castle and run to my husband.

I'm coming, Oziel, and I will save you.

CHAPTER 39
ISABELLE

I don't let the guards come in when I enter Oziel's study. No one needs to see him like this. I only allow Allarick and Erin to join me because I don't want to be alone at this moment. Just staring up at the large statue of my husband nearly brings me to my knees. It would have if Erin wasn't there to hold me up when my legs buckled.

"I got you," she whispers, and once again I'm struck with amazement at how far this woman has come. This isn't the same Erin from Grym Hollow. Her gaze is strong, fierce, but friendly. She holds herself like the queen she is. "I know this is hard. I was in your position not so long ago. I thought I lost Allarick."

"How did you get him back?" My voice is soft, sounding much more like a scared little girl than the demon queen. Oziel would want me to stand tall and regal, but he's not fucking here, so I don't give a damn what he thinks. I didn't realize how much I relied on him until he was taken away from me.

"My love for him combined with a bit of stubbornness." She smiles. "I had help from the other queens of Mescos, who are both from Grym Hollow as well. They helped me when I needed them the most, and I want to be the same support for you. Do what you think needs to be done."

I nod once, and soon Erin pulls away from me, taking a step back. She's here, but she also wants to give me my space, which I appreciate. I take a step closer, looking up at the anger in Oziel's eyes. Even in stone, he looks powerful and otherworldly. I reach up, pressing my hand to his cold cheek. I hate the way he feels. He should be warm, his skin hot to the touch.

With a trembling hand, I lift the vial, its contents sloshing gently inside. The liquid glows a deep red. The river water looks to be tainted with blood, shimmering with flecks of gold that catch the dim light. I collected as much as I could, praying it would be enough. It *has* to be enough.

Before unscrewing the cap, I scan the room and spot a sturdy wooden chair in the corner. I drag it in front of Oziel, its legs scraping against the floor, then climb onto it. I need the extra height. If this is going to work, I need to pour the potion directly over his head, letting every drop seep into him.

Tilting my hand, I let the River Hel pour over Oziel. Water, way more than it seems like this vial can hold, wets the statue. The stone's gray hue darkens, and energy ripples around him. It's nearly overpowering.

I wait with bated breath for the change to happen. For stone to make way for flesh. For gray eyes to turn gold. For his lips to curl up into a smirk and say something that will have me rolling my eyes.

I wait a minute. Then another. I wait for a breath. A word. *Anything.* I don't even blink because I don't want to miss a single second. But Oziel remains unmoving. He's no less a statue than he was a moment ago.

I failed.

A strangled cry leaves my lips, and I bring my fist down hard on his stone chest. It hurts, but the pain of losing him hurts more.

"Isabelle..." Erin says my name softly from behind me, but I can't look at her right now. Because she's standing next to her husband, while mine remains lost to me.

I slam my fists against his chest again and again, my knuckles splitting open against the unyielding stone of his skin. The pain barely registers because nothing could hurt worse than this. Than losing him. Than knowing he's gone.

"I fucking hate you!" I scream, my voice raw, cracking under the weight of my grief. I don't care that I have an audience. I don't care that I look like a madwoman, throwing a tantrum over a man who will never hear me again. I don't care about anything except the unbearable ache hollowing out my chest, breaking my heart into unfixable fragments.

"I told you I didn't want to love you! You didn't want to love me either, remember? We fought it. We swore we wouldn't. But guess what, asshole?" My breath hitches as tears blur my vision. "I love you. I fucking love you. And I hate how much I love you. I hate how much you matter to me. How much you changed me. And now you're just...gone."

A sob rips from my throat as I press my forehead against his chest, my fingers curling uselessly against his lifeless hand. "Fuck you, Oziel," I whisper, the words breaking apart as they leave me, my tears falling freely down upon him. "Fuck you for making me love you... and fuck you for leaving me."

The room falls into silence, my anger swallowed by the crushing weight of my grief.

I don't know how long I stay like this. How long my tears fall. I feel like they are never-ending. A gentle, feminine hand touches the center of my back. I don't need to turn to know it's Erin. She sniffles as if crying herself. "We will keep trying. Come. Let's get you down."

I want to argue with her. Tell her there's no use in trying, because this should have worked. Tell her how I don't want to get my hopes up again. But I don't say any of those things because I'll either take my anger out on her, which she doesn't deserve, or become a sobbing mess...well, more of a sobbing mess.

Like a zombie, I let Erin help me off the chair and allow her to steer me toward the door. I feel like I'm walking through heavy snow, each step harder than the last. Or maybe that's just my failure weighing me down. I want to lie in bed and sleep until it doesn't hurt anymore. Until I can mend my broken heart.

Erin's hand is on the door, fingers curled around the handle, ready to push it open, when a soft sound breaks the silence—a faint scattering, like pebbles tumbling to the floor. My entire body locks up, every muscle tensing.

A chill runs down my spine, and for a moment, I'm trapped in place, frozen in time.

I can't move. I can't even bring myself to turn around. I'm not even sure I'm breathing. The air in the room feels heavier, charged with something unseen yet undeniable.

Then, a deliberate throat-clearing slices through the quiet, sending a shiver through me. I'm left wondering if this is a dream.

"Kitten," a voice I never expected to hear again purrs, smooth as velvet. "Leaving so soon?"

CHAPTER 40
OZIEL

My mind hangs in a precarious balance. I'm myself, but I'm also not. Stone. He turned me to stone. The sensation of having your body change should be painful, but the curse took me over so quickly, the pain never had a chance to register.

Betrayed by my courtier. Garvan. I don't think the revelation will ever stop wounding me. I pride myself on knowing everything that goes on in my kingdom and being a good judge of character. I'm not sure how Garvan managed to slither past all my defenses. The last thing I saw was his triumphant smirk when the curse took over.

But my last thought was of Isabelle. Of wanting to tell her to run, to leave before she got hurt by him. But I was helpless, just a man forever encased in his stone tomb. This was to be my legacy.

My mind drifted, protecting me from an eternity of being stuck. I thought of nothing but her, even if it pained me. Her voice. The way she rolled her eyes when she pretended to be annoyed with me, but really I knew she liked it. She was easier to read than she thought. One just had to pay attention.

Even now I can hear her voice. Though it's not a happy one. No, Isabelle's voice is full of heartbreak and pain, a pain I've never heard come from her before. She's screaming at me, but I can't quite make out all the words. Until one thing sticks.

I love you.

I fucking love you.

Those words aren't delivered like a woman in love. She's pissed. As if I made her fall in love with me against her will. Perhaps I did, but I can't bring myself to regret it. Never.

But then her voice abruptly stops, and all I'm left with is her pain. I can't comfort her, and it's too fucking much. I will my body to move, to do anything but remain still, but of course I don't have the power to counteract the curse.

Just as that thought begins to form, a rippling sensation takes over my body. A tingle at first, then the invisible restraints that kept me in place begin to crumble one by one. I can do nothing but watch as my body morphs once again. This time, the experience is unpleasant. Like I'm trying to fit my body through a tiny cave, sharp rocks digging into my sides. Breathing is hard, and my vision goes blurry.

Then...

I stumble.

I sway like a drunk sap who saw the end of too many bottles. My stomach lurches, feeling the strangest sensation as I breathe in deeply, filling my lungs with oxygen once again. And that's when I see her. My queen. She's walking away from me, led by a woman I don't know. The man, however, I know well. The kraken king. But why is the kraken out of water?

I can't let Isabelle leave. I need to know this is real and not some cruel nightmare the curse is torturing me with. "Kitten," I purr, my voice feeling like a stranger's. "Leaving so soon?"

Isabelle and the woman pushing her toward the door —whom I imagine is Erin, Allarick's wife—stop dead in their tracks. Erin is the first to turn, her eyes wide when she sees me as me and not the stone statue. But Isabelle is slower to turn around, like she too believes she's in some kind of fucked-up dream, which gives me the opportunity to look over her body.

I see blood and bruises along her arms and legs. Her hair is wild, barely contained in the braid that winds down her back. But it's the sadness in her eyes that makes me want to burn everything to the fucking ground until I rid the world of all who wronged her. She stares at me as if she's seeing an apparition. She takes a step forward, but then hesitates, too afraid or stunned to move forward.

So I do it for her.

My muscles are sore, and my legs protest with each step closer. I would crawl with broken bones and bloody wounds if it meant she'd be in my arms. "Kitten," I say again, needing to reach her. "Come here."

Then, as if a fire has been lit within her, Isabelle throws herself at me, arms going around my neck while her legs wrap around my torso. I barely keep us upright, gathering my bearings from my abrupt change. Still, my arms wrap tightly around her slight frame, pulling her even closer. It's not close enough though. I need her with the intensity of a hundred burning suns because my Isabelle did it. There's no other way I'd be here right now if she didn't just save my kingdom.

"You bastard," she cries into my chest, hitting her bloody knuckles against my shoulder. "You fucking bastard."

"Never claimed to be anything different." That earns me another thump of her fist. She tilts her head up, trying to look pissed at me. But I know her secret. "You love me," I whisper, lips curling into a smile so wide it hurts.

"I also said I hate you." She sniffles, but I ignore her and capture her lips with my own. I kiss her with wild abandon, not caring in the least that we have an audience. That's never stopped me before, and it most certainly won't stop me now.

But Isabelle breaking the kiss stops me, her eyes glossy with unshed tears, lips wet with my kiss. "It's really you," she murmurs, reaching up to stroke the side of my face.

"It's really me, Kitten." I know she needs to hear it. "And I love you too. Your darkness calls to mine." Once the words "I love you" would have filled me with rage and sadness, a reminder of what happens when you give your heart away. It exploits your biggest weakness to your enemies. But perhaps I've been looking at this all wrong. Isabelle isn't my biggest weakness. No, this woman is my strength and resilience, and now that she's saved my kingdom, our people will see that as well.

"You saved us all. We all owe you a great debt." I want to know everything that happened since Garvan cursed me until now. I'll get the story soon enough, preferably after a night of rough fucking.

"I don't care about that. I care that you're okay, you foolish man," she chides. "You don't get to leave me after you made me love you."

Her words strike something within me. A memory of our first encounter, when she was nothing more than a human woman. Her words from the start of our marriage ring in my brain. Once this is all done, she wants to be set free. I can't cage my wife forever, even if she loves me and I her. I won't go back on my promise.

"Instead, you'll be leaving me." I watch as her face scrunches up in confusion.

Realization dawns a moment later, and she shakes her head adamantly. "I don't want that anymore. That was before I..."

"Before what, Kitten?" I prompt.

She bites her lip, and I want nothing more than to suck it into my mouth and kiss her until she knows nothing but desire. "Before I fell in love with you, asshole."

"You have the sweetest nicknames for me, Miss Sinclair." I laugh, and Isabelle cracks a smile. She pulls me down and presses her forehead against mine, eyes closing.

"Don't leave me again," she whispers.

"Not even death will keep me from you, Wife," I vow.

And we stay like that, her body wrapped around mine, our foreheads together, as we bask in each other's presence. I'm not sure how much time goes by before someone clears their throat. "It's good to see you're not dead, Oziel," Allarick's gruff voice cuts through the silence.

Unfortunately, this pulls Isabelle away from me. Her arms unwrap from around my neck, followed by her legs from my waist, and I ease her down. She doesn't stray far from me though, tucking herself into my side, where she belongs.

"Thank you. Both of you. I couldn't have done it without your help," Isabelle says.

I take in the kraken king and his wife. I'm not one to show my gratitude, especially to those I consider outsiders. But I can't deny that Allarick and Erin helped Isabelle when I couldn't. That alone means I'm in their debt. "You have my gratitude. Both of you."

"Don't be going soft on us now, Demon King." Allarick grins, and I instantly want to take back my words. I don't, because I'm a good fucking demon. At least today.

Erin handles him for me by playfully hitting his chest, letting her hand linger a moment longer than appropriate. She then fixes her attention on my wife. "I'm glad we could be here. If there's anything you need, please reach out. Us Grym Hollow girls have to stick together, right?" She winks.

"Right," Isabelle agrees as something passes between them. Something I will never understand because I'm not human.

"Allarick and I should head out—"

"Wait!" Isabelle says frantically, moving away from me. I don't let her get far though, keeping my hand interlocked with hers. She doesn't try to pull out of my grip, hopefully finding the same security in it as I feel. Erin raises a brow, confusion etched along her features.

"I mean...it's just...I need to talk to you," Isabelle finally manages to say. She then looks at Allarick before looking back at me. "I need to talk to her alone."

I don't like it. Not because I don't trust Erin, but rather because I don't particularly want my wife out of my sight right now. Judging from the looks of it, Allarick doesn't seem keen on leaving either.

"You can wait just outside the room. I need ten minutes alone with Erin. Please." Isabelle looks between the two of us.

Erin squeezes Allarick's arm, reaching up to give him a quick kiss on the lips. "I'll be fine, my love. Just ten minutes and you'll be right outside the door. Put Delmare outside to guard the window, if that'll make you feel better."

"It would actually," he murmurs. I don't tell him that I agree.

Isabelle pulls me closer, and I stop once her chest touches mine. She looks up at me with big brown eyes, and I know at this moment I will do anything for her. "Just ten minutes."

"Just ten minutes," I agree. "But I'll be waiting right outside the door."

"And I'll run into your arms once I'm done. I just need this," she says gently. I know why she does. She's been keeping this secret for a long time, and I won't be the one to stand in her way.

I press a gentle kiss to her forehead and nod once. "Come to me when you're done. We have a lot to talk about." With one final glance, I follow Allarick out to the hall as the door closes behind us with a resounding thud.

CHAPTER 41

ISABELLE

I've always prided myself on being able to have hard conversations. I may not always deliver the message in the correct tone, but I always get my point across. Never once have I been at a loss for what to say, fearful of what the other person might think of me. But that's exactly how I feel when the door shuts on our husbands and I'm alone with Erin.

The woman smiles kindly at me, completely unaware of the terrible—yet necessary—thing I have done. Will she hate me when she finds out? Distance herself from a killer?

"Something is bothering you," Erin says after I've been quiet for too long. Normally, the warm room wouldn't bother me, but sweat coats my brow as I stare down the woman I've known longer than she's known me. "Whatever it is, you can tell me," she adds gently.

I take a deep breath, centering myself and calling upon my courage. This needs to be done, and she needs

329

to know. So, without a preamble, I begin, "I knew you back in Grym Hollow."

Erin's brows knit together, and she tilts her head to the side, assessing me. "You did? I'm sorry, but I don't remember you," she says apologetically.

"You didn't know me. But we had something in common." I pause, knowing the next thing I say will hurt her. "I knew James," I whisper.

For a moment, Erin reverts to the timid, scared woman James forced her to be. Her body shakes, and it appears she's doing everything she can to keep her breathing even and her nerves in check. Her eyes dart around the room as if James is going to walk out from the shadows. "Oh?" she finally says.

And then I tell her everything. Everything I've been dying to tell her since I've arrived. I tell her about Anna, my sweet sister, and the torment she experienced with James. The hell he put my family through. How my sister became a shell of the woman she once was. How I couldn't save her, and how the day I found her dead in her bedroom was the day a part of me died too.

"James killed her?" Erin's voice is unsteady as tears roll down her eyes. My own cheeks are wet with emotions I can't hold back.

"Yes," I explain, "not by his own hand, but it may as well have been. He led my sister to an early grave. I hated him for what he did to her. And I hated him for doing it to you too. I couldn't let the cycle continue, Erin. I really couldn't. He would only pick a new victim."

Erin gives a single nod, her expression tightening. A flicker of anticipation flashes in her eyes almost like she's expecting the news yet still steeling herself for the weight of it. Her shoulders tense, and she inhales slowly, as if preparing for a blow she knows is coming but still hopes won't land as hard as she fears. Her voice is quiet, measured. "Isabelle...what happened to James when I left?"

And there's the question I've been most dreading. Not because I regret my actions. I would kill James over and over again, even though it won't ever bring back my sister. I just never wanted him to do that to another girl again.

"I killed him, Erin. I watched his blood stain the ground and reveled in the terror in his eyes. Because I knew that's how Anna felt every time he struck her. I wanted him to get a dose of his own medicine, and for him to never harm another person again. I watched the light go out of his eyes, and I regret nothing."

Erin is quiet, standing completely emotionless. I don't know if I want her to yell or punch me, but I definitely don't want her to be quiet. It's far worse than the alternatives.

"I'm so sorry, Erin. Not that I killed him, but that you weren't the one to do it."

"I would have never been able to kill James," she says at last. "I thought about it. Daily, but I knew I couldn't take the life of another person, even one as cruel and horrid as James."

Tears stream down Erin's face as she reaches for me, her fingers trembling. I don't hesitate. My hands find hers, our grip firm as unspoken understanding passes between us. We just stare at each other, two women forever bound by the horrors of the same man, though our suffering took different forms.

Her voice is thick with emotion when she finally speaks. "Thank you for telling me." She exhales, as if releasing a weight she's carried for far too long. I do the same, my body unburdening itself at last. "James got the ending he deserved, and I no longer have to live in fear that he'll hurt anyone else."

The finality of those words lingers between us for a heartbeat. And then, as if pulled by an invisible force, we crash into each other's arms, clinging to the shared relief, the grief, and the unspoken strength that has carried us both to this moment.

We are no longer the girls who left Grym Hollow, running from a past that threatened to swallow us whole. No, we stand with each other as queens, loved by men who truly deserve our love.

An unbreakable bond tethers us, and I know Erin will be a part of the rest of my life. I want to get to know her. The real her, and I want to finally have a friend.

Ten minutes must have passed because a knock sounds at the door just before Allarick and Oziel barge in, completely unapologetic about their abrupt and uncere-monious entrance. Erin and I exchange a glance before dissolving into high-pitched giggles, the kind that comes from a mix of overwhelming emotions and sheer exhaus-tion. Our eyes are red and puffy, and our cheeks streaked with tears, but we make no effort to hide it.

Our husbands pause, scanning us with a mix of concern and bewilderment, as if we've completely lost our minds. Maybe to them we have—and that's okay.

They'll never truly understand this moment—it belongs to Erin and me alone.

"Sweet Girl, Atina is waiting for us," Allarick says gently, as if nervous to separate us.

Erin squeezes my hand one last time. "Let's not be strangers. How about dinner soon? I can introduce you to the other girls."

I've never been one to make many friends, so the thought sounds appealing, if somewhat nerve-racking. I nod. "I would love that."

We share one last look before Erin goes back to Allarick, murmuring to him how she'll fill him in later about what we just discussed. She smiles politely at Oziel, who dips his head slightly in respect. He and Allarick share a handshake, nodding at one another. Allarick lets go and offers me a smile before heading out with Erin.

They barely make it out of the room before Oziel is on me, crushing me against his firm body. "I want to know everything, but before we start, tell me Garvan is dead," he says, eyes flashing black.

I laugh softly, suddenly feeling exhausted. "Very dead. Dagger to the throat by Delmare. I might have helped a little too."

"How disappointing," Oziel murmurs. I can only imagine the type of horrors my husband would exact upon him.

"I will tell you everything," I wrap my arms around his neck, "but first I need you to carry me to bed, strip us, and fuck me." I don't care that I'm tired or that my body hurts. I won't be able to truly sleep well without feeling Oziel inside of me. I need it desperately. I need him.

Without another word, Oziel lifts me up, and shadows form around us. I grin. "Your shadows are back." They never truly left, but they were weakened. He seems to be growing stronger, which means the River Hel is truly healed.

Oziel's shadows curl around us, enveloping me in their cool embrace as they weave through the air like living tendrils. Their touch is both comforting and possessive, a silent promise of protection—one I know Oziel will keep until his dying breath. I lean into him, feeling the solid warmth of his body against mine. He presses a gentle kiss to my forehead, his lips lingering for a moment longer than necessary.

"Let's go, Wife," he murmurs, his voice a low command laced with something deeper. Something meant only for me.

And just like that, the world fades away until there is nothing but him.

CHAPTER 42

OZIEL

2 Weeks Later

The kingdom is far busier than it has been in a while, mainly because there are more demons walking amongst us now. Since the night Isabelle restored the River Hel back to its former glory, we've been diligently working on curing all the cursed. The task is slightly more challenging than we anticipated because the curse can only be cured in two ways. Either they are completely submerged into the river, or someone with strong feelings for the cursed frees them with only a vial of river water, something we discovered by sheer accident.

Now, all of our people are cured.

We haven't had a single demon succumb to the curse since that night. Nephilim still wander outside our borders, but they are no longer an immediate threat with the restoration of our magic—thanks to my beautiful wife. Our people recognize this because Isabelle gets stopped a lot by demons now, all wanting to get into her good graces.

I know we simply won the battle and that a war still brews, but for now, I can breathe a little easier. Rest and prepare for the future. The future that will have my wife next to me. Whatever war we face, it'll be together. The kingdom feels safer with Isabelle by my side.

In the meantime, I have not given up on persuading the other kings of the merit in their wives attempting to communicate with the Nephilim. I understand their hesitancy—I'm not keen on risking Isabelle's safety, but she also agrees it's a risk she's willing to take to learn more about our enemies. Any information can help us win, and seeing as the last great war nearly wiped out Mescos entirely, we need all the leverage.

Isabelle is currently getting ready for her evening dinner with Erin. The two women have seen each other twice since the night in my study and are quickly becoming friends. Tonight, Isabelle is hosting a dinner— which she's reminded me I'm not invited to nearly every night since she planned it—and has arranged for a three-course meal our kitchen staff is currently preparing. I'm allowed to eat the food...just not with them.

Luckily, I won't be forced to idly chat with Allarick, because he won't be joining Erin tonight. How the woman convinced her husband to attend without him is beyond me. I suppose she possesses a power I never will. However, in return, she's agreed to bring Delmare, and I've agreed to not kill or torture him for my amusement.

Progress all around.

My head bowed, busy at my desk with correspondence with the fae kings, I nearly miss the soft tap of the door hitting the wall, followed by footfalls. I look up just in time to see Isabelle enter, wearing only a satin robe and a mischievous smile on her face. Seeing her creamy skin on display awakens something carnal deep within me.

"You're supposed to be getting ready, Kitten. Or have you forgotten you banished me to my study until your friend leaves?" I raise a brow.

Isabelle moves closer, her hips swinging seductively with each step. "I didn't banish you. I simply threatened no sex if you interrupted my girl time."

"Yes, quite the torturous queen you are. More wicked than even me," I tease, an easy smile on my lips.

Isabelle only laughs, like she finds my suffering amusing. In truth, she probably does, and she takes some sweet satisfaction in my pain. "Well, I may have been a tad overbearing these last few days."

"Haven't noticed," I say, which earns me a glare.

"But I'm not completely wicked. I've come to make it up to you before dinner," she says, catching my attention.

"Is that so? Tell me, Kitten, what prize do I get for being a good boy?" I watch the way her cheeks flush at my words. For a seductive temptress, she certainly blushes easily, and I take great pleasure in that fact.

Isabelle reaches for the tie around her waist, tugging on one end until it falls loose, opening her robe. I suck in a deep breath upon seeing my wife's naked body. It doesn't matter how many times I see her, I'll never get accustomed to her beauty. If this is my prize, I will gladly take my banishment.

My wife moves to my desk, pushing all the stacks of paper and books off, sending them crashing to the ground. She lets the robe slip down her body before crawling on top of my desk, slowly making her way toward me. My cock painfully hardens in the confines of my pants. It's a good pain. One I welcome, since I can usually put it to good use...multiple times.

"I thought I'd let you have dessert before dinner. You know, since you've been such a good husband. And I did save your ass, so this is also a treat for me." She grins wickedly. My little Kitten has found her claws. She reminds me daily how she's saved my ass, but it doesn't bother me. She deserves the praise, and I'm happy to show her my gratitude.

"I definitely deserve my dessert now," I say as she comes to sit at the edge of my desk, her legs fanning out to straddle my thighs. She places her feet on each armrest. She's completely exposed to me, her pretty pink pussy glistening with her arousal.

"Eat," she commands, grabbing both of my horns and pulling me down between her legs. Her spicy scent has me groaning, and the first lick of my tongue across her seam has her arching her back, pressing herself harder against me. If her plan is to suffocate me, I might just let her.

"Oziel," she moans my name, the lustful sound going straight to my cock. With one hand, I use my pointer finger and middle finger to part her, kissing her sweet pussy. She's receptive to my touch—I love that about her. She isn't shy when it comes to her pleasure, and she shouldn't be.

"Tonight, I'm riding your cock in the showers," she says breathlessly as I tease her clit. Her body jolts forward, riding my face with wild abandon. My free hand snakes to the ties on the front of my pants, loosening them enough for my cock to spring free.

I wrap my hand around my shaft, squeezing it, though it pales in comparison to how her pussy feels around me. With slow, deliberate pumps, I work my hand up and down my shaft, adding pressure with each pass. She continues to hold on to my horns, a sensitive body part for demons, stroking them the same way I stroke my own cock, driving me fucking crazy.

At this rate, I'm not going to last. One would think it's been ages since I've fucked my wife, even though I buried myself deep inside her sweet heat the moment we woke up this morning. My hunger for her will never be quenched, only burning brighter with time. I've seen couples fizzle out until their passion extinguishes, but that's never going to happen to Isabelle and me—I simply won't allow it.

Isabelle pushes my head down again, and I take her clit into my mouth, earning a scream from her as she rides my face, chasing her pleasure. "Don't fucking stop," she hisses, as if I'm capable of denying her pleasure. I've tried it once, and I think I hated it more than her.

My fist pumps faster on my cock, wanting to find my own release alongside her. I continue to lap, tease, and suck at the bundle of nerves until her legs tense, and her thighs squeeze around my head in a punishing grip. She comes beautifully, and I follow close behind, coming into my hand like a fucking teenage demon. Doesn't matter. I'll finish in her tonight.

I lap at her release until Isabelle giggles and pushes me away, complaining about being late. "If you were worried about being late, you wouldn't have come in here offering me dessert, Kitten."

She only rolls her eyes, something I've come to love about her. It is more a sign of affection than anything. Isabelle pushes herself up, still panting and flushed from her orgasm. She looks freshly fucked, and if I had more time, I'd make sure to give her more. But I won't keep her from her evening with Erin.

She leans down, capturing my lips in a deep kiss. The taste of herself lingers on my tongue as she moans softly into my mouth. A sly smirk plays on her lips as she hums, "Insatiable demon."

That's exactly what I am, and I'll not deny it. But she's no better than I am.

"Enjoy your dinner, Wife. Come find me in our room when you're done." I watch as she slides off my desk and leans down to grab her robe. She ties it hastily around herself, covering up all my favorite parts.

"I'll always find you, Demon King." Of that, I have no doubt. Isabelle blows a kiss at me. "I love you, Oziel."

We've probably said those words a hundred times since the night she broke my curse, but each time feels like the first time. I now understand the love my parents had. The love they died for. If it ever came to it, I would lay down my life for Isabelle, no questions asked.

"I love you too. Now go, before I drag you back here and sit you on my cock." Not much of a threat, but it works. She giggles, and I watch as she leaves my study.

The world is far from perfect. But for this one moment, it certainly seems that way.

CHAPTER 43

EPILOGUE
THE GUARDIAN

Redemption is near.

The nectar of salvation is sweet on my tongue, welcoming me home like a long-lost friend. I have been in the shadows for too long, suffering in agonizing pain. It's part of me. Baggage I carry wherever I go.

There's a certain comfort in embracing what you know. Even if all you know is pain and darkness. But if that's all one has ever experienced, it makes the light feel like an unforgiving fire. Just the smallest kindness will burn you from the inside out.

Pain hasn't been my entire life, but it has been since I lost *her*.

Her presence haunts me. Her face is a reminder of a time when things were simpler. When I was simpler and had no delusions of grandeur. My pride, the one thing I put above all else—above everything else—took me down a road I didn't know how to come back from.

Looking back, I don't think I would have. Not even for her.

I stand in the small bathroom at my house with nothing but a towel on. Something has changed after Isabelle. She was the fourth girl. Only two more remain. My body feels foreign, and anything I try to put on feels like a million sharp knives rubbing against my skin. My back feels tight, full of knots I cannot relieve.

Something is happening. Another punishment? Or something else?

Just as the thought takes up residence in my brain, a sharp, hot pain erupts in my back. It takes me by surprise, and I drop to my knees. The pain grows more intense and becomes all-consuming. I grip the bathroom counter hard enough for my knuckles to turn white. It's the only thing keeping me up.

A low, guttural growl escapes my throat as pain rips through my back, sharp and searing. My body arches as a wave of nausea hits me with the intensity of a thousand suns. I buckle over with a gasp. The contents of my earlier breakfast rise in my throat, and I vomit all over the floral rug. Specs of blood splatter below, and my mouth fills with the taste of bile and copper.

Is this death? Was this all some cruel joke to present me with the hope of salvation and ability to find her, only for it all to be taken away from me when I'm so close? Only two girls left. Just two. So close to finding pieces of my heart to make me whole once again.

No, it can't be. This is...

Pain erupts in my back again, and I roar. My screams

thunder around me, and in this distress-induced fog, my brain is slow to realize the transformation taking place.

My body trembles as the first jagged spines push through my skin.

My nails rake the tile beneath me, leaving deep gouges as another scream tears from my lips—a sound equal parts agony and triumph. Triumph because the gods have not yet forsaken me. No, this is a gift.

I accept the pain, letting my screams mix with the laughter of a schoolboy. If anyone were to walk in, they would think me deranged. I certainly feel deranged as my laughter takes on a manic tone while the transformation continues.

My wings—yes, wings, limbs that were taken from me the day of my punishment. I still remember the terrible tearing sound and the raw pain that made me pass out, only to awake missing a huge part of me.

The wings begin to take form—raw, skeletal frames that stretch outward, dripping with dark blood. Feathers, likely as gray as a stormy cloud, sprout slowly, painfully. Each one a testament to the price I'm paying for redemption. The muscles in my back twist and spasm as the wings grow, unfurling inch by agonizing inch, until they loom above me, massive and beautiful.

My breaths came in ragged pants, chest heaving as I collapse against the sink, body trembling. The pain lingers with me for a long time, and I sit in my bathroom embracing it. The pain is progress. A gift.

Soon, it subsides to a dull ache, replaced by a strange, nearly alien sensation. I've forgotten what the weight of wings feels like. It has been centuries since I lost them, though I've lost count of the exact number of years. Learning how to use the muscles again for long periods of time won't be an easy task. Flying is complex and takes time to perfect. As a child, it was easier. I weighed less and feared nothing.

With shaky legs, I pull myself off the bathroom floor. For the first time in years, I look directly at my reflection in the mirror. I'm quite a sight to behold, vomit and blood splattered across my chest. Naked as the day I was born because somehow between now and the transformation, the small towel covering my body fell free. But it's not the nakedness or the mess on my body that I care about. No, it's the magnificent, otherworldly wings protruding from my back.

They are nearly identical to my old wings. Gray, but with black feathers as dark as obsidian sprinkled throughout. They are heavy, but it's a comfortable weight, like an old blanket draped around me on a cold night. They feel both brand-new and like I haven't been apart from them a day in my life.

Tentatively, I flex the massive appendages. The sound of the wings moving, leathery and sharp, echo in the bathroom. It's music to my ears. But this bathroom is small, far too cramped to truly experience the full effect of my wings. I stumble out of the bathroom to grab pants, lacking all the grace and poise I typically possess, and make my way out of the house.

The moment I'm out in the open, I spread my wings out as far as they'll go. They ache, but it's a good ache. It means they're as strong as my old ones. But that has yet to be tested. Humans have a saying I once found quite odd. They always compare a vastly unrelated task to riding a bike. It took me a great deal to understand what that meant, but I think I finally do.

It's all muscle memory. Things you don't learn, but rather come as naturally as breathing. I hope this rings true now. I access the muscles that have been lost to me for so long. It's painful, but like I said before, I'm not a stranger to pain. It's easy to ignore.

The leathery wings began to thrash until I'm able to control the speed to a simple flutter. My eyes close, feeling the sensation of the wind and world around me. Listening to the sounds of the restless forest and smelling the cedar of the trees, mixed with toxic gasoline from the cars in town.

When I open my eyes, my cottage is below me. The lush expanse of the forest is for my viewing. A curious bird flies close but quickly retreats from the strange gray man in his skies. I'm so overcome with emotions that tears stain my cheeks. Crying is something I never do, but it seems like the only logical response to such a tremendous and world-changing gift.

I'm no longer grounded on earth. The skies are open to me once again.

A battle cry forms in my core, and I shout to the heavens, for once praising the mercy of gods instead of scorning. But my job is far from done. I still have two more girls to go. If this is my prize for four, she most certainly will be my prize for six.

With thoughts of a life that could potentially be mine once again, I take flight to the next destination—to find the new future fae queen.

TO BE CONTINUED...

WANT MORE?

Want sneak peaks of the next Grym Hollow couple? Sign up for my newsletter here or head to Instagram and click the link in my bio.

Also by Tati B. Alvarez

<u>Grym Hollow</u>

1. The Dragon's Rose

1.5 Tallie's Secret

2. The Wolf's Mate

3. The Kraken's Queen

4. The Demon's Beauty

5. The Fae's Promise

THANK YOU FOR READING!

I can't thank you enough for picking up my book. I hope you enjoyed it as much as I enjoyed writing it! If you did and are willing please consider leaving a review on your favorite book sites. This helps out small authors like me so much. Thank you for your continued support!

About the Author

Tati B. Alvarez lives in Austin, Texas with her family. She spends most days lost in her own head, creating stories. When she is not writing, you can find her vacationing at Disney World.